In *Confessions to a Stranger*, Danielle Grandinetti weaves a tale that is at once mysterious, suspenseful, romantic, and inspiring ... Filled with truths that made me ponder my own life, this novel is a lovely start to what is sure to be a wonderful series!

—Heidi Chiavaroli,
Carol Award-Winning Author of *The Orchard House*

Danielle Grandinetti has crafted a wonderful tale of suspense and romance that will keep you on the edge of your seat. With well-drawn characters authentic to the era, a gripping plot, and a strong message of hope, *Confessions to a Stranger* is a read I recommend!

—Misty M. Beller,
USA Today bestselling author of the Sisters of the Rockies

*A Strike to the Heart* is a compelling story. From the very first page, I was immersed into the thrilling action and remained gripped with intrigue until the satisfying ending. The romance escalated right along with the winding plot, creating a layered mystery that is sure to delight readers.

—Rachel Scott McDaniel,
Award-winning author of *The Mobster's Daughter*

Riveting from the first scene, *As Silent as the Night* offers a unique, edge-of-your-seat Christmas read ... A beautiful, gripping, and romantically suspenseful Christmas story you wouldn't be able to put down if you tried.

—Chautona Havig,<br>
Author of *The Stars of New Cheltenham*

*The Neighbor and the Gifts* is a poignant tale that transforms a familiar carol into a stirring journey of faith, love, and danger ... For readers who love historical romance, mystery, and want a deeper meaning in their holiday stories—this one's for you.

—Natalie Walters,<br>
bestselling and award-winning author of *Living Lies* and the *SNAP Agency* series

# Sheltered by the Doctor

**Discover the Foundation
of Danielle's Bookish World**


**Harbored in Crow's Nest**
Confessions to a Stranger
Refuge for the Archaeologist
Escape with the Prodigal
Relying on the Enemy
Sheltered by the Doctor
Investigation of a Journalist


Bridge: His Boss's Little Sister


**Unexpected Protectors**
To Stand in the Breach
A Strike to the Heart
As Silent as the Night


For a complete list, visit
daniellegrandinetti.com/books

# Sheltered by the Doctor

### Danielle Grandinetti

Hearth Spot Press

In memory of my grandma
who, after raising twelve children
while tending to her neighbor,
returned to school to become a nurse.


And to those medical professionals
whose listening and care make a difference to so many,
especially the nurses in my family.

From the end of the earth will
I cry unto thee, when my heart
is overwhelmed: lead me to the
rock that is higher than I. For
thou hast been a shelter for me,
and a strong tower from the
enemy.


Psalm 61:2-3, KJV

# CHAPTER ONE

*Friday, June 5, 1931*
*Crow's Nest, Wisconsin*

A certain smiling blonde waitress had nothing to do with why Dr. Nick Matrone detoured to the Wharfside Cafe that morning. He needed coffee before seeing his first patient. The cantankerous Mrs. Bindle. An older widow who came into the clinic at least once a week complaining of one malady or another. However, in his professional medical opinion, Nick believed the woman was simply lonely. He could relate.

The sun glared off the glassy water to his left as his shoes clumped on the wooden boards of the wharf. The fishing boats were all out on Lake Michigan at this time of the morning. He'd learned enough from rooming with David Martins, a fishing captain, that such calm conditions made for poor fishing. He whispered a prayer for his friend. The man was engaged and needed the income during these lean times. Not that God listened. Nick just couldn't shake the habit of bringing every worry to Him.

He turned his face away from the brightness as his mood darkened.

He tightened his grip on his satchel. Beginning a day in a grouchy mood never ended well. His patients needed him to be positive, encouraging, to foster healing. A perspective that had been increasingly difficult over the last six months. Today's newspaper headline only added to the problem.

Coffee.

Nick plowed through the empty outdoor seating and pulled open the door to the Wharfside. He spotted several of the retired captains sitting at a table in the middle of the room and promptly spun around. He didn't want to talk. Didn't want to be jovial. The gregarious Italian. He barely restrained a muttered Italian phrase that would have had his mamma crossing herself.

Sometimes he wished his skin tone was several shades lighter. His nose, not so straight. His hair, not so black. Then people would see him as a doctor. Not as someone related to Al Capone, whose indictment for tax evasion dominated the front page of today's *Crow's Nest Gazette*. Just because Nick was also Italian. No matter that he had never been to Chicago, except to travel through on his way from New York City.

Yes. He needed coffee. Lots of it.

"Dr. Matrone?" Melinda "Mindy" Zahn stepped out of the Wharfside door wearing a serviceable gray dress and white apron, her blonde hair in her usual ponytail. A beautiful, albeit questioning, smile on her fair face. She always said his name correctly, with the emphasis on the first part and the *ay* at the end. It tripped off her tongue in a lilting way he could listen to all day.

"Uh, hi." He shook his head. Being attracted to someone like Mindy wouldn't end well. A guy who looked like him didn't marry a girl who looked like her. He cleared his throat and dredged up his professional voice. "Might I get a cup of coffee while I sit out here?"

"Certainly." Her smile grew. "I'll be back in a moment."

Nick set his satchel down beside a chair and unbuttoned his suit coat. A warm breeze slipped underneath. It promised to be one of the warmest days yet, as expected, seeing that summer would officially arrive in a couple weeks.

"Did you pick a seat?" Mindy returned with a cup balanced on a saucer.

"This okay?" He waved at the table he'd chosen and tucked his thumbs into his vest pockets.

"It's a beautiful morning." She set the coffee cup on the table, then shielded her eyes as she looked out across the water. "I love early summer days. The sun feels like a warm hug, and the warmth is welcome after the winter. It's like a sheep shedding its winter coat. All the weight is gone. It's delightful."

Nick watched her, as he'd done since he met her. She was rarely static. Though she didn't talk with her hands like Nick's mother and sister, her whole body swayed as she talked, her eyes animated with her expressions. If he had a thousand years, he doubted he could read her fully. However, he loved to read.

"What is your favorite season?" She turned her wide hazel eyes on him.

"Can't say as I have one." Certainly not like she did. "New York winters are full of dirty slush. Summers, the heat is trapped in overpopulated apartments. Central Park is pretty in the fall. I never really noticed spring."

She cocked her head, her ponytail swishing over her shoulder. "I don't think I could live in a big city if that's the way the seasons went. It doesn't sound as if there is any fresh air to—Oh no." Her fingers wrapped around the edge of her apron.

Nick followed her gaze, and his stomach knotted. Joe Spelding. A chore of a man who made it his mission to seduce Mindy, or any other woman gullible enough to fall for his charms while he waited for Mindy to come around. Not that Mindy ever would. Nick had heard of their first run-in last summer, knew Mindy wanted to keep as far away from the man as she could. However, Nick knew men like Spelding. Knew they wouldn't give up easily, that their snake-oil words could weave an enchantment over the strongest of people.

"I best ..." Mindy thumbed toward the door, her hand trembling.

"Mindy." Nick stepped toward her. He hated that there seemed no solution, that Spelding didn't take a hint—or an obvious rejection. "What can I do?"

"Nothing." She grazed her fingers along his arm, so lightly he could barely feel her touch through his coat sleeve. It strengthened his resolve to do whatever he could to protect her from the scoundrel. "I avoid him when I can. When he's a customer ..."

She shrugged and slipped away. Nick worked his jaw as his mind sorted through scenarios. He'd bring it up to David tonight. There had to be something they could do. No woman should feel unsafe like this in her own community.

"Morning, Matrone." Spelding turned into the outdoor seating of the Wharfside. The man had the decency to mostly say Nick's surname as it was meant, just with the hard *n* sound at the end. Like how most people said his name. "You come here for the food or the scenery?"

Nick closed his fist at the innuendo in Spelding's voice. *Uno, due, tre* ... "Coffee."

Spelding laughed.

"If you'll excuse me." Without waiting for a response, Nick dropped into his chair and lifted his satchel to his lap. He didn't plan to look over patient files while drinking his coffee, but he needed a physical barrier to keep people—Spelding—from talking to him.

Spelding's chuckling finally ended as the door closed behind him.

Nick removed his glasses and rubbed the bridge of his nose. He was tired. So very tired. The weariness dragged his shoulders down. Even the coffee couldn't infuse his body with energy. How was he going to be kind to Mrs. Bindle with this grouchy feeling stealing any lightness inside? The sun was shining, summer was coming, he was away from the dirty city. Hope should buoy him up. Why couldn't he find his life raft?

A small figure caught his attention. A young girl in a dirty tan dress that came to her knees. Beat up shoes. Messy blonde hair. She walked almost like a ghost. Wandering. Meandering. Nick shifted, ready to react if she went too close to the edge of the wharf and the water. Instead, she turned into the cafe seating area, dragging a carpet bag behind her. Her gaze passed over him to the sign above the doorway, yet she stayed still. Strangely still.

Nick searched the wharf for anyone connected to this child. She couldn't be over eight years old. Surely there was a parent nearby. Or other relative. However, the wharf maintained its early morning quiet.

Slowly, so as not to startle the child, Nick rose from his table. Five careful steps brought him to her and he knelt. "Hi. My name is Dr. Matrone. What's your name?"

She cocked her head, reminding him so much of Mindy.

Nick's pulse picked up. "Where are your parents?"

One thin shoulder rose and fell.

"Are you looking for someone?" Nick's medical training pounded in his ears. The girl's gaunt face, questioning gaze, overly thin frame ... and the fact she showed no signs of desiring to talk ... he shoved his medical instincts aside. For the moment. He needed to find her people. He followed his suspicions. "Are you looking for Mindy?"

The little girl's eyes brightened. He eased out the breath that wanted to whoosh out. This child was connected to Mindy. Somehow.

"Can I help you find Mindy?" Nick held out a hand. She laid bony fingers, pale against his dark skin, in his palm. His heart constricted with a fierce protectiveness.

Mindy straightened her spine as she brought Joe Spelding his fish sandwich. He'd been back in Crow's Nest for several months now, and she managed to avoid him. Except when he came into the Wharfside.

"Here is your meal." She tried to keep a pleasant tone, not just because her boss expected it, but because she didn't want Joe to know how much his presence affected her.

"Thank you, doll." Joe winked, sending a shudder down Mindy's spine. She stepped out of reach in case he tried to grab her hand or attempt any other type of inappropriate touch, which he always tried to get away with. She hated it. Hated that she'd agreed to let him take her out on a date last summer. He thought that gave him a license she didn't want him to have.

Not that he was the only man to think that because she was a waitress, she was an easy woman. If only she didn't need this job to support her family.

"Will that be all?" she asked Joe as she gathered bowls from the table beside his.

The light in his eye warned that something lascivious was about to come out of his mouth. Mindy braced, praying her pale cheeks wouldn't turn red. Then the door opened. A murmured prayer wisped up from her heart.

Nick Matrone didn't look like the knights in shining armor that she imagined as a little girl, with his dark hair, glasses, and general bookish appearance. In this moment, she could almost image his lanky frame covered in chain mail instead of a suit, and a shield on his arm instead of a ... her gaze caught sight of the little girl clasping Nick's hand.

"Mabel?" She set the bowls on a table with an unceremonious clatter and rushed forward. She dropped to her knees in front of her baby sister. "What's wrong? Where are Mother and Father?"

Her sister looked back at her with bright blue eyes. Mindy willed her to finally speak. Yet, Mabel's lips didn't move. Then she realized Mabel's little hand was still in Nick's larger one. Her gaze ran up his arm to connect with his. She found question there, and concern. But no judgment.

"Can you come outside?" He nodded toward the door.

Mindy glanced over her shoulder and realized the entire cafe was staring at them. Heat flared up her neck, and she pushed to her feet, desperately needing to get her sister away from so many prying eyes. Her toe caught on her skirt, and Nick caught her elbow. The touch went straight to her heart. It was respectful, protective. He held the door as he ushered them outside.

"Mabel arrived alone?" Mindy searched the wharf for any sign of her parents. Her pulse pounded in her throat. Where were they? Had Mabel wandered so far from the farm? She barely left the house.

"She came with a carpetbag." He pointed to the flowered bag, which sat on the ground beside his satchel.

Mindy pressed a hand to her chest, a bad feeling welling inside. Mabel tugged Nick toward her bag, opened it, and pulled out a folded paper. She turned her wide eyes toward Mindy and held it out. Mindy took the paper, stared, unseeing, at it. Her heart hammered. Her ears filled with rushing. Then Nick was beside her, leading her toward a chair. He pressed fingers to her wrist, then raised her chin to look into her eyes. She latched onto their brown depths as if they could pull her from the spinning world.

"Sit here while I get Mabel settled." Nick ordered in his doctor tone, except he trailed his thumb along her jaw before he stepped away. It grounded her, made her feel the hard chair, the firm ground.

Yet worry sank deep as she watched Nick return from inside with a muffin for Mabel and a coffee for Mindy. How Mindy wished her sister would speak. Could speak. Never had her sweet little sister uttered a single word. Her parents refused to investigate why. Was it her hearing, her shyness, something else? Mindy would have paid for a doctor's visit herself, if only her father allowed it. Instead, her parents kept Mabel sequestered away on the farm. Hidden from the world as if she would shame the family. It broke Mindy's heart.

So how did Mabel get here, alone, and with baggage? Where were their parents? The paper crinkled in her fingers, and she caught sight of her mother's script. Father didn't approve of Mindy having a job, said the unwelcome male attention she received was because she worked as a waitress. Yet farming didn't bring enough money when her father bought bootlegged whiskey. Not a drunk like David Martin's father, he still overindulged during the slower seasons. Of course, Father would never hear of Mindy sending them money, so she secreted it to Mother. How Mother explained the money, she didn't know, though Mother gratefully made it stretch as needed.

Nick slid a chair beside her. "Do you want me to read it aloud?"

She turned away from him, so he wouldn't learn her secret. Even her mother didn't know. David did. He was the only one. Shame washed over her. If only the words didn't jump all over the page as she tried to read. She could decipher enough to get by ... however, to read a letter in front of Nick?

He covered her hands, slid the crushed paper from them. "Close your eyes, Mindy, and just listen."

She nodded, hating how much she appreciated Nick taking the decision from her. She felt like a tiny boat set out in a stormy sea and Nick the lighthouse, pulling her into a safe harbor.

"Melinda," her name rolled from him like a warm breeze. Mother never called her *Mindy*. "There is no time to say this gently. The corn crop failed. Your father has decided we will go west at once, and we cannot take Mabel with us. Please take care of her. Keep her safe. Use the money you would send me to see to her. I will write again when we settle. I love you, daughter."

Mindy stared at her sister. Her sweet, gentle, kind sister. Mabel sat at a nearby table eating the muffin as if she hadn't eaten well in days. How could she take care of her? She couldn't leave her alone in her apartment above The Barn, the local bakery. Did Mindy make enough as a waitress to provide the food and clothing Mabel needed? Did she send her to school in the fall?

"I'm sorry, Mindy." Nick's voice tugged her gaze to his. "Your parents didn't even say goodbye to you, did they?"

Her shoulders fell. So focused on Mabel, she hadn't even realized what this meant for her. Would she see her mother again?

"Do you have to finish your shift?" Nick squeezed her hands, then stood. "Never mind. As your doctor, I'm telling your boss you're taking the day off."

"Wait." She stopped him. "I can't afford to miss a shift. Especially not now."

Nick's jaw firmed, eyes narrowed. "Are you sure? You're reeling from this news. Grieving."

How did he understand emotions she had yet to identify in herself? "I need this job, Nick. I've spent too much time out here as it is. Mr. Clifford won't give me a lunch break now. No, I have to work or I'll lose my job. You understand, don't you?"

"Okay, Mindy. Yes, I understand." Nick's expression softened. "Then may I take Mabel to the clinic with me?"

"Heavens, why?" Sure, she was so silent most people didn't notice her presence, yet no one had ever volunteered to spend time with Mabel. "What's your angle, Dr. Matrone? Do you plan to fix her? Dissect her? Evaluate—"

"Mindy." He caught her shoulders. "No. Mabel doesn't need to be fixed. She's not an engine that's broken. She's a little girl whose parents left her, who no longer has a home. Like you."

Mindy blinked, and her nose tingled. "No one has ever said that before. They always wonder what's wrong with Mabel." *With me.*

Nick turned to stand beside Mindy as they both looked at her sister. "I'll ask my sister to come by to keep Mabel company. Bella loves practicing her English. And don't worry, she won't make a big deal if Mabel doesn't say anything. She's used to me letting her chatter with barely a nod in reply."

Mindy couldn't help a smile. Nick spoke so ... normally. The defensive, protective fight died right out of her, and a smile took its place. She could picture Nick with a book, rolling his eyes as Bella animatedly told a story. From what she'd seen over the past few months, they got along easily. Their teasing and lighthearted relationship was a joy to watch. It was as if they'd never been apart, though Mindy knew they hadn't seen each other in years. Bella only recently left Italy, whereas Nick had lived in New York City since he was a child.

She couldn't imagine being separated from Mabel for that long and was suddenly grateful her parents had left Mabel with her instead of taking her west with them. Though how a parent left a child behind, she didn't know. Couldn't fathom. She opened her mouth to ask—because Nick's parents had brought him with them to America when they left Italy, yet had left Bella behind with her grandmother. However, something within the cafe caught Nick's attention. In one fluid movement, he'd scooped up his satchel and Mabel's carpetbag.

"Don't worry about a thing, Mindy." His doctor's tone was back. "Focus on being a wonderful waitress, and we'll talk when you come by the clinic later."

Mindy nodded. Grateful. "All right. Thank you, Nick. Truly. I—"

Joe emerged from the cafe, calculating eyes taking in the scene. What did he think about what was going on? What assumptions did he make? Her palms turned clammy, yet she put herself between him and her sister. "Was your meal satisfactory, Mr. Spelding?"

"It would have been improved by your presence." He stepped into her personal space. Mindy raised her chin. Why did he have to be so familiar with her? "Go out with me tonight."

"No." Mindy glared at him, hoping anger could hide her quivers. "Good day, Mr. Spelding."

"You will say yes eventually, Mindy Zahn." Joe leaned forward so quickly, she barely had time to turn her head before his kiss landed on her skin. "No one tells me no for long."

Mindy kept herself from slapping the man. She needed her job too much to risk it.

She felt Nick's gaze. Would he think her loose like everyone else? Needing to know, even as she feared the truth, she raised her eyes. Not judgment. Deep concern warred with anger. Did she want him to step in or stay beside her sister? She subtly shook her head and squared off with Joe. Mabel was more important. A minor discomfort was worth keeping Joe's focus and avoiding a further scene with Mabel at the center. Mindy was used to being mistreated.

"I need to return to work." Mindy backed toward the door, wishing she could tell Mabel all would be okay. "Good day, Mr. Spelding."

Prayer didn't come naturally, yet as she entered the dim interior of the Wharfside, one poured out. She thanked God for Nick, then begged God to protect Mabel and their parents. She needed wisdom and the ability to provide for her sister. A customer called, and while she went through the motions of work, she silently added to her requests, hoping God was listening to a woman like her. Her friend Adaleigh said God heard her. Mindy Zahn. How she hoped Adaleigh was right, because Mindy never wanted her prayers answered as much as she did this day.

The morning slogged into afternoon. She repeated prayer after prayer. Demands and innuendos fell aside. They were nothing compared to the growing whirlwind of thoughts in her mind. The reality that Mabel now depended upon her. How would Mindy be what her sister needed? She'd made so many mistakes. She wasn't smart or savvy or book-learned. It seemed her smile and pretty face were her only assets. At least according to Willie Clifford, the Wharfside owner, and most of the customers.

Would that be enough? It had to be. She wouldn't fail her sister. Right now, she needed to trust Nick to keep her little sister safe.

# CHAPTER TWO

Later that afternoon, Nick leaned against the doorframe leading to the waiting area of his clinic, watching his sister interact with Mabel. Two opposites in every way. Bella moved constantly, her hands, her body, her mouth. She was tall and lean like him, a long, thick braid hung over her shoulder. She wore a simple, bland dress—showing their family's lack of financial standing—the only item not dynamic about her. Even though she'd just arrived from Italy, she jumped at the chance to accompany him to Wisconsin. While their parents had hoped to have both children close by for the first time in almost two decades, New York City tenements were no place for a vibrant young woman like Bella.

Over the course of the day, Bella had lapsed into Italian. The musical tones made Nick smile. He missed hearing it every day and all around him. For all the challenges that came with his heritage, he was proud of it. He was born into an Italian family and could thank God for that. He loved the emphasis on family and community. Admired his parents for their determination and sacrifice in leaving the homeland to give their children a better life. Even if Bella didn't get to join them until last fall. A few bad apples, who newspapers and bigots used to paint the entire Italian community, shouldn't make him ashamed of who God made him.

Mabel didn't seem to mind Bella's change from English to Italian. She sat in her chair, perfectly still, wide eyes watching Bella's every move. Though he told Mindy he didn't invite the little girl here to analyze her, he couldn't turn that part of his medical mind off. He watched Mabel's gaze, attempting to pinpoint exactly what she looked for in Bella.

From Nick's angle, it seemed like the little girl watched Bella's eyes most of all. That encouraged him. He'd seen a dozen mute children over the years. Many times it was because of deafness or disinterest in the world around them. With Mabel, she watched too closely, tense yet not wanting to draw any notice. He wanted to ask Mindy questions about her sister. Had she ever spoken before? Had she gone to school? Did she read?

He wouldn't, though. It didn't take a mathematician to see that she was incredibly protective of her little sister, and in no way did Nick want to break the trust she placed in him this morning. However, perhaps he could earn Mindy's confidence enough that she would eventually seek his medical advice about her sister. Not that he was an expert or thought he had a cure, but perhaps together they could help Mabel find her voice.

The door opened and his standing three o'clock appointment walked in. Nick straightened, as he always did when in the company of Buck Wilson, head of the Crow's Nest Conglomerate. The man was impeccably dressed in a finely tailored suit. He commanded authority wherever he went, yet he kept a relaxed air that said he had everything under control.

Bella's story slowed as she watched Buck cross the room. The man offered a congenial smile, gaze darting to Mabel, before he returned his attention to Nick. Bella waited another beat before continuing the story she was telling Mabel. Nick hadn't made an opinion of Buck yet, but he was grateful the man didn't seem interested in his sister. Bella, however, watched all the bachelor men in town, making Nick itch at the thought of someone asking her on a date.

"I'll hold my questions." Buck shook Nick's hand, drawing Nick away from his brotherly protectiveness. Nick nodded, then raised his arm in an invitation to go down the hall to his office.

The clinic was originally operated by Dr. Thompson, a hawkish man stuck in the old ways. The man's prejudice against Nick was obvious the first time they met. He looked down his nose at Nick's heritage, his youth, his newfangled ideas. Used to being judged by his nationality, Nick had expected it when he first approached Dr. Thompson. He downplayed himself to a point just shy of groveling. It was enough that Dr. Thompson allowed him to work beside him in the clinic to see a few patients, particularly the ones Dr. Thompson hadn't wanted to treat. Nick put up with it because it was a temporary arrangement and allowed him to help his friends.

Upon his return to New York City this past Christmas, he saw his old partner in a new light thanks to Dr. Thompson's treatment. It sank into his hide like a thorn. So when he was again needed in Crow's Nest, he sold his half of the business and moved permanently to Crow's Nest. Then with Dr. Thompson's recent nefarious activities, Nick inherited the practice in full.

However, not everyone liked having an Italian doctor, or a younger doctor, or a new doctor. It was partly why Buck had set up these appointments. He wanted the town to know he approved of Nick. Though Nick couldn't quite understand why the man went out of his way to make such a point.

Instead of following Nick's direction, Buck turned into the last exam room across from Nick's office. Surprised, Nick followed him in and closed the door. "Are we not discussing your attempt at finding the mole within the Conglomerate?"

Buck lifted himself to the exam table and shook his head. "I need some medical advice." A pinkish hue covered his ears.

"You came to the right place." Nick purposefully relaxed, hoping it would set Buck at ease.

"Since my step-brother returned from prison, I haven't been sleeping." Buck pressed his palms to the table on either side of his body, as if voicing this was physically painful. "Joe is a criminal and having him in my house ..."

Only practice kept Nick from reacting. Buck's step-brother was none other than Joe Spelding, and after seeing the way the scoundrel treated Mindy today, he wanted to do more than simply express his complete agreement that the man was a criminal.

"I don't trust him." Buck sagged. "When he's in my house, my ears are attuned to every movement. When he's gone, I'm waiting for bad news."

Nick nodded to keep Buck talking.

When the man raised his head, Nick nearly gaped. Buck's mask was gone. Haggard lines marred his face. Black shadows showed beneath his eyes. The man was exhausted.

"Having Joe close allows me to keep an eye on him. It's taking its toll. I can't remember the last time I slept a whole night. Then this morning, I experienced this tightness around my ribs. I'm not one to run to the doctor ..." Buck's chin dropped to his chest.

"There's nothing to be ashamed of for seeking medical help, Buck." Nick had told many a man that, though so often they came to him when it was too late. "Let's give you an exam, then go from there."

Buck gave a defeated sigh. "Thanks, Doc."

Twenty minutes later, he'd detected no medical reason for Buck's condition. "I could give you a clean bill of health; however, I won't because, if you continue with so little sleep, you'll be back in here with an actual medical condition. That means we need to address the reason you're not sleeping."

"We?" Buck buttoned his shirt, giving Nick a sardonic smirk.

Nick shrugged. "I don't use the term to couch the word *you*. I really mean *we*."

Buck slid from the table. "What do you have against Joe?"

"Picked up on that, did you?" Nick set aside his stethoscope and crossed his arms. "He's harassing Mindy Zahn, and I don't want Bella to catch his eye."

A gleam lit Buck's eyes, washing away the dark circles. "Mindy, hmm? You watch her unlike other men do."

A strange tension crawled up his neck. He lifted his glasses to scrub his face. "I try to catch myself because I know how she feels about the way men treat her. I admit, I do watch her, which means I'm a cad and no better than them."

"Did you not hear me?" Buck shrugged into his suit coat. "*Unlike*, man. *Un-like*. As in you have respect in your eyes. You're not staring at her ... well ... it's not lust that I see. You're curious, like you want to know her as a person."

Nick leaned against the wall, letting it brace him. "I do. She's an amazing woman. She brings laughter and light to those around her. Always selfless and caring. She makes tough days enjoyable just by being."

Buck raised an eyebrow. "You going to ask her out, then?"

"No." Nick shook his head to emphasize what he knew deep down. "I couldn't do that to her."

Buck slid his hands into his pockets, the head of the Conglomerate persona returning. "Want to know why I made this standing appointment? Because you might not like me, you might not trust me, you might believe like everyone else that I am indeed a criminal, but you don't let that get in the way. I can respect that."

Nick pushed from the wall and opened the door, not wanting Buck to see how his words pierced. They should be a compliment, and they were, but it also touched that raw place in his heart. Why he left New York.

"So, is it patient confidentiality, or can you tell me why Mindy's little sister was in your waiting room?"

A laugh jumped from Nick's throat. Buck was back in usual form. However, the glimpse was enough to wonder who the real Buck Wilson happened to be.

Mindy stopped outside the clinic and allowed herself a moment to fold. Her shoulders sank, her vision blurred, her heart bled. Her parents had left. Mabel's care was now hers alone. Was Nick a man she could trust? She hesitated. What if he treated her sister like a curiosity? What if he wanted to dig into why she didn't speak? Sure, Mindy would love to understand, but not at the expense of turning Mabel into a circus act. Right now, she wasn't sure she could take one more disappointment.

The door swung open before Mindy was ready to face what she'd find inside. Laughter drifted out. Female laughter. Surely not her sister's, though she had never heard Mabel laugh.

"Miss Zahn." Buck Wilson held the door open. "I assume you're here for your sister."

Mindy narrowed her gaze at the man. David's uncle was investigating Buck for criminal involvement. Detective O'Connor had yet to find proof and Buck had shown himself willing to help her friends, however Mindy wasn't about to trust that Buck wasn't hiding something. He was Joe Spelding's brother, after all. Mindy had a horrible track record for trusting the right men.

"Dr. Matrone didn't say a word. Neither did Miss Matrone. Your sister looks just like you, so it was an easy guess." Buck's smile was strangely genuine. "If you have need of anything, please tell me."

Mindy cocked her head, trying to understand the reason for Buck's offer. "Did Nick tell you about Mr. Spelding?"

"Only his own reaction to what my step-brother did." Buck slid his hands into his pockets, using his back to keep the door open. "Since I know Joe won't do it, I'd like to extend my own apologies on Joe's behalf."

Mindy stared at him.

"If there was anything I could do to change his behavior, I would." The dapper man sighed. "You have a good day now, and tell me if you need anything."

Mindy watched him until he entered the Conglomerate headquarters a block or so down Main Street, then entered the clinic. Nick was nowhere in sight. Mabel sat on a chair beside Bella Matrone.

Bella's laugh was what she'd heard from outside. The young woman laughed again, then patted Mabel's knee. "*Grazie mille, Paperotta.* I very much enjoyed talking with you."

Mindy took a step back, surprised, not at the sincerity in Bella's tone, but at how grateful she sounded. As if Mabel listening was a blessing to *her*.

Bella leapt to her feet and snagged Mindy's hands, a string of Italian words on her tongue. She broke off and shook her head. "I forget to use English when I am happy. Your sister is delightful, and I do hope I have not bored her with my chattering. Niccolo can only listen for so long. Mabel never took her gaze off of me. She is a sweet brave, little one."

Mindy didn't know what to say. She wholeheartedly agreed. Yet she was usually the only one who thought so, and even then, her desire to protect her sister likely didn't allow Mabel to stretch her wings. However, the world was a cruel place, and she wanted to shield her sister from it for as long as she could.

"Mindy!" Nick emerged from the back, looking relieved. "Did the rest of your day turn out okay?"

She didn't exactly want to talk about it. "It is done." She forced a smile. Nick adjusted his glasses, and she suspected he didn't quite believe her.

Mabel slipped her little hand into Mindy's and leaned her head on Mindy's arm. What was she going to do with her now? They'd go home to the apartment above The Barn ... then what?

The Matrone siblings exchanged a look, then Nick stepped forward. "Would you be willing to discuss ways we could help you?"

Mindy glanced back and forth between the pair. "What do you mean?"

Nick stuck his thumbs into his vest pockets. "I have an idea, but it will take a conversation."

Mindy tapped a tired foot. She really just wanted to get home and take off her shoes. "You're speaking cryptically. Explain?"

Again, Nick looked to his sister. This time, Bella spoke. "Tell her the plan, Niccolo. Then we will get permission from everyone else."

"Everyone else?" Mindy's heart cinched, and she tightened her hold on Mabel's hand.

"I don't want to get your hopes up and then disappoint you." Nick rocked on his heels. "There has been so much house shuffling since Gilbert and Marian left, what with David and I taking Mrs.

Whittlebush's house until he and Adaleigh get married, and Samantha going west so Bella could have her room. With Patrick and Meri living in the Ward's old house, that leaves his room open at the Martins home. Adaleigh lives there, and I know you two are friends. So I thought, perhaps, Mrs. Martins could offer you a place to stay, too. You and Mabel wouldn't even need to share a room."

"Mabel could stay with me while you work," Bella jumped in. "I took *Signora* Whittlebush's seamstress clients, so I occasionally have a customer to speak to. But mostly I sew alone. Maybe Mabel would like to help me."

Mindy looked down at her sister. Would Mabel want to learn to sew? She knelt, noting again how small her sister was, shorter than most children her age, including both of Marian's girls, who were a bit younger than Mabel. "What do you think of the Matrone's plan?" Mindy asked her. Would this be her first word?

"We need to get Mrs. Martins's approval." Nick hedged. Mindy knew the older woman, David's grandmother, and had no doubt she would welcome Mindy and Mabel with open arms.

The more she considered the idea, the more she desired it. To live under Mrs. Martins's roof, to share a home with Adaleigh—until she married. It brought peace to her soul. "Should we stay with David's grandmother?" she asked Mabel again. The little girl had met David a couple times, since he and Mindy were childhood friends.

Mabel's eyes lit up, and she nodded.

Mindy grinned. She pulled Mabel into a hug, hope taking root. Then she remembered her prayers from earlier. Was this God's answer? Had He really heard her? She raised her gaze to Nick. He was watching them with a look of tenderness that stalled her breath. Then he blinked, caught her watching, and looked away.

"Can we move them tonight?" Bella bounced and clapped.

Nick groaned, but his smile betrayed his teasing. "Only if David helps me. It's really up to Mindy."

Bella dropped to her knees to encompass both Mindy and Mabel in her arms. "Say *sí*, do say *sí*!"

"We need to talk to Mrs. Martins, Bella," Nick warned.

Bella waved him off. "You worry too much, *il mio fratello*. *Signora* Martins will love this idea. I know it."

"Your brother does have a point." Mindy pushed to her feet. For the second time that day, Nick caught her elbow to help her stand. She noted he didn't do that for Bella when she jumped to her feet. "It's Friday evening. I work half a day tomorrow. Perhaps afterward, we can move my belongings. Anyway, my lease is week by week, and I've already paid for next week."

"*Signora* Martins will understand." Bella crossed her arms. "Ask her before you make plans."

"A wise idea." Nick reached around the desk that sat in the corner of the waiting room, returning with both his satchel and Mabel's carpetbag. "Allow me to escort everyone to the Martinses' home."

Bella clapped again, then held out a hand toward Mabel. "Walk with me, Paperotta? Or maybe we will skip. It is not *signorile*, ah, being a lady, but I am happy. Let us skip."

Mabel's eyes danced and the hint of a smile peaked out, like a single ray cutting through stormy clouds. It struck Mindy and melted her.

"She's happy." Nick's voice rumbled in her ear. Mindy nodded, unable to speak. He held out his elbow. "May I, Miss Zahn?"

Mindy accepted his escort, surprised at the muscle she felt under his suit coat sleeve. She was used to farmers and fishermen. Braun and muscle, weathered faces and calloused hands. On the surface, Nick didn't appear like any of those things. She wondered now, as he locked up the clinic, whether she had misjudged him. Not that she ever thought ill of him. Quite the opposite. She'd always appreciated him. He seemed to save the day more often than not. A knight for most of her friends. Was Nick all he seemed?

"You never answered my question." Did he move closer to her? "How was your day?"

"Like all my others." The truth in that made her cringe. "I'm grateful for my job. Remember how Marian couldn't find one? I shouldn't complain."

He gave a noncommittal hum. "Do you enjoy working as a waitress?"

Ahead of them, Bella was indeed skipping. Mindy had never discovered how old Nick's sister was. One minute she seemed all beauty and sophistication, the next she was skipping like a little girl. Mabel walked beside her, hand-in-hand, Bella skipping slow enough that Mabel didn't need to even trot to keep up.

"Mindy?" Nick's laugh tangled with her name.

"I don't know how to answer." Mindy shrugged. What else could she do? "I've never considered enjoying my job to have anything to do with doing it."

But the question made her think of a conversation she'd had with Adaleigh last year. She'd told Adaleigh that she dreamed of opening her own cafe one day. A dream, that's all it was.

"Girls like me don't have the choices others might, and now I have my sister to consider." The bitterness that seeped through made her eyes sting. "And you? Why did you leave your practice in New York to live in little old Crow's Nest?"

They turned toward Lake Michigan. The clanging of boats mixed with the caw of seagulls. The breeze had picked up since this morning, causing ripples to spread out from shore and providing relief from the heat. After a long winter, it felt like the perfect day. Her feet slowed of their own accord, Nick coming to a halt beside her. She couldn't help closing her eyes, and for just a moment, breathing in the fishy air.

"Perhaps this is why I chose to return." Nick broke into the moment, not disrupting it, adding to it. "The city is close, cloying, dirty. Here is fresh air and peace."

"You've found peace?" Mindy wanted it, wasn't sure she'd ever had it.

"Not yet." He lowered his arm, her hand slipping away. She felt the loss. Was he purposefully putting distance between them? Was she being too forward? Then he wove his fingers between hers. "I'm searching for it, and this seemed like the place to find it."

"Do you think it can be found?" She didn't dare move, afraid he'd realize he held her hand as he did, yet needing to know. "Do you think God hears us?"

Nick was silent for a long time. Bella and Mabel were nearly out of sight now. Still, Mindy didn't want the moment to end. Wanted to know Nick's answer. Did he think her foolish? Maybe she should—

Nick squeezed her fingers. "I pray the answer is yes, or we'll be searching for a lifetime."

# CHAPTER THREE

Why had he taken Mindy's hand?

Nick backed into a corner of Mrs. Martins's kitchen to stay out of the flurry of females. As he expected, Mrs. Martins opened her home to Mindy and Mabel with great enthusiasm. The short, round older lady reminded him of his own nonna. Late nonna. She hadn't survived last year's earthquake in Italy. Before that, he'd harbored no hopes of seeing her again, yet she'd always been there. A person to write. A person who prayed. Again it reminded him of Mrs. Martins.

Another commonality she had with his nonna was her smile, which bloomed when Mrs. Martins learned Mindy wished to move into her home. Nonna would have felt the same, her aged face wrinkling with years of laughter and difficulty. Where Mrs. Martins had a bob of silvery hair, the last he saw of Nonna, she'd had black curls with just a hint of gray threads. It'd been a long time.

"Help yourself to coffee, Dr. Matrone." Mrs. Martins waved at her electric stove. Adaleigh's Christmas gift to her soon-to-be grandmother-in-law. "It will take me a few minutes to get the girls settled. Don't you dare rush off. You will stay for supper."

Nick winked. "I wouldn't dream of it, Signora Martins."

"Good." She gave a decisive nod. "You don't eat here enough. Even with your sister living here."

"Sí, signora." Nick bowed his head, knowing when to defer, thanks to his own mamma's training.

Mrs. Martins snorted, then narrowed her eyes. "You put up no fight. Why?"

"It is because he knows better, *Signora* Martins." Bella came to his rescue, hooking her arm through Mrs. Martins's. "When it comes to food, Mamma is queen."

An odd light lit in the older lady's eye. The kind of sparkle that put Nick on alert. She patted Bella's hand. "Is that so?"

Bella tossed her head back with a laugh. "If you tell him to appear for a meal, he will be here. Unless a patient needs him."

"Bella," Nick groaned. It was a half-hearted protest. Honestly? He was lonely, and the idea of sharing meals with a large family, especially if Mindy happened to be a part of the gathering, held too much of a draw. More than was good for him.

"It is settled, then." Mrs. Martins wagged a finger at him. "You will eat supper here every day."

Bella grinned like a cat who had gotten her way. Nick folded his arms and watched the pair disappear up the stairs, where Adaleigh had led Mindy and Mabel. What was Bella—and Mrs. Martins—up to that they considered Nick's presence at supper a triumph?

Silence settled until the front door opened and closed. The footsteps were familiar to him since he heard them every morning well before even the summer sun rose. David Martins halted as he reached his grandmother's kitchen. "I wasn't expecting to see you here. Did Grandma finally convince you to stay for supper?"

Nick frowned. "I didn't realize she'd been asking." Is that why Bella and Mrs. Martins were so thrilled?

David crossed to the breadbox and pulled out a loaf. "She's been asking me why I don't bring you more often. I'm sorry I haven't. I suppose I've been distracted." Red crept up his clean-shaved face.

Nearly as lean as Nick, they could be brothers, except David was brown-haired and, while weathered from fishing the open waters day after day, rather fair compared to Nick's dark skin. Nick couldn't help glancing at his own hands before shoving them into his pockets. He wasn't ashamed of being Italian. He just wished others didn't jump to conclusions based simply on his coloring.

"You okay?" David sliced off a piece of bread. "What brings you here, anyway?"

Nick shook off the hurts of the past. "Mindy and her sister are moving in upstairs."

David held the knife in one hand, bread in the other. "Her sister? Mabel? She's here?"

"You know her?" Nick shouldn't be surprised. Mindy and David were well-known as friends. In fact, from what Nick had gathered, most townspeople were surprised the two had never married. Though, when they met Adaleigh and saw her and David together, wise nods ensued. David had chosen well. Nick hadn't decided if it was a slight against Mindy. She deserved to have an honorable man choose her, too.

"Mabel?" David put away the loaf and knife. "I've met her a few times. Adorable and sweet. She hasn't left the Zahn farm in years."

"Why not?"

David leaned a hip on the table close to Nick and lowered his voice. "Because she doesn't speak. Her parents sequestered her on the farm."

Nick bristled. "That's not how to help her. There's usually a reason a child doesn't talk. From my observation today, it's not—"

"You promised you wouldn't evaluate my sister." Mindy's voice sliced into his words. She stormed across the living space and into the kitchen area, fire in her eyes. "I trusted you! You told me you'd look out for her. Not treat her like a ... a ..."

"Specimen under a microscope?" Nick folded his arms against the sting of her words. "I didn't. But I can't help my medical training. I can't just shut it off. If you'd let me finish."

"No." Her eyes turned watery. "David, escort him out."

"Mindy."

She stomped away. Nick sighed and stared at the ceiling. If she'd have let him finish, he would have told her how he thought Mabel was smart. Observant. She saw much more than anyone thought she did. It wasn't that she could not physically speak. She did not speak for another reason, and Nick couldn't deny wanting to know why.

"You don't have to leave." David had finished his bread, concern turned to worry. "That wasn't like Mindy, but her sister is a sore spot for her. She's protective of her."

"I don't want to upset either of them." Nick made his way down the hall, David at his heels. "I have a feeling now she won't ask for my help in moving her belongings. If you need a hand, I'll make myself available."

David clapped him on the shoulder. "I'm sorry, Nick."

Nick shrugged as if it didn't hurt. Said goodbye as if the old pain didn't rear its head. He wandered alone to a bench overlooking Lake Michigan. He'd sat here a couple of times before. Now the horizon called to him like it did back in New York City. As if he could see Italy across the water. He was young when his parents brought him to the United States. Most days he didn't even sound Italian. Of course Mamma could only speak Italian, so he was fluent in both his old and new languages. He could still remember Nonna's house back in the old country. When he became heartsore, he longed for those idyllic days most of all.

He'd hoped moving to Crow's Nest, with its small town community and friendly neighbors, would offset what had happened back in New York. He also couldn't deny that Mindy was another reason he'd wanted to return. She intrigued him. More than he should allow. He wasn't the man for her. Wasn't worthy of her. If he doubted it, his failure to abide by her wishes confirmed it.

Of course, he hadn't intentionally broken his promise. That was the crux of the matter. He didn't intentionally do anything of which he was accused. It was simply inherent to *who* he was. He was simply too dark. Too not-American. Too much of a physician. *He* was too much of the wrong things.

As the evening sky turned purple overhead, the lake before him reflected the beauty of the sunset. Mindy had asked him if God heard them. He had no doubt God heard Mindy. She was sweetness itself. Would God listen to the likes of him?

He rested his elbows on his knees, head in his hands. "*Padre nostro,* I ask for the peace only You can give. I'm not worthy, but You never asked us to be worthy. I need You tonight. To heal me. To strengthen me. Be with Mindy and Mabel. Amen."

He didn't move. Let the warm night air wash over him. As if on the wind, he could hear his mamma's voice reciting a verse from the Bible. *Quindi, non siate tristi, non abbiate paura. Don't be sad. Don't be afraid.* Nick breathed out, ran his hands down his face, and looked out over the water. It had turned black as night settled over Crow's Nest.

Peace did not settle in his heart. If anything, an urgency lit his spirit. He knew this feeling, had experienced it before. It was a warning. More trouble was coming to Crow's Nest. As the lone doctor in town, he needed to be ready.

Mindy ran her fingers over Mabel's blonde hair as she sat beside her on the soft bed in what used to be Patrick's room. Her sister had finally fallen asleep. Still, Mindy couldn't leave her. While Mabel hadn't shed a tear, she tossed and turned, her little brow furrowed, and an odd murmur slipping from her usually silent lips. Was she trying to speak in her restlessness?

With Mabel's chest falling in an ever deepening rhythm, Mindy finally convinced herself to rise. Crossing the hall to Samantha's old room, she lifted the letter her mother had sent with Mabel. She wanted to read it again. If only the letters didn't jump on the page under the lantern light. Tossing the paper aside, she unfolded the nightgown Adaleigh had left for her.

"Mindy?" Before she could change, Adaleigh's voice came through the closed door, followed by a soft knock.

Mindy wanted to ignore her friend, yet couldn't turn away the kindness. Especially after the way she had treated Nick. She'd probably overreacted. At least, David thought she had. Adaleigh hadn't offered an opinion over supper. Bella had remained strangely quiet. Mrs. Martins covered the awkwardness with conversation.

"Mindy?" Adaleigh opened the door. "I was listening for you to leave Mabel's room. It took so long, I thought maybe you'd fallen asleep in there."

Adaleigh was strong, friendly, confident ... all the things Mindy wished she could be. Frankly, it would be easy to envy her friend if the woman hadn't arrived looking so lost. Of course, she'd tried to hide it that day Mindy met her. Sitting in the Wharfside with David's great uncle, Detective O'Connor, after she saved a little boy from drowning. Sopping wet and determined to speak for herself. Mindy recognized the look in her eye. When David had shown interest in Adaleigh, Mindy made an effort to be Adaleigh's friend.

What Mindy hadn't expected was how much Adaleigh appreciated being her friend in return.

They couldn't be more different. Adaleigh's brown hair to Mindy's blonde. Adaleigh's penchant for pushing limits, riding a motorcycle, and having absolutely no figure that men could ogle. Unlike Mindy, who seemed to draw unwanted attention like sugar drew bees.

"Is this the letter you mentioned at supper?" Adaleigh picked up the paper Mindy had tossed aside.

Instead of snatching it away from her friend, she nodded. Perhaps Adaleigh would read it aloud without Mindy having to ask for help.

"The corn crop failed." Adaleigh tapped the letter. "Were your parents that hard off that they couldn't recover from that?"

"We've had lean years. It's why I work at the cafe. Father drinks, but not like Mr. Martins." Mindy sank onto the bed. "I didn't realize they were even considering moving."

Adaleigh sat beside her, brows furrowed. Again, she tapped the letter. "Why would your mom specifically ask you to keep your sister safe?"

"It's what Mabel needs us to do. She can't talk." Mindy's ire rose. "People don't understand."

Adaleigh was shaking her head. "I'm sorry, Mindy, I think Nick was right. It's not that Mabel can't talk. Something is stopping her."

Mindy stared at her friend. "You're taking his side? You examined Mabel, too?"

Adaleigh set the paper down on the bed and grabbed Mindy's hands.

"Nick and I ... we have training. We went to school. We—"

"You're smarter than me. I get it." Mindy jumped to her feet to hide the sheen of tears that blurred her vision. "I'm just a dumb waitress whose only use is for men to desire me, then toss me aside."

"This isn't like you. Where's this coming from?"

"I'm going home." Mindy snatched up her purse and stuffed the letter inside. "I'll try to return before Mabel wakes up in the morning."

Adaleigh followed her down the steps. "Just stay here, Mindy. There's no reason to go anywhere. Not this late."

Mindy ignored her, too churned up inside to listen. Why she felt betrayed, she couldn't quite understand. That made her feel even less intelligent than her inability to read her mother's letter. Remembering the letter made her feel even lower. Her parents hadn't even bothered to say goodbye.

Adaleigh slipped in front of her, barring the front door. "You can't go without an escort."

A humorless laugh escaped her throat. "You go out all the time without an escort. Why can't I?" Then she pushed past her so-called friend.

More tears blurred her path as she navigated the darkness toward The Barn. She knew she was wrong. Knew the reason she snapped at Adaleigh was because she was right. David was right. Nick was right. But the pain in Mindy's heart hurt so much she couldn't help lashing out at them. Couldn't stop the intense need to shelter her sister. Their parents had abandoned them. She would never, *never* do that to her sister.

Her feet hit the wooden boards of the wharf, and she laughed. Never abandon her sister? Lord have mercy. What was she doing this very instant?

The tears dripped down her cheeks, and the warm summer breeze caressed them away. As her mother would have done when Mindy was a child. Yet Mindy was no longer a child. No matter that she was acting like one.

But her parents didn't even say goodbye.

A sob caught her unawares. She hiccupped as it shook her shoulders. Boats bobbed on the water to her left. Light filtered from the Lightning Bug to her right. Her father would have liked the Lightning Bug. A place everyone knew sold Prohibition alcohol. Even the most honest detective she knew, David's great uncle, Detective O'Connor, didn't stop it.

The darkness pressed in. Shoving away her friends was not the way to combat this situation. She needed to rely on them. Trust them to have her back the way she had theirs over the last year. Being a waitress put her in a strategic position to hear gossip and spread the truth. It was time to let her friends return the favor.

If they'd be willing after the way Mindy pushed them away.

Is that why Mother and Father left without a word? Had she pushed them away so that they wanted nothing to do with her anymore? Had they told her about the financial struggles on the farm, and she not heard them? She couldn't send any more money home than she did or she would have tried. She would have taken a second job if there was one to be had. Why not tell her? Why leave Mabel behind? Did they think Mindy—an unmarried waitress—could provide for her mute sister any better than they could?

Though math wasn't any more her subject than reading, even she could see something didn't add up right. Like someone ordering a coffee and muffin and only paying for the coffee. She could add that math in her head, like she remembered every order. Things with her parents did not equal the correct amount.

What could she do about it? Other than not allowing the hurt to impact her friendships. She had a lot of apologies to make in the morning.

Equilibrium returning, she looked up and down the wharf. Did she return to the Martinses' home or go to her own? She was halfway between them both. Home made the most sense. She could begin packing her things, continue working through the muddle in her mind, then return to see her sister before Mabel woke. She could sleep tomorrow after her shift.

Decision made, and feeling calmer because of it, she continued along the wharf. Past the Wharfside and David's fishing shanty next door. Past Sweetie's Ice Cream parlor. She'd have to take Mabel there. She reached The Barn, the town's bakery, and slipped down the shadowy alley to the rear stairs that led to the upper rooms. The rickety steps climbed the outside wall, allowing entrance after hours, although there was another entrance inside since Mrs. Collins, the plump older woman who owned The Barn, also lived upstairs, along with a handful of other unmarried women.

She liked Mrs. Collins. The boisterous widow of a dairy farmer, she treated her customers like the children she never had. Mindy had never doubted her welcome. For Mabel's sake, she'd give up her apartment.

Hand on the railing, foot on the first step, the hairs on the back of her neck rose. Weird. Joe Spelding and the handsy customers aside, she'd never actually felt unsafe living here, essentially alone. Sure, the last year had seen its share of danger and crime, but most of it had been brought in or churned up by those who did not live in Crow's Nest. Like Adaleigh. And the Wards, who had all moved to Montana, surely took any trouble with them. Except there was Joe. He was a criminal.

The thought of the sleazy man sneaking up on her in the middle of the night snapped her into motion. Up the stairs, she flew. Only for someone to grab her arm and fling her down the five steps she'd climbed.

She covered her head as her body bounced down the stairs. Each bump created a bruise along her back and sides. Hitting the bottom was blessed relief, though the world around her spun.

"Where is your father?" Someone—a man wearing a bandana over his face and a stocking cap pulled low to hide his hair—yanked her to her feet, gripping her bruised arms in the strongest grip she'd ever felt. He shook her. "Tell me where to find your father."

She whimpered. "He went west."

The brute lifted her off her feet. "Then where is that little girl? The one always skulking about where she shouldn't be?"

Mabel? This man wanted Mabel?

"Useless woman." The man threw her to the ground. Her hip, then her shoulder, then her head hit the dirt, sending pain ricocheting through her body. The man followed it up with a kick to her stomach. "Tell me where to find your father."

Mindy struggled to draw in a breath as he kicked her again.

"Where is the girl?" the man demanded in time with another steel toe to her ribs.

Mindy curled in on herself, covering her head and hiding her belly.

"She doesn't know anything." Another man spoke behind her. "Just leave her."

"Boss won't like it if we don't return with answers." He kicked at her shins. Stepped over her as if she were only a stone in the street. "I will get answers."

"Suit yourself." The second man sounded as if he didn't care what the brute did. "If you kill her, you'll never get answers."

*Kill her?* Mindy tried to think through the pain and fear. She couldn't leave Mabel unprotected. She couldn't abandon her sister any more than she already had because of her own foolishness. How could she escape these men alive?

"Then leave, if my methods disgust your sensibilities." The brute kicked her back, causing her to arch in pain. She'd never forget his voice. His vicious determination. "Tell me where the girl is, or you die."

*Lord, please render me unconscious to keep me quiet. Mute, like Mabel, to protect my baby sister.*

It was the oddest prayer she ever thought she'd pray, yet she repeated it over and over as the man's kicks became stronger, more frustrated. She had no hope of a rescue, not after the way she'd treated her friends. They didn't even know where to find her, or that trouble had found her.

Wait. Was this what her mother meant by keeping Mabel safe? Had their parents fled the farm, not because the crop failed, but because her father got in trouble with the wrong people? Then why desert their girls to face the consequences alone?

Alone.

Alone.

Not alone. *God, are you the One Who Hears? Will you answer my prayer?*

Her body was all sharp, pounding pain. Her ears rushed, and the world spun so that she'd ceased to keep her eyes open.

"You absolutely worthless woman!" The man spat on her, and then leveled the hard toe of his shoe directly into her cheek.

*Thank you, Lord* ... The whisper of gratitude seeped from her heart as she let her body drift into unconscious darkness. God had heard.

# CHAPTER FOUR

The ringing of the telephone broke into their conversation.

After Nick's time by the lake, he'd returned to Mrs. Whittlebush's former house to find David already there waiting for him. They sat in Mrs. Whittlebush's kitchen—it would always be Mrs. Whittlebush's to Nick—and talked about superficial things. The warm weather. How the fish were biting. The latest news from Montana.

Silas, David's cowboy friend, and Cora, Mrs. Whittlebush's great niece, were expecting their first baby. After Cora's health struggles, Nick couldn't be happier for them. Would Silas's sister-in-law and her new husband, Gilbert Cox, be next to give her two little girls a sibling? David had also sent his little sister Samantha with the Cox Family and Mrs. Whittlebush for a new start out west. He hid his concern for his sister well, yet Nick saw through him.

David stood to answer the telephone. "At this time of night, whoever is calling is probably looking for you." Usually David was sound asleep by now, since he had to rise so early to captain his fishing boat. Nick suspected David stayed up since Nick's mood had turned so dark. And Nick didn't have the heart to send his friend away.

Nick leaned back in his chair. "If it's your brother, asking if that little boy of his should still be waking them every two hours, tell him a healthy six-week old needs to eat." While the child, baby Samuel, wasn't Patrick's by natural means, the former irresponsible Martins brother had taken to fatherhood with all the enthusiasm Patrick had been lacking. Much to Nick's amusement and occasional annoyance. The man asked more questions than Meri, who adapted to all the monumental changes in her life with surprising grace.

David chuckled and answered the telephone, leaning close to the cone sticking out of the wooden box, ear cone close to his ear. "Adaleigh, darling, slow down. What is it?"

Nick sat up, watching his friend closely for what action would be needed. David made eye contact with him, the kind that said an emergency played out. He grabbed the keys to Mrs. Whittlebush's car, once again grateful the older lady had sold Adaleigh so many of her belongings and that Adaleigh could afford to purchase them.

"Nick is getting his medical bag, and we'll be out the door." David leaned close to the telephone. "I love you."

An ache twisted Nick's heart. The surety in David's tone, that someone loved him as much as he loved her, it increased the lonely feeling that had been growing over the last year. Instead of dwelling on it, he allowed his medical training to take over. All efficient business. He had his bag and was halfway to the car by the time David jogged up beside him.

"It's Mindy." David clasped Nick's shoulder to draw him to a halt. "She was attacked outside her apartment."

"What?" For the first time since he witnessed his first death as a doctor, Nick froze.

"She and Adaleigh had a fight, and Mindy went home alone." David's jaw clenched. "My fault. I shouldn't have pushed Mindy."

"About how she treated me?" Nick lifted his glasses to squeeze the bridge of his nose. He shouldn't have let her pain get to him, either.

"Adaleigh followed her, arrived as the muggers ran away."

Nick absorbed the words, knew he needed to get moving, however something held him. Something—he pointed at David with the hand that held the keys. "I'm dropping you off at your grandmother's. Call your uncle to meet me at the clinic." Then he was in motion again.

David slid into the passenger seat as Nick started the old Ford. "You think her mom's letter meant to keep her sister safe in a literal sense?"

Nick nodded, accelerating along the dark, empty streets, the two round headlights slicing through the shadows. "It's bothered me since I read it. The whole letter did. I thought I was too close to it. I'm not so sure now."

"You are close to it, Nick." David pressed a hand on the door as Nick took a turn too sharply. "Wanna slow down so you can get to her in one piece?"

Nick ignored him, though he eased up on the accelerator. "Mabel knows you and seems to get along with Bella. I know you want to see Adaleigh. Mindy needs her and Mabel—"

"I know," David interrupted him. "I know. Adaleigh does, too. She won't leave Mindy's side, and I'll stick close. Patrick can take the boat out in the morning if it comes to that."

Nick slammed to a stop in front of David's grandmother's house, emotion clogging his chest. "Grazie."

David met his gaze in the dim light. "Go save our girl." Then he was gone, and Nick sped toward the other end of town.

Ten years of doctoring in the poorest areas of New York City didn't prepare him to see Mindy's injuries. Probably because he knew her and couldn't distance himself like usual.

He held his medical bag in a death grip as he took in the scene.

Adaleigh sitting on the ground beside Mindy's head, her legs tucked under her simple brown skirt. She looked up, and the fear in her eyes danced like flames in the lantern light. A lantern held aloft by Mrs. Collins. The lady stood over Mindy and Adaleigh with a wrap covering her nightgown. Despite the older lady's roundness and the warm evening, Nick's medical eye caught the shivers that occasionally shook her.

All three women needed him to be the professional he'd trained to be. Dr. Matrone. Not Nick. Which meant he needed to put his personal feelings for Mindy—whatever they were exactly—aside and treat her as he would any other young woman who had been mugged on the streets of New York City.

"Thank you both." Nick forced the words out calmly and confidently. "Has she woken since you found her?"

Adaleigh shook her head. She opened her mouth to speak, her chin trembled, and she pinned her lips together.

"I asked David to stay with Mabel." Nick offered her what he hoped was a comforting smile.

"Can we move Mindy off the street?" Mrs. Collins asked as one of those shivers shook the lantern light. "This is no place for a decent young lady like her."

"I'd like to take her to the clinic." Nick knelt, beginning to take stock of the visible injuries. His stomach turned at the bruising already covering her bare arms, shins, and face. He took her wrist to count her pulse. Surprisingly strong, which eased his worry.

"Not alone." Mrs. Collins's tone brooked no argument. "She struggles enough with unwanted attention, I won't let this destroy what reputation she has left."

"That's why I'm hoping Miss Sirland will accompany us." Nick glanced between the two women. "Detective O'Connor will be joining us as well."

"Oh. Okay." Mrs. Collins deflated.

Nick jumped to his feet as she swayed. "Allow Adaleigh to help you inside while I get Mindy settled in the car. Don't you worry about Adaleigh's reputation either. These ladies are safe with me."

"You're a respectable man, Dr. Matrone." She patted his arm. "Too young and handsome to be a doctor, but a respectable man. Now, if we can get you married ..."

*Mamma Mia.* The matchmakers would never leave him alone. "I need to help Mindy, Mrs. Collins."

She ran her gaze over him with a calculating gleam he'd seen in a few too many nonna's eyes, then she nodded. "I'll visit her tomorrow at the clinic."

"Good." He left Mrs. Collins in Adaleigh's care, then once again knelt beside Mindy. He waited until the women were focused on climbing the steps before he brushed Mindy's swollen cheek. "Oh, sweet Mindy, who would do this to you?"

She didn't stir. He didn't like the idea of moving her before he understood all her injuries, however, he couldn't assess her properly in a dark alley behind a small town bakery either. Nothing told him she required emergency treatment that couldn't wait until he had all his equipment at hand back at the clinic.

A breeze swept by, swirling leaves around them. Gently, he eased his arms under her shoulders and knees. A soft groan slipped from her lips. Being unconscious for long was a bad sign, but neither did he want her waking to the pain too early. The wind caught a piece of paper, or maybe that was currency, and carried it toward the lake. Oh well, he couldn't chase after it.

Instead, he rose to his feet, his thighs burning with the action. Mindy wasn't large or heavy, but he hadn't been sparring like he used to do in the city. It had been the only way to clear his mind. Perhaps that's why he'd been more muddled since moving here. The wind laid a piece of blonde hair on Mindy's cheek, making her appear even more vulnerable. It hit him squarely in the chest.

"I'll bring your bag." Adaleigh was beside him then, opening car doors, helping him situate Mindy in the backseat as carefully and modestly as they could. They reversed the process when he parked on Main Street, outside the clinic. All the shops, the post and telegraph office, the Conglomerate headquarters ... all the buildings were closed and dark as today inched toward tomorrow.

Adaleigh flicked on the electric light in the waiting area of the clinic, then the light in the first exam room.

Nick carefully laid Mindy on the table. "Can you lock the front door and turn off the waiting room light? I don't want curiosity seekers. Detective O'Connor will knock."

Adaleigh obeyed without comment, quickly returning. "Where do we start, Dr. Matrone?"

Hearing his title settled his nerves. "Will you make notes as I catalog her injuries? There's paper and ink in my office." He handed her his ring of keys.

She stopped in the doorway. "Do you have a mechanical pencil? I find them more efficient for things like this."

"I don't." He hadn't considered it. They were expensive.

"I'll get you one." Then she took off down the hallway at a fast clip.

"You have a wonderful friend, Mindy." He adjusted her head so he could examine her lovely, marred face. Would it leave scars? He could see the shape of a shoe already forming along her cheekbone. It had broken the skin and swelled her eye shut. Her bottom lip was cracked. She had a gash on the opposite temple.

Mindy's eyes fluttered, and she moaned

"Shh, Mindy, it's Nick." He glanced behind him as Adaleigh nearly ran through the door. "And Adaleigh. You're safe. Mabel is safe."

Mindy relaxed.

"I need to see all the places where you were injured." His biggest concerns were her ribs and stomach. Was there internal bleeding? Lacerations that would require surgery? He wasn't fully equipped for that here, which meant he'd need to call the county ambulance. More time, more jostling. He'd make that decision if needed. First, he'd see what they were facing.

Mindy had never been in so much pain. Ever. It consumed her. Flames crawled over her body. Surrounded her ribs. Ate at her stomach. Covered her face. Even her legs. Nothing didn't hurt.

Still, she knew she had to wake up. Had to fight through it. Mabel needed her. She had to protect her little sister from men who would beat a person just to get answers. Men who seemed to enjoy inflicting pain.

"Nick, she's waking up." Adaleigh's voice sounded both near and far away. It drove a spike through Mindy's head.

"Mindy?" Nick's voice rumbled, causing painful vibrations in her chest. "Can you open your eyes?"

She tried to shake her head. The pain was too much.

"Turn off the electric light." Nick instructed. Heels tapped the floor like nails drilled into her head, and then darkness fell, broken only by the flickering of lantern light against her eyelids. She sighed with relief. Nick chuckled. "Better?"

Despite all the pain, she couldn't be all that hurt if Nick could find the humor in her situation. Because she knew he would never laugh at a patient unless he felt relief, he must have thought her in worse shape. Wasn't that a cheery thought, considering how much she hurt?

"Where?" The word caught in her throat like hair in a spider's web. Panic threatened. Pain slashed through her.

"Where are you?" Nick's calm soothed. Until a large hand circled her wrist. She flinched, then relaxed when she sensed how gentle the touch was. Nick's touch? "You're back at Mrs. Martins's house. You've been in and out of consciousness, fighting a fever for a few days."

Nausea churned her stomach. She needed to find and protect Mabel. Unable to move, with this much pain, she'd have to ask for help. Nick would help her. So would Adaleigh. Then she could go back to sleep. Yes, sleep.

Wait. She needed to tell them about her sister first. "Mabel?" The word croaked as if it came from someone else, except for the discomfort of speaking.

"Mabel is doing wonderfully well. Brought you this exquisite drawing as a get-well card." The smile in Nick's voice eased her worry. "She's taken to my sister, and Bella is thrilled to have a friend willing to listen to her chatter. Mabel can't seem to stop watching Bella, and follows her around the house."

"Good." Mindy sighed. Her head lolled to the side. A cool, soft pillow meeting her sore face. "And men?"

"The men who attacked you?" Nick ran his thumb over her wrist. Comforting, secure. "Detective O'Connor is investigating. We can't do much until we hear your side of the story, though not until you're ready.

I'm your doctor, and I won't let the detective push you."

She tried to smile ... It hurt too much.

"Time for you to rest again." He released her arm, and she immediately felt the loss. Panic squeezed. "I'll have Mrs. Martins warm you a cup of soup for when you wake again."

"Wait." The word came out too loudly, too painfully. A tear leaked from her left eye.

"What is it, Mindy?" He touched her shoulder. Gently, oh so gently. "You're safe here, and you need more rest. You've been through an ordeal."

"Stay?" She turned away from him, not wanting him to see how much she hated to be alone right now. Yet how could she ask this of him after how she'd treated him? She remembered their argument in vivid detail, and she'd planned to apologize to him. Would now, except her strength ebbed. She should ask Adaleigh to stay, but she wanted Nick.

"Of course I will." His hand left her shoulder, then came the scrape of a chair. She wanted his touch again, to know without opening her eyes that he was there. "Shall I read to you? If you're not opposed, I can continue reading in the Bible where I left off."

He'd read the Bible to her? She'd never actually read it, only listened to what she heard in church or what she could remember when someone quoted it. "Yes, please."

"Then rest, Mindy. You're safe. Mabel is safe. And I won't leave."

She would have nodded had it not been too painful. Instead, she held out her hand toward him. He must have understood her unspoken question because he wrapped her fingers with his. She instantly relaxed, let his words drift over her like a bank of clouds, and fell asleep.

When she woke up again, the room was dark, lit only by the flickering of lantern light. Her head was clearing, and her body had less pulsing pain. She wiggled her fingers, finding them still within Nick's grasp. It gave her courage to fight the lingering pain and fully open her eyes. Her gaze immediately landed on him.

Seated on a hardback chair beside her bed, her right hand in his left. His feet stretched out, crossed at the ankles. Coatless, shirtsleeves rolled to the elbows, tie askew. His glasses had slipped down his nose, his scruffy chin rested on his chest, which moved in constant rhythm. As grateful as she was to have his vigil these last hours—days? She had no sense of time—when was the last time Nick had slept?

She didn't want to pull her hand away. With her pain lessened, however, she wouldn't lean on Nick. Plus, she needed to apologize for taking her fear out on him. Perhaps doubly so, since she kept him in that hard chair. Yet, as much as she knew she should release him, she didn't want to. With him, she felt strong, brave, ready to face her pain and everything else.

Enough. What she actually needed was to find her sister. Who knew how long Mindy had been laid up? Her sister must be worried sick. Did Bella, Mrs. Martins, or whoever else have the patience to care for a mute child as Mabel deserved? Of course Mrs. Martins did. She was David's grandmother, after all. But Bella? She didn't know Bella.

She wiggled her fingers to free them from Nick's grasp. He tightened his hold, brought his feet underneath his chair as if he were about to stand. Did she wake him? She tugged her fingers, only for them to be trapped in a punishing grip that caused a whimper to seep out.

Nick's eyes shot open, and he immediately released her. "I'm so sorry. I'm ..." He looked at her with half-crazed eyes, breathing heavy. Then he shook his head, and the emotion cleared from his unkempt face.

"Nightmare?" She didn't want to delve into his personal life, yet she couldn't *not* ask.

He swallowed, his scruffy Adam's apple popping with the motion. "Sometimes I remember things no one should see. It's the plight of a doctor, I suppose. Never mind me. You are looking much improved. Color in your cheeks. Not as much pain hiding behind your eyes. Good." He flipped her hand to press his fingers to her wrist.

"How long have I been here? And Mabel. Where is she? How is she? Does she know I'm here?" The questions poured out.

Nick silently counted her pulse as he checked his watch. Then he snapped it closed with a nod and released her. "Mabel is wonderful. She's peeked in a few times over the past days, leaving you a few more drawings. I didn't want her to become fearful, so she doesn't know the extent of your injuries."

"She's safe, then?" And drawings? Since when had her sister begun drawing? Where did she get the supplies?

Nick nodded. "David and Detective O'Connor have taken turns being here so that we always have two men on the premises. Samson has taken a shine to your sister. I believe the feeling is mutual." He chuckled.

Mindy tried to picture Detective O'Connor's humongous mastiff next to her little sister. Mabel was usually so shy and skittish. Samson was large and loud, especially when someone came to the door. The lumbering beast would charge the newcomer with foundation-shaking barks. Mindy had no doubt Samson would defend those under his protection if necessary. A benefit for Mabel, even if they seemed an unlikely pair.

"Adaleigh and Mrs. Martins have been attending to your other needs." Nick's olive skin darkened. "Including spooning broth into you. You haven't had a proper meal in a while. Feel up for a little toast today? We need to get your strength back."

"How long have I been here?" She whispered the question, afraid of the answer.

"Almost two weeks."

"What?" She tried to sit up, then groaned.

"Mindy ..." Nick removed his glasses and scrubbed his face with his free hand.

"It was bad." She could see it in the weary lines he couldn't hide. "What, uh, what injuries do I have?"

Nick replaced his glasses. "Are you sure you want to know everything?"

No. Yes. She nodded.

He rested his elbows on his knees. "Severe concussion. Contusions and bruising on your face, arms, legs, torso. Laceration along your orbital—eye—bone. Three broken ribs, five bruised ribs. Bruised kidneys. One cracked rib punctured your spleen."

She stared at him, unable to absorb that all those injuries belonged to *her*. How was she alive?

"Your spleen ruptured after Adaleigh and I got you to the clinic. No time to get you to the hospital, so I operated. Then we moved you here. Infection set in, and I conferred with a doctor at the hospital in Hawk's River. He wouldn't have done anything differently. Time was of the essence. Had we transported you directly to the hospital, it may have ruptured along the way, and we wouldn't have had a clean environment to operate."

She would have died.

"Still, infection set in." Sorrow weighed him down. "Didn't think you'd make it."

"It wouldn't have been your fault." She clenched her teeth against the pain in her middle—the ribs or the surgery?—in order to touch him, but she couldn't reach. She laid back against her pillow. "You saved my life,

Nick. I owe you everything."

He rubbed his thighs, straightened his shoulders, shedding the moment of vulnerability, then stood. "I'll have Mrs. Martins bring you food and help you with any other needs you have."

"Nick."

He leaned over her, pressed cool lips to her forehead. "In the meantime, rest."

Then he was gone, leaving her heart in a tumultuous mess she didn't have the energy to sort out. Except that she wanted him to stay by her side. A feeling she wouldn't act on now that her strength was returning. Though all indications were that Nick was one of the honorable men. Still, what would a learned doctor want with an illiterate waitress like her?

She closed her eyes, sinking into the bed with the feel of his lips on her skin. Heaven help her, she wanted someone who would love her like that until the end of her days. Which may come sooner than she imagined if she aimed to keep her sister safe from whomever willingly beat her senseless just to get at Mabel and their father.

# CHAPTER FIVE

*Friday, June 19*

As the noon sun beat down on him, Nick couldn't wait to sleep in his own bed tonight. He finally felt confident Mindy was out of the woods enough that he didn't need to keep vigil.

First, Mrs. Bindle had another appointment. The sore back she complained of two weeks ago now included a sore knee, which meant this wasn't one of her usual hypochondriac maladies. Perhaps this unusually warm weather was causing a problem? He would ask more specific questions this time.

He turned onto Main Street, toward his clinic, and the memory of the desperation he'd felt when he realized Mindy did indeed have internal bleeding hit him anew. The purple bruising on her abdomen. Her cool, clammy skin, rapid breathing, and pulse. His medical training had kicked in, and she wasn't Mindy any more, simply a patient who needed a doctor's care.

Yet, he couldn't help appreciating how Adaleigh had assisted him. No squeamishness, as he would have expected from someone with a wealthy background like hers. She rose to the occasion, and he couldn't have saved Mindy without her help.

It was enough to prompt an idea for the future. A nebulous plan that was more fog than reality. He needed to discuss it with her and David. Perhaps Buck Wilson as well. Because it wouldn't move forward without their backing.

Speaking of Buck, he needed to follow up with him about whether his sleep had improved. Nick tugged out his pocket watch. He had time before Mrs. Bindle's appointment. He returned the watch to its pocket and crossed the street.

The Conglomerate Headquarters had been destroyed last year during a tornado that ripped through the town. By the time Nick first arrived in Crow's Nest, it had already been rebuilt. Most of Main Street had been, thanks to Buck and Adaleigh. He'd tried to poke at David during their occasional evening chats to see how he felt about Adaleigh working with Buck, had yet to get a powerful reaction. Other than absolute certainty that David trusted Adaleigh with every ounce of his being and distrusted Buck Wilson equally so.

From what Nick gathered, being an outsider to Crow's Nest, the Conglomerate started with positive intentions. About a decade ago, some man named Perry Baxter brought together several small businesses to create a type of union. The businesses, including shops, mechanics, even fishermen, paid into the Conglomerate for help with legal fees, or whatever type of protection they needed.

When Nick had first heard about that exchange, it raised concerns. Back in New York City, he knew how situations like that worked. It had nearly gotten him killed a time or two. It was also part of the reason he'd chosen to sell his half of his practice. Whether the Conglomerate would prove as corrupt as what he'd experienced back in New York remained to be seen.

He pushed open the wooden door, the warm air following him into the dim, stuffy interior. The small room held several chairs and a small table with a bell. No receptionist.

"Dr. Matrone." Buck emerged from a back office, hand extended in greeting. "A pleasure to see you this morning."

It'd been about two years since Buck Wilson took over for Perry Baxter. According to David's uncle, Detective O'Connor, who was actively investigating the Conglomerate, Buck had turned it into a power-hungry organism with some questionable practices. Rumor was, he expected members of the Conglomerate to pay higher dues, but if anyone wanted out, he ran their business into the ground.

While that wouldn't surprise Nick, he had been on the wrong end of preconceived notions most of his life, and so withheld judgment until he had proof. Which is why he could return Buck's greeting with genuine kindness. "I'm sorry I needed to cancel our standing appointment last week, so I wanted to check on you."

Surprise flashed across Buck's face. Tall and about the same age as Nick, he dressed in a tailored pinstripe suit that hung open to reveal a matching vest, starched white shirt, and red tie. "I ... um ..." Buck glanced over his shoulder in the way he'd seen his former medical partner do. A tell. Buck couldn't or wouldn't talk freely.

Nick raised his eyebrows. Never had he seen the polished man anything but smooth. He'd give him a way out of the situation, see what he did with it. "Walk with me to the clinic?"

"Most grateful." Buck didn't give the back room a second glance. Instead, he sped out the door.

The heat hit Nick like a wall. "Has to be the hottest day this year."

Buck didn't reply. Yes, something was definitely going on with the man. Was it his brother? The business? Something personal? For a moment, Nick wondered whether he wanted to get involved. He was friends with David and Adaleigh, and others who considered Buck a criminal. Yet Adaleigh worked with him. This past winter, Gilbert Cox, an accountant, couldn't find anything crooked in Buck's books.

Nick barely held in a sigh as he checked for traffic before crossing the street to the clinic. No matter what his friends believed, whether or not Buck Wilson was a criminal, Nick was a doctor and a Christian. It was not his to judge actions or character, rather to heal and prevent illness regardless of creed, behavior, skin color, gender, wealth, or age. *Padre nostro, grant me grace to be Your hands. To bring compassion and mercy to the hurting.*

He barely finished his prayer when certainty struck. "I have an appointment in ten minutes, then we're having luncheon together at the Wharfside."

Buck stopped in the middle of the street. Realized a car was headed toward him and jogged the rest of the way. "What do you need to meet about?"

Nick unbuttoned his suit coat, wishing society allowed for fewer layers in heat like this, and tucked his thumbs in his vest pockets. "Not meeting about anything, Buck. I'm your physician, and today's prescription is to have luncheon … with a friend."

Was that a sheen in the man's eyes? No. Couldn't be. Buck cleared his throat. "I'd be honored to share a meal with you, Dr. Matrone."

"Sharing a meal?" The voice came from behind them, and Nick wanted to bolt. How had Greg Alistar crept up on them?

"It's what businessmen do." Buck stuck his hands in his trouser pockets, an easy grin in place. "What can I do for you today?"

Nick edged away from them, hoping Mrs. Bindle would be early so he had an excuse to escape the nosy reporter. Alistar worked for the *Crow's*

*Nest Gazette.* With short brownish-blond hair, closely shaved scruff, and a dopey expression, the man looked like many of the reporters Nick had run into in New York City. Nondescript and slightly unkempt. What set this particular reporter apart from any other Nick had met was how skilled he was at skirting journalistic ethics with sensational stories that hinted at rumor, even flat out lies. Adaleigh and Buck had been trying to get him fired for years, but Alistar knew the line and walked it perfectly.

"I'd like a statement from Dr. Matrone regarding Mindy Zahn's injuries two weeks ago. I'm doing a follow-up article." Alistar pulled out a notebook. "I understand she was … on a date when the man had to fend off her advances?"

Nick didn't think. He simply drew back his fist and aimed it squarely at Alistar's nose. Fortunately, Buck intercepted the blow before it landed on the slimy reporter.

"I trust you have chased down your facts, Greg." Buck placed himself between Nick and Alistar. "Have you actually spoken to the witnesses?"

Alistar raised his chin. "I spoke to the man who was attacked."

Buck backed into Nick, obviously keeping him from showing Alistar what the word *attacked* actually meant.

"Greg," Buck spoke with annoying calm. "The truth is, that man attacked Mindy. If you know who he is, I encourage you to come forward with the information. She deserves to be protected."

"A waitress like her deserves exactly what she got." Greg slid his notepad into his breast pocket. "Everyone knows she's easy. It was just a matter of time before she took it too far. Waitresses ask for it, and her most of all."

This time, Buck fisted his hand and Nick caught his arm. "Mr. Alistar, Buck and I have a meeting. Good day."

"You know I'm right!" Alistar called after them.

"Waitresses are not prostitutes." Buck ground out the words, showing more anger than Nick had ever seen from him. "Mindy is most definitely not that. She's innocent, naïve, and, as I said, deserves to be protected. What happened to her is unconscionable. I will find out who Alistar's source is, and make sure O'Connor can prosecute him to the fullest extent of the law."

Nick unlocked the clinic door and waited until it closed behind him and Buck before he spoke. "You're passionate about defending her." He couldn't bring himself to voice the real question that had entered his mind. Was Joe the only brother that carried a torch for Mindy Zahn?

Buck rocked on his heels, studied Nick a moment, then grinned. "I approve." Then he laughed and slapped Nick's shoulder.

Before Nick could ask what the man meant, Mrs. Bindle limped into the clinic.

Mindy needed fresh air. She needed to get back to work. Two whole weeks she had missed! She couldn't afford that while living on her own, let alone now with Mabel to care for. A glance at the beautiful pictures Mabel had given—when had her sister learn to draw with such artistry?—gave her courage to face the pain getting out of bed would cause.

She swung her feet out from under the quilt. She'd go into the Wharfside this afternoon, explain to her boss what had happened, and sign up for a shift tomorrow. Too soon to return to work, she was sure, which is why she waited until Nick left and the house quieted before enacting her plan.

Adaleigh had left Mindy a change of clothes this morning, suggesting getting out of her nightgown would help Mindy's spirits. With Bella keeping Mabel occupied and Samson on protection detail, Mindy knew now was the time to slip out.

Getting dressed took more time than she hoped. Adaleigh usually spent the day in David's fishing shanty doing whatever it was she did there. Mindy didn't pretend to follow all the business arrangements Adaleigh facilitated. Mrs. Martins had a church ladies' meeting or something. It all boiled down to the fact that Mindy needed to get moving, and fast, before everyone returned to look in on her.

The stairs proved painful, but the determination to provide for her sister drove Mindy on. She shuffled and held her side, wishing for an arm to lean on. Nick's arm. She wouldn't though. He deserved better than her. Her sister depended on her, so she couldn't allow herself to get distracted with pretty fairytale dreams of knights in shining armor.

Outside, the heat slowed her steps so that she was sure a snail or turtle would get to the Wharfside faster than she could. By the time she limped into the outdoor seating area of the Wharfside, the luncheon crush was past. Probably a wise thing. Fewer people to witness her pain. Entering the cafe, she stayed against the wall, head down, as she worked her way to the back.

"Miss Zahn." Her boss, owner Willie Clifford, planted his hands on his hips. "Where have you been? You missed two weeks of shifts, and you look awful."

Mindy raised her chin. The large man expected friendly service for his customers and had no time for excuses. "I was injured, Mr. Clifford. But I'm back on my feet and ready to return."

"It's too late." He waved a meaty hand between them. "There are plenty of workers to replace those who don't show up for work. When I heard you got yourself injured, I replaced you."

She stared at him, not quite comprehending. "But this wasn't my fault."

"First, it doesn't matter. Second, that's not what I heard. Third, I wouldn't let you return to work with a face looking like that. I need pretty waitresses. Not ..." He grimaced. No, it was disgust.

Mindy shrank. "I need this job, Mr. Clifford."

"Not my problem, Miss Zahn." He folded his arms. "Now, remove yourself from my kitchen."

If she could have run from the cafe, she would have. The determination that got her here drained away with her failure. Again, she hugged the outside of the main dining area, yet it felt as if every eye watched her labored steps. She wished she could blink and be gone from here. Or that a knight in shining armor would rescue her. As if a knight would choose to rescue the likes of her.

Tears pricked. Shame stole her hope.

"You look as if you need an arm." Joe Spelding hooked his arm around her waist.

Of course, her knight would be this creep. Why wouldn't he just leave her alone? She shoved away from him, pain shooting through her middle. "Go away, Mr. Spelding. I don't need your help."

He followed her into the heat. It rose from the ground like a stovetop. It beat down from overhead. Even the air took more effort to breathe than her ribs allowed. She needed to get away from Joe before her body gave out. She shouldn't have left the Martinses' house today. Once she made it back, she might never leave again. It was too far away to offer refuge right now.

So, instead of turning north on the wharf, she turned south. Toward The Barn, and her room above the bakery. Though revisiting the place where she was attacked made her want to head the other way. Still, seeing Mrs. Collins would be a comfort.

"Why do you insist on pushing me away?" Spelding kept pace with her. An easy feat with his long steps and her shuffling ones.

"Because I'm not interested," she ground out. *Go away. Just ... Go. Away.*

"Of course you're interested. You already accepted my offer of a date." He slung his arm over her shoulder, nearly making her stumble. "Or did my wrongful stint in lockup turn you against me?"

"Yeah, that's it." She ducked out from under his arm. Only two more blocks. Mrs. Collins would send Joe away.

"You think you're better than me, huh?" A hard edge sharpened his words. It sent a skitter down Mindy's back. "I'll make sure everyone knows you're not some saint, so don't toy with me, doll."

For a moment, Mindy considered giving in. Appeasing the brute beside her. That thought led directly to the brute who attacked her, nearly killed her. If she could live through that, then she was strong enough to reject Joe. How, she didn't know. Or maybe she did. She couldn't have survived her injuries without Nick Matrone. Perhaps she'd tell him about Joe.

"Mindy," Joe growled.

No, she needed his aid sooner than she'd next see him. "I'm already spoken for, Mr. Spelding, or haven't you heard?" It was impulsive and reckless, yet the hope it sprouted strengthened her.

"What do you mean?" Joe spun her around by her arm. Mindy bit back a wince.

"I mean that someone is already calling on me. Nick would not take kindly to having someone try to steal his girl away." A mix of truth and lie, that, but she knew without a doubt that Nick would defend whomever his girl would be. Not that it would ever be her, especially not after this breach of their acquaintance.

"Why you two-timing—" He drew back as if to slap her, and Mindy bolted. Pain arched through her torso, causing stars to dance before her eyes. She pushed into The Barn, dashed behind the counter and into the back.

"Mindy!" Mrs. Collins stared at her, a sifter in one hand and a half-powdered pan of something in front of her.

"I need to hide from Joe Spelding." Mindy searched for the perfect corner. "He's being forward."

Mrs. Collins huffed. Her baker landlady hated ungentlemanly men with a passion. "Duck down over here. He won't get past me."

None too soon, Mindy crouched at Mrs. Collins's feet. Pain had her swaying. She exercised her new prayer muscles, thanking God that her knight in disguise was a baker. Joe stormed into the kitchen, and just as quickly, Mrs. Collins sent him away. Then Mrs. Collins helped Mindy into the older woman's personal living area, settling her on the couch.

Mindy sank into the firm cushion, exhausted. Mrs. Collins didn't seem to mind. "Thank you, Mrs. Collins."

"You're welcome, sweet one." She smiled at Mindy. "I wish I could do more. David already gathered your things, and I let your room, or I'd take you there instead."

What?

"Your rent was due." Mrs. Collins looked near tears. "I couldn't wait to see how long your recovery might be."

Mindy struggled to sit up. "I could work for rent. Mr. Clifford wouldn't rehire me today, so I could work for you at the bakery."

"Oh, Mindy." Mrs. Collins sat beside her. "I'd hire you if I could. I need the rent money just to stay afloat. A loan from the Conglomerate."

"I'm sorry, Mrs. Collins." Mindy lay back and closed her eyes. Fortunately, Mrs. Collins said no more as she bustled about. Mindy might have dozed off, but instantly came awake when a male voice intruded into the silence.

"I need to speak with her, Mrs. Collins." Buck Wilson? Why was he here? Defending his brother? Mindy's heart rate increased.

"You, especially, may not." Mrs. Collins spoke with all the authority of a mother bear. "Please leave."

Buck huffed. "Fine. Call Miss Sirland to meet me here and we'll escort Miss Zahn back to the Martinses' house together."

"Only if she arrives with David."

"Deal."

Mrs. Collins muttered something, then her footsteps led away. The telephone box was situated at the rear of the customer area so anyone could use it. Mindy leaned back again, grateful someone else would fight her battle.

"Psst, Mindy?" Buck stuck his head into the room. "I need a minute of your time. May I enter?"

Surprised, Mindy nodded.

Buck, even with his similarly tailored suit and same color hair, looked nothing like his step-brother. As she met his worried gaze, she realized why. Buck was concerned for her. Joe wanted to use her. It struck her, the opposite nature of the two men. So why had Joe gotten out of prison, and why did David's uncle—and everyone else—want to put Buck behind bars?

He knelt on one knee beside the couch. "First, I'm terribly sorry for Joe's behavior. It was wrong of him. I wish I had followed you right away so I could have stopped him."

Mindy skipped over the apology. "What do you mean, followed right away?"

"Nick and I shared lunch at the Wharfside. I stayed after he left and heard ..." Buck cringed. "Well, I heard what Willie Clifford said to you and tried to convince him to take you back. I'm sorry, I couldn't."

"Go on." Everything about this was strange. She'd never noticed this side of Buck before. It was as if he dropped a mask. She didn't want to dwell on Nick at the moment. She cringed at what she imagined his reaction would be when he learned she claimed they were an item.

Buck didn't seem to notice. "I sent him home and stayed to pay the bill and speak with a few folks, so I overheard your conversation with Willie."

"And?" Where was he going with this story? "Best hurry before Mrs. Collins finds you here."

"Skirting the line is what I do best." Buck grinned, then sobered. "I couldn't convince Willie to rehire you. Perhaps I shouldn't have tried. Nick might not tell you this, but I need to be blunt. Until your visible injuries heal, I wouldn't count on finding a job."

Mindy fingered the stitches that ran from her temple to her still-swollen cheekbone.

"I have an opening for a secretary. Can you type?"

Mindy shook her head. She couldn't read. Not that she would tell Buck Wilson that.

"I have another idea that I think would fit you better, however, I wanted to offer my own opportunity first. Because this other one could get ... complicated."

"What do you mean?" Mindy held a hand to her side as she tried to sit up.

Buck pressed her shoulder to keep her from moving. "That's why I sent for Adaleigh. She's the more suitable person to tell you. I'll make sure Nick pays you a call later today, too."

Heat danced up her cheeks.

Buck chuckled. "Yes, I meant that both ways, Miss Zahn. I don't think he'll be as put out by your claim as you think."

The heat spread. "How many people know already?"

Buck glanced over at the door. "Considering Joe shouted the news at me on the wharf. Plenty."

"I just wanted him to stop." Mindy fingered the cuff of her sleeve.

"I know. I'm confident Nick would have given you permission had he known you needed it."

"Why are you being so nice to me?"

"I have my reasons, Miss Zahn." Buck stood, stuffed his hands into his pockets and returned to the relaxed cockiness that made everyone believe he hid criminal behavior. "I shall leave you in the capable hands of—"

"Out!" Mrs. Collins growled as she stomped into the room. Mindy couldn't help a smile as Buck dodged his way right out the door.

# CHAPTER SIX

Something shook Nick out of a dream that twisted his last weeks in New York City into more of a nightmare than it had actually been. Mostly because Mindy had made an appearance and Nick hadn't been able to save her.

"Matrone!"

Nick gasped and sat up. "*Cosa?*"

David crossed his arms. "You are a hard man to wake up. It's suppertime. Were you planning to sleep all night?"

"You could have let me," Nick grumbled. He swung his legs out from the blankets and stuck his fingers through his hair. Where were his spectacles?

"Nope, I couldn't." A smirk lifted the corner of David's mouth. "Mindy needs you."

Nick threw his pillow at the boat captain. "Some friend. Don't tease."

David tossed it back and sobered. "Actually, she does need you. As both a doctor and a friend."

Nick stuffed his legs into his trousers. "Is she all right? Why didn't you wake me sooner?"

"Because she needed rest as much as you did." David rocked on his heels.

The lack of urgency in his stance said this wasn't an emergency, but what did the man know? Nick was the doctor. What if Mindy was bleeding internally again? He buttoned his shirt and snapped up his suspenders in record time.

"She's fine, Nick." David cut through Nick's haze. "You're too close to this."

Nick plopped back on the bed. "I know. I've never been this …" What? Invested? Emotional? That made him sound like a horrible doctor. Was that what went wrong in New York?

"You've never liked a girl like Mindy." David shrugged. "That's actually good in this case, because she needs you to like her."

"My brain must still be half-asleep. What are you talking about?"

That one-sided smirk again. "It's selfish of me to be the only one to see your reaction when you find out. If I wasn't such a good friend of Mindy's, I'd tell you, but she deserves to see the raw look on your face."

"*Non ho capito.*" Nick shook his head, sleep mixing his languages. "I don't understand."

"Then I'll show you." David nodded toward the door. "Let's go."

Nick followed obediently, grabbing his medical bag on the way out the door. Thankfully, David stayed silent, keeping his cryptic words to himself. Because Nick had plenty to sort through on the brief walk to David's nonna's residence.

From the first moment Nick met Mindy, he thought her beautiful. Not that it meant much. He suspected most men thought her pretty. Then he saw how she helped Silas and Cora during Nick's first visit to Crow's Nest. She defended them. Helped spread truth to combat deceptive rumors. Respect drew him to her, and he discovered he enjoyed conversing with her. She was easy to speak with and never pointed out his occasional Italian language slip-ups.

Then he returned to New York.

She hadn't been far from his thoughts, especially as things spiraled. Perhaps the dichotomy of her easy acceptance of him made the barbs more obvious. When the opportunity came to return to Crow's Nest, Nick knew Mindy was a big reason why he made the move permanent.

However, it wasn't fair to either of them. Not really. They could be nothing except friends. Nick respected Mindy too much to open her to the arrows thrown his way because of his nationality. Being an Italian these days was hard, and getting harder. Now, not only were his people looked down on at best, lynched at worst, for being immigrants, for being poor, for being swarthy-skinned, but also for being criminals.

Even  for the sole reason of keeping the likes of him out of the US. Things weren't looking to improve with the rise of Benito Mussolini back in the homeland. Nick tried to stay out of politics, yet made the mistake of speaking against Mussolini and the way Italians were being treated by the Blackshirts. Nick was labeled and condemned as a communist, and escaped from New York fortunate enough to have been able to sell his portion of his clinic.

How could he offer a non-Italian woman—any woman, really—that type of life? Unless she was willing to stand beside him against the mistreatment of people? Whether by government or arrogance or ignorance. Something told him Mindy would; however, he respected her too much to go down that path. She deserved a life of happiness, not one tied to a man who rarely received the benefit of the doubt because of his nationality.

"You finished brooding?" David bumped his shoulder, bringing an awareness of their surroundings. They'd reached the Martinses' house.

Nick took a deep breath. *Padre nostro* ... The words flowed in Italian as he begged God to give him peace, wisdom, and strength for whatever task was placed before him. That, above all, he could protect Mindy's heart. And his own.

Samson's booming bark greeted them as David led the way up the front walk and into the house. The big dog rubbed up against David's legs, then shoved his massive head under Nick's hand. Nick couldn't help a smile as he scratched behind the dog's ears. Then Samson trotted back toward the kitchen. Obviously following his nose because an amazing garlicky scent wafted from the back of the house. He'd recognize that childhood smell anywhere.

"What is your nonna making?" Nick shed his hat and suit coat. After the last few weeks, Mrs. Martins's house had become a second home, and the need to stay formally dressed, especially with the summer heat, made little sense.

David grinned. "Fish were biting this morning, so I brought home a couple of salmon. Grandma's garden is producing faster than the girls can keep up harvesting it, so they have a spread laid out for us."

"I wish I had something to offer." Nick slipped his hands into his pockets, strangely unsure of himself.

David rounded on him, lowered his voice. "You do, Nick. More than any of us. As Mindy's friend, I'm glad circumstances brought you back to Crow's Nest. A piece of advice: don't get in God's way, thinking you know what's best for yourself or Mindy." David bounced his brows, then turned on his heel.

Nick stayed still, absorbing David's words. Lighthearted greetings filtered from the kitchen.

"Signora Martins, David kisses Adaleigh in your kitchen." Bella's laugh echoed in the house. "They are supposed to sneak away for such things."

"They're in love, let them be." Mrs. Martins's chuckle joined Bella's. "You'll have your turn soon enough."

Nick rubbed his temples. Nope, he didn't want to think about a gentleman whisking Bella off her feet. She was a true romantic.

"They could at least wait until after supper," Detective O'Connor groused. "Or hurry up and get married so they can have their own house."

"Oh, you put up with us fine while we were up north, Uncle Mike," David said around the scraping of a chair. David had been injured over the winter, and Detective O'Connor and Adaleigh helped him convalesce.

"I see that smile peeking out from under your mustache." Adaleigh's scolding held a teasing note. "You know you can't hide facial expressions from me. I'm learning all your tells."

"Insufferable children," Detective O'Connor muttered, barely loud enough for Nick to catch.

"You love them, Michael." Mrs. Martins chuckled. "Don't you deny it by being a grouchy old man."

"Who are you calling old?" Detective O'Connor laughed like he did only when his sister teased him.

Nick dropped his chin to his chest, enjoying the picture of family the Martinses created. Yes, they were missing Patrick, his new wife Meri, and their little baby, plus the brothers' younger sister Samantha, who had moved out to Montana with Silas and Cora, but they were still a family and had welcomed Bella and Nick into their lives, their home. Mindy and Mabel, too. Though Mindy's voice was conspicuously absent. He needed to put on his doctor's perspective and make sure she was okay.

Little footsteps mixed with padded ones. He looked up to find Mabel and Samson coming down the hall towards him.

He squatted down. "Hi Mabel. How are you today?"

She pressed her lips together, though Nick willed her to speak.

"Do you like talking to Bella?" he asked.

Mabel nodded, her braids swinging.

"Is she teaching you words to say in *Italiano*?"

The sparkle entered her brown eyes.

"I'm sure she's teaching you all the sweet words, isn't she?" Nick grinned, infusing his voice with humor. "Like *caramelle* and *torta* and *dolce*."

"*Bella*, too." Bella herself appeared in the hall. She smiled down at Mabel and placed a hand on the little girl's shoulder. "I'm not the only bella. Mabel is *motlo* bella. Isn't that right, Paperotta?"

Mabel's cheeks pinked, drawing Nick's attention to her appearance. From that day when they first met, she appeared drawn, pale, almost hollow. In the last weeks, her face appeared rounder, her chin higher, her frame less scrawny. His medical eye recognized the change for what it was. Mabel was healthier now, which begged another question. What was her home life like before her parents left her with Mindy? He'd seen plenty of children mistreated back in New York, however that wasn't the only reason for a child to look malnourished. Poverty among the immigrants with whom he worked came to families filled with love as much as those filled with hate. Either way, it tore his heart to pieces.

"You help Signora Martins while I take il mio fratello to see *la tua sorella*," Bella said, her hurry causing her to lapse into Italian.

Mabel must have understood because she returned to the kitchen without protest. They watched Mabel disappear, then Bella hooked her arm around Nick's and led him out the front door.

"We insisted Mindy rest outside. She was cold and the sun would do her good." Speaking in rapid Italian, Bella explained all that had happened from luncheon until now. Mindy's lost job, Spelding's wretched behavior, Buck hinting at the idea Nick and Adaleigh had been bandying about since her return from the Northwoods, and doubly so since Mindy's attack.

"If I hadn't listened to Buck and left the Wharfside early, I would have been there." Yes, that was his takeaway from all Bella told him. It was easier to blame himself than feel the painful empathy for what Mindy suffered in just a few short hours.

Bella, like a usual baby sister, scoffed and scolded, her Italian flying as fast as her hands. "She needs you to be strong for her, brother mine. Be her rock, someone she can lean on and depend on. Be her shelter. She needs someone to look out for her, and I think you're the perfect person to do so."

"She's a strong woman, Bella. She doesn't *need* me or any man."

Bella muttered under her breath an Italian phrase that would have Mamma swatting her with her apron. "It's not about how strong or not strong she is. Right now she's in a storm and could really use a lighthouse. Go be that for her." Bella gave him a shove.

Nick let his sister propel him a few feet, then turned back to her. "What if my troubles only make the waves worse for her?"

"You mean your old medical partner?" Bella frowned. "He's old news, Niccolo. Mamma told me he isn't even treating Italian immigrants any more. Before you think you should return, don't forget that it was our neighbors, our fellow Italians, who turned on you after your partner blabbered what you had told him in private. Move on, brother mine. There's a pretty woman who needs you right now. Go."

That is why he loved his sister. Even across an ocean, she'd never minced words as they wrote letters to one another each week. He was the man he became because of her. Their mamma, too. Strong women who could point out his weaknesses and then bolster him to do better. Be better.

Nick snagged Bella's hand, swung her toward him, and smacked a kiss on her cheek. "Grazie mille, il mio Bella." Then he ruffled her curls in that way he'd learned she hated when they finally saw each other face-to-face again last year.

Bella rolled her eyes and stuck out her tongue, then returned to the front of the house.

Nick took a breath to tamp down on his brotherly love for his sister and turn to the serious matter of Mindy's situation. His smile in check, he turned. To find Mindy leaning against the corner of the house, laughter in her eyes.

"David and I might not be blood siblings like you and Bella, but he used to tease me the same way. Still does occasionally." She rested her head against the wall. "I'm glad Bella came with you to Crow's Nest. She's a sweet woman and Mabel adores her."

"Should you be standing?" Nick reached her in three steps. "Let's get you settled again."

Her face turned a bright pink. "I heard you and ... well ..." She shrugged, the pink turning to red.

"You wanted to see me?" He couldn't quite believe it.

She scuffed the toe of her black shoe on the ground. "I didn't want you to leave."

"Come on." He gently tugged her away from the wall and tucked her under his arm to lead her to the back of the house where the Martinses had rocking chairs set out. "I don't know how much time we have until supper. Let's talk until then."

He barely resisted swinging his other arm around her and stopping just to hold her. His sister's encouragement to take care of Mindy had his guard dropping, which wasn't good. Yet, he had no interest in raising it again.

Mindy had never desired to learn a language other than English until today. English was hard enough. But seeing Nick and Bella interact, she wanted to know what they said to one another. It had begun as an intense conversation and yet they ended with teasing. Then again, if they hadn't been speaking a language she couldn't understand, she would have felt horrible for eavesdropping.

She didn't know why the pair had come outside, however, she didn't want Nick to leave without an opportunity to talk to him. She had to tell him about the rumor going around, that they were an item. Then she could decide whether to bring up Buck's suggestion. If only Adaleigh had been willing to explain Buck's idea. Instead, she sent David to get Nick. Mindy couldn't decide if her friend was matchmaking or if Nick really was the best person to tell her about whatever it was.

Worse, she had no idea what *it* was. Adaleigh had been even more cryptic than Buck, which was highly unusual for her friend.

Nick helped her sit in the rocking chair she'd been in when she first heard his voice. Lowering into it caused an ache within her whole torso. Her activity today had definitely aggravated her injuries.

"Hey." Nick raised her chin so their eyes could meet. "I know you're in pain. Is it physical or emotional? Or both? Remember, I'm a doctor. I can help."

She wanted the physical pain gone. But she also wanted her wits about her, and anything he could give her for the pain made her sleep.

Nick dashed his thumb along her cheek. "I'm your friend, too." Then he abruptly spun away and brought the other rocking chair to her side.

She watched him. What would his reaction be to what she'd say? When she first met him, he had an air of authority about him, sweeping in to save the day, no matter the danger involved. He'd been willing to marry Cora, a woman he'd never met, at the request of a mutual friend. As soon as he realized Silas Ward had feelings for Cora, Nick switched to being their friend. That type of selflessness could be easily used. Mindy knew all about being used. She'd never want to do that to Nick.

"Are you in physical pain?" He turned that medical gaze of his on her. It made her squirm. "Be honest Mindy. I won't think less of you."

"I shouldn't have left the house." For more reasons than this.

Nick didn't react, that she could tell. "That wasn't what I asked, Mindy. Allow me to rephrase. Does your head hurt?"

She touched the stitched up wound. "I suppose."

"Meaning you hurt more elsewhere." He gave a nod, as if he expected that answer. "Do you have pain in your back?"

"I don't know." How could she not know? He must think her dumb. She shifted in her chair to see if that caused pain in her back.

"Hey." He reached across the space between them and touched her forearm. "Don't hurt yourself to tell me what you think I want to hear."

She looked down at where his dark fingers rested on her white skin. She wore a simple light blue cotton dress with cap sleeves. It added to the contrast between them.

He snatched his hand away. "How do your ribs feel? Sharp pain? Achy pain? Pain when you move? When you're still?"

She scrunched her nose, still stuck on why he pulled away. "I rarely like when customers touch me. They think because I'm a waitress, they have a license to do so. More often than not, they aren't gentlemanly about it."

"Mindy, I didn't mean—" The earnest pain in his voice had her waving him quiet.

"I know that." It's what made his actions stand out to her. "I have never felt that way with you."

"Okay ..." Nick sounded as if he expected a lecture from her. It brought her gaze to his. The confusion she saw echoed her own.

"Why did you pull your hand away?" She wanted to know because something told her it mattered.

"What?" He looked from his fingers to her arm, then out toward Mrs. Martins's garden. "Oh. No reason."

"I don't have Adaleigh's skills, yet even I can tell that's a flat out lie." There was a reason, a deep one, if she didn't miss her guess. "It's not because you're a doctor and I'm your patient. We're friends, like you said."

His jaw worked. Perhaps he needed a little push. She ignored the discomfort from her ribs and stitches, reached across the divide, and wove her fingers between his. It was forward. Brazen, even. Exactly the type of action she'd been accused of. But somehow, with Nick, it didn't feel that way. It felt comforting, safe. Like her hand belonged in his.

She didn't understand it. No, she did. It just made little sense. It certainly couldn't lead to a genuine relationship beyond that of friends. She had nothing to offer him. Unintelligent, illiterate, with a reputation in tatters, a mute sister to care for, and scars that took away her one asset, her beauty. Not that she thought herself beautiful. It was just that everyone seemed to think she had a pretty face. Not anymore.

Asking this of Nick wasn't fair to him. She tried to tug her hand free. He tightened his hold.

"I left New York under a cloud." He still didn't look at her. "Not because of my medical experience. Because I spoke up against mistreatment. Because I'm Italian."

"You think I would treat you like that?" It hurt to consider it.

"No. No. Definitely not." He squeezed her fingers. She waited for him to explain. Except, instead of speaking, he brought the back of her hand to his lips. Her belly flipped.

"Nick ..." She had to tell him the lie she told Joe before he told her something they couldn't unsay to each other. Before he thought she was using him for her own gain. The words caught in her throat as he turned his dark eyes on her.

"I care about you, Mindy. You're strong, capable, beautiful." He smiled a sad sort of smile. "It's forward of me to tell you this. To say how I admire you, respect you."

The *but* in his words screamed at her. Tears burned her eyes. He brought her hand to his lips once more, and a tear slipped down her cheek.

"I wish I had something to offer you, Mindy. I don't. I would only bring you into a mess you don't deserve."

"Wait, what?" Her tears vanished, her heart pounded. "You're an incredible man, Nick. I'm the one who doesn't deserve you. What in the world does touching my arm have to do with any of this?"

He stared at her. "Of course you deserve an honorable man, Mindy. Why would you think otherwise?"

"Arm, Nick." She pulled free of him. "Explain. Now."

"I did. I'm Italian. *Swarthy.*" He spat the word like it was a swear word.

"Handsome." This made no sense.

"You think I'm handsome?" The man looked incredulous.

Mindy rolled her eyes. "I cannot believe we're having this conversation."

"Fine." He removed his spectacles, pinched the bridge of his nose, then replaced the frames. "But it doesn't change the fact that we can't be more than friends."

"Well, tough." Mindy crossed her arms. "I already told Joe Spelding that you've been calling on me. By now, the entire town of Crow's Nest knows we're an item. Or is our imaginary relationship over before it starts?"

# CHAPTER SEVEN

Nick stared at Mindy. For all his years of study to become a medical doctor, he felt incredibly dense just now. "Imaginary relationship?" Why wasn't the evening cooling down yet? This heat was oppressive. He tugged at his tie.

Mindy sighed. Before she could explain—if she indeed would—Samson's barks echoed from inside the house. Mindy sat up, her face brightening with a gorgeous smile that went right to his heart.

"Adaleigh said they were waiting on dinner for Patrick and Meri." Mindy rubbed her hands together, then pushed to her feet. "I've been wanting to get my hands on that adorable baby of theirs. Every time I see those little chubby cheeks, I ..."

She stared at him, pink once again infusing her own cheeks.

"What, Mindy?" He rose, stood in front of her. Too close, but after their conversation, it seemed appropriate. Not that he knew what to do with any of it just yet.

She tilted her head back to look him in the eyes. Her gaze took in one eye, then the other, as she assessed him. What did she see? He wanted to be worthy of a woman like her. Was having integrity enough when it also got a person labeled and tossed out of town?

But Mindy said nothing. Uncharacteristic of her, and that made him worry. He caught her fingers as she went around him, toward the back door to Mrs. Martins's home.

"Mindy." He tugged her to a stop, and she didn't fight him. "We aren't finished talking yet."

"I know." Her words were a whisper. "Detective O'Connor and David won't let this rest, either. Let's eat first. I'm ... I'm tired."

He squinted at her. Assessing the cause of her weariness. Causes, really. That was his professional opinion.

"Stop working, Dr. Matrone." She cast him a compassionate smile. "No doctoring until after supper."

"Yes, ma'am." His stomach did a flip. He released her hand and followed her inside.

The whirlwind that was the Martins family caught them into its chaos. The noise and chatter reminded him of home. Watching his sister come alive with the activity did his heart good. Bella had seemed aimless since leaving Italy and arriving in America. He knew she still grieved the loss of their nonna. Their home too, though he knew Bella received letters from her friends. Nevertheless, it cheered him to see her helping Mrs. Martins, tickling baby Samuel under his chin, and hugging Mabel.

Mindy stayed near the edges of the room, obviously trying to stay out of the way, but her injuries had her moving slowly. Nick wanted to shield her from being bumped except several people stood between them and making such an effort would single her out too much. After their conversation, he wasn't sure what to do. Their friendship was comfortable, and as much as he liked Mindy, more than friendship couldn't be an option. So a fake relationship?

"Conversation not go well?" David sidled up to him.

"I'm not sure how it went." Nick frowned. Adaleigh settled Mindy in a chair, Meri set baby Samuel in her arms, and Mabel stood at her elbow. The scene did something to him. Made him wish for something that couldn't be. How could they pretend to be an item and not actually become one? Nick didn't think he could do it. So why did Mindy suggest it? "Just how dangerous is Spelding to Mindy?"

"You're catching on." David crossed his arms, lowered his voice. The action must have caught his uncle's attention, because Detective O'Connor's mustache twitched as he watched them.

"Is putting on a front enough?" Nick turned his shoulder so Mindy wouldn't catch the intensity he wanted to show David. "Or does she need the protection of a husband?"

David's brows rose. "You like offering that solution."

"Liking has nothing to do with it." Nick couldn't help remembering the speed with which he'd made his way to Crow's Nest that first time around, when Bella had brought a message about the danger Cora Davis Ward faced. He hadn't needed to act on the offer of marrying her—a woman he hadn't met before—since Silas already had her protection and heart in hand. The idea of someone beating him to protect Mindy in such a way did not leave him with the peace or relief as when he'd noted Silas's intentions.

"Time for supper, boys." Mrs. Martins passed by them, giving them a look only a mother—or grandmother—could give. They were to put their serious talk aside and eat. She also situated Nick next to Mindy with the same expression. *Yes, ma'am,* was the only reply she'd accept.

The conversation flowed easily around the table. David and Patrick shared fishing stories. Nick was pleased to see how the winter had healed the relationship between the brothers. Mrs. Martins and Adaleigh included Meri as if she was a long-lost relative. Being her doctor, Meri and Patrick had confided in him the way they met, and the truth of Samuel's father. He wondered whether the women knew, too. Patrick made it clear he was claiming Samuel as his own and had no desire for anyone to think otherwise.

Mindy moved her food around her plate. Had she eaten anything? He leaned closer to her. "You can take your supper up to your room."

"I know." She used her fork to pull salmon meat from the skin. On her other side, Mabel watched them.

"Let me give you something for the pain, Mindy." It hurt him to see her hurting.

She chewed her lip. Conversation continued, as if the others were oblivious to them. That was okay to Nick's way of thinking. He didn't want to draw attention to Mindy's weakness. She had enough to worry about without an entire host of people fretting over her. Anyway, *he* wanted to help her and didn't like the idea of being usurped by well-meaning females. Which said more about his feelings toward Mindy, and why this faux relationship idea was a foolish one.

Time to be a doctor, not a friend. "I'm prescribing rest, Mindy. I'll have Adaleigh take you upstairs. I'll visit tomorrow to finish our conversation."

Mabel slipped out of her chair, and the table fell quiet. She circled around to Nick, looked up at him with her wide eyes. Then she tugged his sleeve. He let her pull his arm toward her until she held his hand. His large one in her small one. Then she took Mindy's hand and put it in his. Nick shot his gaze to Mindy's only to find worry there. What was Mabel asking of him? Of them?

Detective O'Connor cleared his throat. "Nick, Mindy, David, and Adaleigh, might I speak with you all outside for a moment?"

By unspoken mutual agreement, all four of them followed the detective out the back door. Nick didn't miss the concern on his sister's face, or Meri's whispered words. "He's in good hands with that group on his side."

The truth of her statement sank in. He didn't have a group on his side back in New York. Here, amid people who were strangers a year ago, he found community. It caused emotion to swell in his chest. Gratefulness, as well as the fight to do everything he could to see these friends stayed healthy to live long, prosperous lives, as far as the Lord willed it.

Mindy sank into the rocking chair she'd been in most of the late afternoon. Her body hurt more than she wanted to admit, especially with Nick hovering close. She should tell her doctor, listen to his medical advice, but there was too much left unsaid between them. She could still feel the warmth of his hand around hers after Mabel joined them. What did her sister mean by such an action? It worried her.

Adaleigh took the rocking chair beside her, leaving the men to stand. A few more minutes, then she could ask her friend to take her upstairs.

Detective O'Connor crossed his arms. "I'm tired of this dancing about. You young'uns can't get out of your own way, so I'm doing it for you."

She gaped at him.

"Mindy is in danger from multiple sides. We're going to create a plan to keep her and Mabel safe." Detective O'Connor looked from one to the next of them. "First is her physical safety. The men who attacked you, I still haven't found them. That means they could return."

"Do we know who they are?" David leaned against Adaleigh's rocking chair. "Or why they attacked Mindy and threatened Mabel?"

Mindy shuddered at the memory. Nick rested his hand on her shoulder.

Detective O'Connor shook his head. "They vanished. I did learn that your father, Mindy, mortgaged the farm. Severely."

"I was sending money home to help." Why hadn't they told her? Surely she could have done more.

"It wasn't because of the farm. Your father had debts to the wrong people. Taking out the loan was a way to pay them." Detective O'Connor didn't flinch as he delivered the next blow. "Your father had secrets, Mindy. They aren't pretty. Drink was the best of his vices. He gambled and lost a lot. A neighbor told me that your mother knew. Last year, she asked the neighbor to hide money for her, especially what you sent. Your father caught wind and stole it. Your mother never asked her again."

One of her attacker's kicks hurt as much as that knowledge. Mindy held just a thread of hope. "Are you sure? Absolutely sure?"

"I'm sorry, Mindy." Detective O'Connor's compassion brought tears to Mindy's eyes. "I only tell you because I believe that vice is the reason for your attack."

Mindy bent over her knees. Her body hurt. Her heart hurt. Everything was a cloud of pain.

"This is too much." Nick's voice was stern, yet held too much emotion to be his medical opinion. "Can't we protect her without these details?"

"Nick." She wove their fingers together, tugged him down beside her. He knelt, bringing his face level with hers. "I need to know what I'm up against."

"You are not fighting this alone." Those brown eyes wrapped around her like the smell of freshly ground coffee beans in the morning.

"I know. So hush up and let Detective O'Connor finish." She tightened her hold on his hand. He squeezed back and stayed kneeling beside her.

"My current inquiry is into the identity of the loan shark, as well as who your father's gambling partners tended to be. He moved around and didn't visit places close to the farm to avoid the risk of being noticed. The secrecy is making the lead difficult, but I'll keep at it."

"Thank you, Detective." And she was grateful.

"As for protecting you from them, the plan is twofold. Find them and arrest them. In the meantime, I don't recommend you or Mabel go anywhere alone. You have more than enough friends who will gladly keep you company."

"And, don't think you're being difficult, *Melinda*." David shot her that big brother look he'd perfected when they were kids. He only called her by her full name when he used "the look." She rolled her eyes. She knew the truth behind his tease.

"That same plan will also deter the problem of Joe Spelding." This time, Detective O'Connor sighed and waved to Adaleigh. "You want to explain this one?"

Adaleigh smiled. "Gladly."

"She's entirely too happy about this plan." David chuckled, casting a fond look at his fiancée, then a wink past Mindy's head. She glanced at Nick to find his skin darkening. What was that about?

"It's a wonderful idea. Of course I'm happy." Adaleigh turned her attention solely on Mindy. "You losing your job today is incredibly fortuitous. Instead of us taking up residence at the Wharfside while you work, you can join us. Me and Nick, that is. And possibly Buck, if the detective will get off his case in this matter."

"He's hiding something," Detective O'Connor growled. "Just because his books weren't cooked doesn't mean there isn't criminal activity somewhere in that organization."

"I believe there is, too." Adaleigh shrugged. "But Buck is willing to see to the welfare of this community, so I'll trust him that far."

"What does that have to do with me?" Mindy asked. "How does that help me stay away from Joe?"

Nick rubbed his thumb along her knuckles. "After the medical issues that have arisen the last year, and me now being the town doctor, Adaleigh, Buck, and I have come up with an idea."

"I've been wanting to invest a significant portion of my finances into bettering the community that gave me a home." Adaleigh picked up the story. "It took me until Nick's return to figure out what. Mrs. Whittlebush agreed. It's part of why she sold me her house. We're going to turn it into a small hospital clinic."

"After your injuries," Nick's voice was gruff, "we moved up the plan."

"So you and David won't live there when you're married?" Mindy looked at her friends.

"That was never the arrangement." David toyed with one of Adaleigh's loose strands of hair and she batted him away.

"It wasn't. Grandma Martins needs us. David will move back in after the wedding. This will be our home." Adaleigh looked smitten with the idea.

"Bella and David are going to swap places after the wedding. That way, I can live at the clinic," Nick explained. "Bella, however, is enjoying being a seamstress, which means I'm lacking a nurse."

"You think I could be a nurse?" Mindy squeaked.

"You'd be perfect." Nick showed no doubt, yet he couldn't be more wrong.

"I can't, Nick. I can't ..." *read*.

"Mindy." David broke the moment. "I know why you think you can't."

"David, don't." Panic set in.

Adaleigh pressed her palm to David's chest. "It fits with your fake relationship idea, Mindy. Why wouldn't your man give you a position working with him? It'll sell the idea, and it's a wise one. It will make Spelding ridiculously angry, of course, but everyone else will cheer on an item like you two. That will be added protection from him and the thugs who attacked you."

"This is such a mess." Mindy tried to free herself from Nick's hold. He wouldn't let go.

"I don't know how we can pretend to be a couple," Nick said, "but if it means keeping you safe from a man like Spelding, then I'm all in."

"He'd marry you," David chuckled.

*What?* Mindy shot her head up to find everyone staring daggers at David.

"What?" David shrugged. "He offered that solution to Cora, and would have offered it to Marian if Gilbert hadn't already done so. Third time's a charm, isn't that what they say?"

Detective O'Connor snorted a laugh that echoed in Mindy's chest.

"Oh, you two brutes!" Adaleigh grinned as she rolled her eyes at Mindy. "I'm taking them inside. You two work out the details. I'm coming back in five minutes to help you up the stairs."

The woman was a force to be reckoned with when she wanted to be, and the two men let her herd them through the back door. The scent of berries wafted out in return.

"Mrs. Martins is baking dessert." Mindy stated the obvious to fill the silence.

Nick kept hold of her hand as he brought Adaleigh's rocking chair closer and sat. "David was teasing, but he's right. I will marry you if that would help you at all."

"Nick, you wouldn't be marrying me for the right reasons. Sure, it worked well for Marian and Gilbert. I won't do that to you.

An imaginary relationship is trouble enough. I shouldn't have even suggested it."

"You did it to protect yourself." He rested a knuckle under her chin. "I want you to promise me you'll do it again. If you ever feel unsafe, use my name. Claim anything you need from me."

"Nick." Something in his tone suggested this was more personal than the other times he offered aid, and her stomach twisted.

"I mean it." His jaw worked. "I can't bear to see you hurt like this again."

Emotion swelled. This was personal to him. Why? Who was she that a man like Dr. Nick Matrone would sacrifice himself to shelter her? David did, like a brother would. Nick's reaction did not make her feel sisterly at all. It made her feel ... cherished. Made her want to protect him, too. "All right, Nick. But I can't work for you. You need a capable nurse helping, and that's not me."

"Capable? You are very capable. I've seen you as a waitress. I've encountered few doctors with a bed-side manner as wonderful as yours. Your smile itself would heal a patient, I'm sure. If it's the actual nursing care, then you can be my secretary."

"Nick." A secretary was the last thing she could be.

"Or is it because we'd be a couple? A fictitious one, sure. But, you know. Propriety. We could figure that out, though." He was rambling, and she needed to stop him.

"It's not that." Could she tell him? She had to. He wouldn't understand otherwise. She sucked in as big a breath as her ribs allowed and spilled her secret before Nick could start up his ideas again. "I can't read."

"Okay?" Nick shook his head. "Why does that mean you can't work at the clinic?"

The man was intelligent, so why did he need her to make the connection for him? "You heard me, right? Words jump around. I memorize orders, make my own type of symbols to get by as a waitress, but a nurse? A secretary? I couldn't read your mail. I couldn't leave you a note. I'd make a mess of things and would simply be a burden."

"You would never be a burden." Nick glared at her, then softened. "Not being able to read is easily remedied. I could teach you."

"It's not that simple, Nick. Don't you think David tried? He helped me get through school, until I dropped out to work."

Nick's mouth flattened, yet she could see the determination building in his eyes. He wasn't about to take her lack of ability to read as a reason not to work at the clinic.

"It's also why we can't be more than friends, even if we pretend to be more until Detective O'Connor finds the people who want to hurt me and Mabel. You're a learned doctor, Nick. I'm an illiterate waitress. An uneducated farm girl, really. I was astonished Adaleigh wanted to be my friend, what with all her book learning. That I could have two such friends is more than I deserve. I—"

Nick growled, an odd sound coming from such a studious-looking man. Fire flashed in his eyes. He was mad. Mad at her? She shrank back as far as the rocking chair would allow. Her heart pounded. Had she said too much? She knew better. Knew not to make men angry. To make them look twice at her. She made that mistake with Joe. Now she'd made it with Nick.

He blinked. Squinted, as if peering deeply into her soul. Mindy crossed her arms, as if she could hide from him. She shouldn't have told him about not being able to read. She'd revealed too much. But he had to understand.

"Dessert is ready." Adaleigh's interruption felt like a life preserver.

"Uh ... it will keep. Finish your conversation."

"We're finished." Mindy knew she sounded desperate.

Adaleigh raised her eyebrow, looked between Mindy and Nick. Mindy's pulse raced.

Then Nick stood, held out his hand to her. "May I help you inside?"

She stared at his hand, shocked at the kindness in his tone. The closing of a door brought her gaze to the house, where Adaleigh had disappeared, then to Nick's face. Compassion had replaced anger. He nodded, giving her permission to take his hand? She did, and he lifted her to her feet. Nick drew her closer than friends should be, yet not too close that she felt uncomfortable.

"I hate it when you put yourself down, Mindy. You are a treasure. Any person would be privileged to know you, to be called your friend."

A sob tangled in her chest.

"I shouldn't." He closed his eyes.

Shouldn't what? "Nick?"

When he opened his brown eyes, warmth emanated from them. More than the warmth of a compassionate doctor, or even a friend. It struck her directly in the heart.

"I—"

He cut her off with a gentle kiss. "Don't."

She touched her lips and stared at him. Bewildered. Men had kissed her before, but not like that. It had always felt like they took something when they kissed her. This? She felt like he gave a piece of his heart to her. Oh how she would take care of it. With all the vehemence she could muster.

"Please let me protect you, Mindy." His voice cracked. "I can't stand by if there's something I can do to keep you safe."

"Okay, Nick." She would. Not for herself, for him.

His shoulders relaxed, and he smiled. Goodness, he was handsome.

"Do we keep up the charade of a pretend relationship?" Did she want to?

"Yes." All vulnerability disappeared from him. He was the decisive doctor again. "That will keep you safe from Spelding. I'll have a word with Buck to see whether he can help us keep his brother away from you."

"Thank you, Nick." She pressed a kiss to his cheek, couldn't help it.

"And," he winked. "I'm going to teach you to read."

Dastardly man. She couldn't help a grin.

# CHAPTER EIGHT

*Friday, June 26*

It had been a week since that night on Mrs. Martins's back porch, and Mindy could not stop thinking about Nick's kiss. It sat, tucked in the corner of her heart, like a warm blanket. She'd pull out the memory at the end of a long day. Or when she grew weary with pain. Or when she despaired over what to do with Mabel.

"She's in good hands, Mindy." Adaleigh broke into her musings, nudging her shoulder as they walked away from Mrs. Martins's house and towards the lake. "Grandma Martins is preserving green beans today and looked delighted to have a helper."

"I know." Mindy adjusted her clutch under her arm. "I worry is all. Usually people become annoyed when Mabel doesn't speak. I know that's not Mrs. Martins in the slightest."

"You've been okay with Bella spending time with Mabel." Adaleigh turned them north, toward Mrs. Whitlebush's house.

"Bella seems to need Mabel as much as Mabel needs a friend." Mindy had been pondering their unusual friendship more and more, especially after that kiss with Nick. "When Bella is tired or emotional, she lapses into Italian. Sometimes she gets her words all mixed up. She uses a lot of words."

Adaleigh chuckled. "Nearly as many as you."

Mindy ignored her warm cheeks. "Mabel seems to hang on every word Bella uses, whether it's English or Italian."

Adaleigh caught Mindy's arm, drawing them to a stop. Beyond the cliff, Lake Michigan stretched out in a slate of glassy blue. "Do you wish Mabel hung on your every word?"

The question startled Mindy. Did she?

"Have you ever asked yourself why you wish Mabel would speak?" Adaleigh linked their arms and restarted their walk.

"Isn't that what's best for her?" Defensiveness came easily.

"Why do you think that?"

"You and your questions," Mindy huffed, not liking the uncomfortable feeling rising in her belly. "You think Mabel is okay, just as she is? That not being able to speak is perfectly acceptable? Then why do people look down on her? Why do they mistreat her?"

"If she did speak, you think they wouldn't?" Adaleigh's tone answered her own question. Of course, people would. Look at how people treated Mindy because she was a waitress.

Then Adaleigh's choice of words hit her. *Did speak*, not *could speak*. "You think Mabel is capable of talking?"

"Absolutely." Adaleigh glanced at her. "Don't take this the wrong way ... Nick does, too."

"You talked about Mabel." Exactly what she didn't want to happen.

"Yes, Mindy, we did. My degree is in psychology and rhetoric. He's a medical doctor. It's completely natural for us to speak about the human condition."

"You think I'm being childish for protecting Mabel."

"I think you're being overprotective. You know full well that Nick and I would never want to see Mabel come to harm. We didn't discuss her like an oddity. We shared our observations and discovered we have similar conclusions."

The rebuke in Adaleigh's words struck hard. "I'm so used to protecting her."

"You're her big sister. Of course you are."

"Then what am I supposed to do?" Case in point, she'd praised Mabel for the beautiful drawings she had given her while she recuperated, but Mabel had shied away from the conversation. As if she didn't want Mindy to know she'd drawn them.

Adaleigh sighed as Mrs. Whittlebush's house came into view. The white house with the wide front porch spoke of comfort and home. Mindy could see why Nick and Adaleigh wanted to turn it into a hospital of sorts. After what she just went through, coming here to heal would have brought about the rest she still needed.

Nick emerged from the house, coat discarded, white shirtsleeves rolled up, olive skin growing darker with each summer day. He raised a hand to them, yet didn't smile.

"You should ask him." Adaleigh nudged Mindy's arm. "About Mabel. We agree that her muteness is not physical. We don't believe she is deaf or has a physical issue preventing her from speaking."

Mindy froze. "You mean she's choosing not to speak. Why?"

"That is the question, isn't it?" Adaleigh tugged her toward the house. "Come on, you don't want to be late for your first day of work."

As if Nick would fire her. She lowered her voice as they grew nearer the house. "How is this supposed to go? Me working for him and him calling on me. Pretending to call on me. Frankly, fake working for him, too."

"You're nervous."

"I am." Could her feet move any slower? With Nick watching them approach, she felt on full display.

They'd seen each other since "the kiss." He hadn't let a day go by without checking on her. It hadn't struck her that his actions were anything except him being an exceptional doctor, seeing that he had visited her every day since the attack. But this last week, she'd regained much of her strength. She didn't need a doctor checking on her every day. So, had he visited because it was expected to maintain such a relationship? Or—

"How are you ladies this morning?" Nick jogged down the porch steps to greet them. "Warm day, yet beautiful. Nothing like fresh air. I could get used to this."

"Fresh air?" Mindy asked.

"In New York City, the buildings are so close, and in the section where my family lived, the people crowded together. Hot days were stifling. This is glorious."

She'd always grown up with wide open spaces and couldn't imagine living in a city. Another thing the two of them did not have in common.

Adaleigh untangled her arm from Mindy's grasp. "I have some paperwork my lawyer expects from me, so I'll be in the kitchen. Behave yourselves." She hurried into the house.

"Spoken like an almost married woman," Nick called after her.

"Don't you forget it!" She laughed, then closed the door.

Mindy clasped her hands together. Nervous was an understatement. She was never like this around people, even the men who made her feel all slimy. Something she didn't miss now that she didn't work at the Wharfside. So what was *this* feeling for and why did it only happen around Nick?

"How are you today?" Nick ran his hand down her arm, then freed her fingers to weave with his own.

Her heart raced. "What are you doing?"

His brown eyes squinted behind his spectacles. He was assessing her. "Do you like when I hold your hand?"

"I ... I don't know." She did and yet ...

He released her. "Perhaps you haven't had a man you trust hold your hand for no other reason than because he wants to be connected to you."

Oh, she couldn't do this. "We can't fake a relationship, can we?"

"Let's have this conversation inside." He touched her back, guiding her forward and into the house. Protective, gentle. David would do something like this, and yet not exactly like this. It confused her.

The house had changed little since Mrs. Whittlebush left with Marian and Gilbert for Montana. To the left was the seamstress room and to the right was the parlor. Deeper into the house was the kitchen and Mrs. Whittlebush's old room. Upstairs were several other rooms.

"I'm planning to leave the seamstress area as is." Nick tucked his thumbs into his vest pockets. "When Bella returns, she can use that space as it was intended. The parlor will be the waiting room, and the bedroom back here will be the exam room."

It sounded like he had it all figured out.

"I'll put a secretary's desk out here. I'm thinking between you and Bella, you can manage it."

"Nick." She couldn't do that.

He turned his back to her. "I wish I had two exam rooms, but I don't want to take the seamstress room. That's my current dilemma."

She followed him. "Why do you need two exam rooms?"

"Because one needs to be a surgery. Minor procedures that don't require a hospital, of course."

She considered her own surgery, the one Nick performed to save her life, and shuddered. "Seems like you'd want it close to the kitchen, with hot water readily accessible."

Nick glanced over his shoulder with an approving smile. "You think like a nurse."

Why did that compliment make her all warm inside?

"Giving the grand tour?" Adaleigh looked up from where she sat at the kitchen table, papers spread out in front of her.

"Debating having an actual surgery room." Nick rubbed his chin.

"How big of a room do you need?" Mindy paced the kitchen. It took up the entire back of the house, if one included the pantry and cellar steps. She tapped a finger against her lips. "If Silas were here, he could build a wall."

"Where would you put it?" Adaleigh pushed away from the table.

"The pantry." Mindy walked the line where she would put a wall. "We would have to push the table into the cooking area, and we would lose pantry space."

"Easily remedied by adding cupboards under the stairs here." Adaleigh pointed to the area across from the sink pump.

"You would have to enter the cellar through the surgery," Mindy shrugged, "but hopefully you won't need to use the cellar all that often."

"You two are brilliant." Nick shook his head. "David and I learned a few techniques before Silas moved west. I'll talk to him tonight."

Adaleigh returned to her chair. "Show her the upstairs. How you want to turn the rooms into in-patient rooms. And the attic."

Nick rubbed his neck. "Shouldn't you join us?"

He was worried about her reputation. Mindy hugged herself, his concern for her wrapping around her chest like a blanket.

Adaleigh waved her hand, already focused on her paper. "You'll be a gentleman or I'll send Mrs. Martins after you. Or Bella."

"That threat has teeth." Nick gave a mock shudder. "My sister has the female Matrone gift for keeping people in line."

Adaleigh laughed. "Get on with you both. I have work to do."

"Shall we, Miss Zahn?" Nick offered her his elbow.

She slipped her hand around his arm, once again surprised at his strength. Not something she should be thinking about. Yet she had to admit, she stayed closer to his side than she needed as he led her upstairs.

"Four small rooms up here. Mrs. Whittlebush had them for the boarders she often invited in." Nick opened one door. "We'll make them simple recovery rooms for patients, like yourself, that need round the clock medical care."

"Will you add curtains and other homey touches?" she asked, thinking how curtains and frills would be more healing than simply a bed and unadorned bureau.

Nick led her down the hall. "Adaleigh has an amount to spend, however I give you freedom to do as you wish."

"Wait, what?" She stopped them.

"What?" A teasing light flashed in his brown eyes. "You're working here, and I can give you a job, can't I?"

"Decorating a room is a job?" That sounded ... enjoyable.

"Of course. We need to make these rooms places of healing. You have firsthand experience with what that means. Who better to make them what they need to be?"

Tears blurred her vision, and a few escaped down her cheeks.

"What is it?" He rubbed a tear away with his thumb. "Don't you like that plan?"

"More than I should." She sniffed.

"If you didn't like it, I wouldn't make you do it." He frowned. "Your last boss. He didn't keep the men from laying their hands on you, did he?"

"I'm a waitress." She shrugged. "Well, I was. I'm not sure what I am now."

"You're a nurse." Nick used gentle pressure to lift her chin so she had to look at him. "My nurse. And I promise to keep you safe from that type of behavior. You tell me if any patient makes you uncomfortable. If *I* make you uncomfortable. Are we clear?"

She nodded, then wrapped her arms around his waist. Inappropriate. Especially here. Alone on the second floor. But she couldn't help it. She felt ... loved. And needed to hide that emotion in the safest place she could think of. Nick's chest.

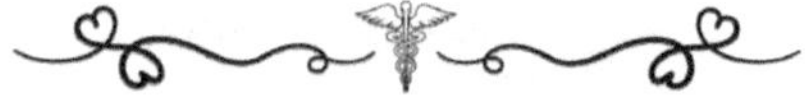

This woman would be his undoing. Nick rested his chin on her head, his hands gently touching her back, giving Mindy the freedom to escape the embrace she initiated. He wanted to tighten his hold on her. Maybe never let go. However, that would scare her. Frankly, he still didn't think they could ever be more than friends. She didn't think so either. So this hug had to be one of friendship.

Yet, it definitely was not. To him at least. This was the second piece of his heart he gave her. At this rate, he wouldn't have anything left by the end of the summer.

"Nick! Buck's here," Adaleigh called from downstairs, the distraction both welcome and unwelcome. Mindy stepped away, shoving loose strands of her hair away from her cheeks.

"We'll be there in a minute," Nick called back. He'd give Mindy a moment to recover before either Buck or Adaleigh saw the emotion she tried to hide. "Come on. I'll show you the attic."

"What's so special about the attic?" Mindy followed him up the steep, narrow steps.

"Right now, nothing. Eventually, I'll divide it into three rooms. One for me, one for Bella, and a guest room." Nick waved to the open expanse that stretched the length and width of the house, rising in a peaked roof. The summer heat radiated through the closed up space. Stifling. It'd be hard to sleep up here, but it was the only place left.

"You'll want to make sure it's a priority, Nick." She stepped through the dust toward the lone window facing east. From this elevation, Lake Michigan stretched in a sparkling blanket of diamonds for as far as the eye could see. Gorgeous. Or maybe that was the wonder that overtook Mindy's face as she peered out. "This view is wasted in an attic."

"I thought I'd give Bella that spot." He shrugged, not wanting to admit that with Mindy here, a longing to give her that room rose swift and strong. That would mean they were more than friends. That they were partners. For life. Husband and—

"No, no. She won't be here for all her days." Mindy crossed back toward him. "Bella is a young woman with a great future ahead of her. She won't stay with you forever, Nick. You need to take that room. Make it your shelter from the heartache, long nights, and death you'll face as a doctor. You need that view."

Wow. "You can teach a lot of things in medicine, but not bedside manner. You, Mindy Zahn, will make an excellent nurse."

"Have you forgotten that I can't read?" She waved him down the steps ahead of her.

"I said I will teach you. I can teach you medicine, too." He glanced over his shoulder at her. "Schooling is not a requirement to be a nurse,

Mindy. Only if you're a registered nurse, which you don't have to be. Unless you'd like to be one day. You could. You're intelligent and you can see what a person needs."

Mindy didn't reply.

The thought picked up steam in Nick's mind. He could see working side-by-side with Mindy, taking care of patients together. He'd begin with verbal instruction, substituted by simple notes that she could learn to read. Most nurses learn in a hospital setting. Why wouldn't this be any different?

He stopped on the first step of the first floor stairs, and spun, bringing him eye level to Mindy. "It's not flattery, if that's why you disagree with me. I've worked with dozens of nurses, and doctors, and you have something special. Something that can't be taught. It's innate in the way you see people, the compassion and care. I should have made the connection sooner."

"What connection?" She hugged herself, her tell for when she was feeling vulnerable. He needed to tread carefully.

"At the cafe. One of the reasons people are drawn to you, listen to you, is because you listen to them." He cupped her shoulders. "That gossip you pick up, the rumors you dispel, it's because of this ability you have to truly see a person for who they are."

"I think you've confused me with Adaleigh." Mindy stepped out of his reach, her eyes a wide mixture of hope and fear.

"Why do you think the two of you get along so well?" Nick held still, so she'd know he wasn't budging on his perspective. "You both listen to each other. Which, as listeners, neither of you experience very often. Where you differ ... Adaleigh can understand the mind of someone, she pulls out their secrets. Like a doctor drawing out an infection. You, Mindy, are the healer. After the doctor has excised a wound, you know how to make it right again."

She blinked rapidly. Nick spotted the moisture.

"You have a gift, Mindy. I'd be honored if you would use it here in my clinic." He bit the corner of his mouth to keep himself from offering anything more than a working relationship. They were already juggling a pretend romantic one that bordered on reality. A doctor to nurse relationship needed to be built on a firmer foundation.

"Matrone!" Buck's holler sliced through the moment. "Get down here. Joe is coming up the walk."

Mindy squeaked. Nick grabbed her hand as they hurried down the steps. "Did you know he was coming over?" Nick demanded.

"No. Haven't seen him all day." Buck peered out the parlor window in a way that kept him from being seen from outside. "I doubt he knows I'm here."

"Have a plan, then?" Nick tucked Mindy close to his side, and she pressed closer.

"Adaleigh, take Mindy to the cellar." Buck stuffed his hands into his pockets. "Nick and I will handle my brother."

The women didn't argue. Nick fortified himself with a prayer. Then opened the door.

And promptly had to dodge a fist flying toward his face.

"Joe!" Buck yanked his brother inside and away from Nick. "What's the meaning of this?"

"He stole my girl." Spelding glared at Nick, then his brother. "You put me in jail so I couldn't fight for her. Well, I'm fighting now."

"She's not your girl." Buck shoved him. "Mindy's with Nick now. Leave her alone."

"You would say that?" Spelding sneered, then advanced on Nick.

Nick took a step back, though his brain screamed at him to hold his ground.

"Why would you think you had any chance with her?" Spelding spat. "You're only a—"

"What do you want from me?" Nick stopped the slur he was sure to find on the tip of Spelding's tongue.

"Bow out." Spelding's broad shoulders loomed large. "She's mine."

"No, I'm not." Mindy stood in the hall, face white, arms wrapped around her stomach.

Nick caught her gaze. *Use my name,* he mouthed. Fear darkened her eyes. He'd give her every tool in his arsenal, will her every ounce of his strength, but this was a battle she needed to fight.

"You're coming with me." Joe turned on her.

Nick wanted to block his path. Buck made a move to do so. Nick held up a hand. Joe wouldn't get out of the house with Mindy. Let her win this.

One more glance at Nick, then Mindy lowered her arms and raised her chin. "I chose Nick."

Joe snarled. "You're going to regret that choice."

"Joe, leave her alone." Buck turned his brother by the shoulder.

"I'm going," Joe shrugged him off. "You don't need to manhandle me."

Now Nick stepped between Mindy and Joe, taking the mantle Mindy had offered. He would protect her, claim her as his girl for as long as she needed.

Joe stopped at the door, hand on the knob, then spun back. In two strides, he loomed over Nick. "You're a dead man, Matrone." Then he leveled a punch directly to Nick's gut.

Nick dropped to his knees, his diaphragm spasming, stealing his breath. He heard the door slam, felt Mindy's hands running down his arm.

"Adaleigh, call Detective O'Connor," Buck demanded. "Nick is pressing charges. No one, not even my brother, assaults a doctor. Not in my town."

"Come on," Mindy's sweet voice was soft in his ear. "You can wait for Detective O'Connor on the couch in the parlor."

Nick let her lead him to the couch, though he was half doubled over. He knew the blow didn't do any damage, and he'd be fine as soon as his muscles eased up. He lay back, let Mindy perform her ministrations. Her sweet, gentleness took his breath away, along with a third piece of his heart. Thinking he'd have even a chunk of it left by the end of the summer was laughable. He'd be fortunate to make it a week. A sacrifice he'd make to keep her safe from a man like Spelding.

He caught her fingers before she could go too far. "Thank you."

"This is my fault." She pressed her free palm to his forehead, concern making her frown.

"Thank you for trusting me to be your protector." He brought the back of her hand to his lips. "And for being my nurse."

# CHAPTER NINE



*Sunday, June 28*

Mindy trailed her hands down her hips, the cotton fabric of her Sunday dress smooth under her palms. Today was a momentous day. She and Nick would arrive at church together. He would sit with her. They'd declare in front of the entire community that they were an item. It was all make believe. And lying in church gave her the willies.

A tug on her skirt brought her around. Mabel took her hand in both of hers. She scrunched her nose. "B—" The soft puff slipped from Mabel's mouth, and her eyes popped open. Fear flashed there, and she ran from the room.

"Mabel, wait!" Mindy's heels prevented her from running after her sister. In the moment it took to kick them off and make chase, Mabel made herself underfoot as Mrs. Martins, Adaleigh, and Bella carried sweet treats to Mrs. Martins's Chevrolet.

Have it her way, Mindy wouldn't press her sister.

She retreated up the stairs, her body protesting her actions. Had Mabel tried to speak? Or was that Mindy's wishful thinking? Most importantly, what was Mabel afraid of? Surely not Mindy. Yet she'd run away from her.

Mindy donned her shoes, cloche, shawl, and clutch. She hadn't followed through on Adaleigh's suggestion to talk to Nick about Mabel's lack of speech. After today, she found he was the first person she wanted to tell. Perhaps he could explain what she saw in her sister's eyes. If they could calm Mabel's fears, would her sister speak? Mindy's heart broke that fear could be the prison holding her sister's voice hostage.

It made her want to talk to Nick even more. She felt safe with him. Of course, they hadn't had a moment to themselves since the tour on Friday. Not a negative thing if they were determined to remain friends, and nothing more. No matter the pretense they put on to keep Joe away from her.

Nick, David, and Buck were framing the surgery area she suggested in the kitchen. It seemed, since Joe's threat, Buck was always around, as if reluctant to allow Nick out of his sight. She and Adaleigh had been at the house all day yesterday, and she couldn't help noting how Buck remained watchful. What did he think his brother would do to Nick?

She shuddered. Yes, this counterfeit relationship could protect Mindy, yet at what cost?

All the questions kept her quiet, even more so as she stood on the front step, watching Mabel ride away with Mrs. Whittlebush and Bella.

Adaleigh paced the walk. "It's unlike David to be late. After everything that's happened the last year, I don't like it. I could have lost him twice now." She fingered the thin, woven twine around her ring finger. Mindy's idea. She'd made it for David to present to Adaleigh as a symbol of their engagement. Mindy knew her friends, knew they needed something tangible to remind each other that they'd never allow Adaleigh's wealth—or anything else—to stand between them.

"Should we walk toward them?" Mindy would not voice the real concern David and Nick's delay brought to mind. Not that danger had found them, as Adaleigh worried, but that Nick had changed his mind. That he didn't want to escort Mindy to church, or pretend to claim her as his girl.

"Yes. Let's go." Adaleigh stalked to Mindy's side, hooked her arm around Mindy's, and tugged her down the walk at a pace that didn't fit with heels. How Adaleigh walked in hers with such confidence, Mindy didn't know. She hated the things. Of course, she had to wear them as a waitress, but she chose Mary Janes with their low heel. For church, it didn't feel right to wear her working shoes. These pumps hurt her feet.

"I'm sure they're fine," Mindy insisted, hoping she could calm her friend. Suggesting they slow down wouldn't help the root cause of Adaleigh's angst.

Her friend simply walked faster.

Mindy dislodged her arm and stopped. "Rushing head-long into whatever is delaying them won't help them."

Adaleigh groaned. "I know. I know. I just …"

"Love David and don't want to lose him." Mindy gripped her friend's forearm. "I don't understand why you're waiting for October to get married."

"We considered a quiet ceremony over the winter, after this past Christmas, but David wanted his grandmother there." Adaleigh shrugged, a light blush pinked her cheeks. "So we decided to wait until the fishing season is over. Then I'm taking him on a honeymoon to see my old house. I want him to see where I came from."

Mindy hugged her friend. She wanted to say something about God. It seemed appropriate here. It's what Adaleigh would do for her. But she couldn't read the Bible, could only recall what she'd memorized from church services over the years. Nothing came to mind. Even if it did, offering it felt awkward.

A car roared up beside them. Mindy and Adaleigh jumped apart. Mindy's pulse raced, her head grew light. Why hadn't they been paying attention to their surroundings? What if her attackers had returned? She couldn't be the reason Adaleigh's wedding wishes didn't come true.

However, David leapt out of the passenger side and Mindy's knees nearly buckled in relief. Adaleigh flung her arms around his neck. David planted a kiss on his fiancé's lips, then waved Mindy toward the still open car door.

"Nick needs you to be his nurse." David kept Adaleigh tucked to his side. "You'll have to present your imaginary relationship at services another time. Off you go."

Mindy opened her mouth to protest. To ask whether this was appropriate. Or any other number of questions that jumped to mind.

Nick leaned across the passenger seat. "Mindy, don't second guess. Please get in the car. I need your help."

His demanding doctor's tone propelled her into the car. David slammed the door and Nick accelerated. Mindy braced a hand on the dash. "What's the emergency?" Because, obviously, it was one.

"Little girl fell out of a tree." Nick took a turn too sharply. "Concussion at best. Family can't afford the hospital."

The poor child! "Who is it?"

Nick glanced at her. "Mary Lou Vashen."

Mindy could picture the precocious child who was the recipient of one of Silas's carpentry projects. She was also the Vashens's only child to survive past her third birthday. "Will she be all right?"

"We won't know anything until I see how bad off she is, or whether she has other injuries." Nick glanced at her. "Like with you, there could be internal injury."

She pressed her fingers against the scar on her side where Nick saved her life. "If anyone can help her, it's you."

Nick shook his head. "I'm an average human doctor. God is the true Physician."

"How do you do that?" Mindy asked as he pulled up to a weathered farmhouse along Crow's Nest Creek. Similar to the Wards's old place—now Patrick and Meri Martins's house—but northwest of town and much smaller.

"Do what?" Nick reached into the back seat for his black medical bag.

"Bring God so easily into the conversation."

He stalled, the twist of his body bringing him close to her. "I've never thought about it." Then he was moving again.

Mindy scrambled out of the car, struggled to keep up with his brisk pace to the Vashens's back door.

Mr. Vashen welcomed them inside. The heat followed them into the kitchen. Little Mary Lou lay on the table, unconscious, her flour-sack dress dirty and torn. Mrs. Vashen looked up from where she kept vigil beside her daughter, her pale cheeks stained with tears.

Instinctively, Mindy went straight to the hurting mother and wrapped her in her arms. The woman sobbed, her free hand clutching Mindy's dress in a desperate grab. As if by holding on tight enough, she could protect her daughter. Mindy's heart cracked in half. There were no words she could say.

"Tell me exactly what you've done since she fell." Nick set his bag beside Mary Lou on the table and bent over the little girl, raising her eyelids one at a time.

"I made sure she was alive," Mr. Vashen's voice quivered. "Then carried her inside. She thrashed so much, I was afraid she'd harm herself more. We keep a bottle of medical whiskey on hand. We got it from Dr.

Thompson. It was legal, wasn't it? We won't get into trouble—"

"Medical whiskey is allowed despite Prohibition." Nick pressed his fingers to Mary Lou's wrist.

"Okay. Okay." Mr. Vashen nodded. "We called you before we gave her the whiskey. I didn't know what else to do."

Mindy hated the man's fear and despair. *God, if you hear me. Save Mary Lou.*

Twenty minutes later, Nick leaned the kitchen chair back on its hind legs and scrubbed his fingers through his hair.

Little Mary Lou still lay on the table. Stable, but unconscious.

There wasn't much else he could do for her other than observe how she fared. And make sure she didn't flail when she woke.

He dropped the chair back on all four legs and pressed his elbows into his thighs. There was no evidence of internal bleeding. She had several bruised bones and one broken one. Fortunately, from what Nick could tell without surgery, the femur break was an oblique fracture. There was a risk of the bones not being set well, though he did his best. The femur fracture concerned him most because it could affect her gait if he hadn't gotten it set straight.

The responsibility of a doctor weighed on him. He felt it most keenly when he worked with children. Their lives in his hands. But as he told Mindy ... not entirely in his hands. In God's hands, too.

He bowed his head. *Padre nostro* ... words of healing and mercy for this little girl poured silently from his lips. He thought of Mindy's question about how easily he turned to prayer, how easily he mentioned God in his conversation.

It had always been that way because Mamma had always been that way. She brought God into everything. If ever a person prayed without ceasing, it was her.

She could be cooking dinner, then suddenly pause for a moment to pray. They would be walking to the grocer's down the street when something would catch her eye that caused her to pause for a moment to pray.

Becoming a doctor, seeing life and death so vividly day in day out, it became second nature to him as well. Because as much as he was a doctor, he was not a healer. God was the healer. Without God's healing mercies, Nick could not cause the healing his patients required.

Again, that was especially true with children.

He raised his gaze to Mary Lou as she moaned and moved her head. She'd done so several times since Mindy took the Vashens outside. Yet the little girl hadn't woken. Didn't now, either.

His thoughts drifted to Mindy. How could he explain his belief that Jesus was a physician who could heal both the body and the soul? Even when—no, especially when—death visited. It was then that Nick clung to that belief even more. And he admitted doubts about God hearing all the prayers he prayed. Especially since his previous medical partner derided him for such thinking.

Would little children like Mary Lou and Mabel have to wait until heaven to be completely healed? If Jesus were here now, how would he respond to Mabel's lack of speech? Jesus, who healed the mute, the deaf, the lame. Who desired the little children to come to Him.

What would Jesus do for Mabel?

Nick checked Mary Lou's forehead for fever, grateful to find it cool.

Would Mindy let Nick talk to Mabel? To ask some of the questions that weighed down his mind. Not whether Mabel could speak, because he was reasonably sure she could physically, but to dig into why she did not. It concerned him that Mindy's beating and whatever held Mabel's speech could be connected. He'd seen children too afraid to speak. What happened that the Zahns thought it safer to leave the girls here without them?

Nick jumped to his feet to pace the house. The Vashens's small downstairs was made up of two rooms: the main room and the bedroom. The upstairs would be where Mary Lou usually slept, though she wouldn't be able to climb the ladder for weeks. He opened the back door, and a wall of heat met him. He marveled at how easily Mindy had ushered Mr. and Mrs. Vashen out of the house.

The morning chores had been forgotten amid Mary Lou's initial injury, so Mindy went out with the Vashens to do the chores while Nick kept vigil. It felt weird to let her go out to do manual labor while he stayed inside. He had never milked a cow or fed chickens. He was a city boy, through and through. He knew how to set a bone, and how to use herbs and concoct poultices. Yet he needed somebody to grow them. Someone like Mindy.

He rested his hands on his waistband, having shed his coat and rolled up his sleeves. It made him think, again, that he and Mindy would make excellent partners. They complimented one another, could easily become a team, unstoppable.

Yet, it would mean tying her to himself. Opening her up to the struggle and pain of the discrimination they could face.

His last name was not as obviously Italian as others, especially since people tended not to say it correctly. So, if she wasn't standing beside his swarthy self, it wouldn't be as obvious that she was connected to an Italian. However, in a small town, would their neighbors eventually turn on him as his own neighbors had back in New York? Would this trouble brewing in Europe spread here and cause even more heartache?

No. He couldn't do that to her. She had such a soft heart, he couldn't subject her to even more criticism than she already faced. He just couldn't do it. It broke his heart to even think of what could happen. That told him even more about how he felt toward her. It was not enough just to look out for her. Wasn't enough just to allow her to use him as the other half of a fictitious relationship. He wanted more.

Behind him, Mary Lou stirred on the table. He closed the door to the heat of the outdoors and crossed to the little girl's side. While he also needed to get a gauge on her pain level, he couldn't give her anything to manage it until she woke. His main concern was to make sure that Mary Lou could walk again. That her gait would be even and that she wouldn't be on crutches for the rest of her life. That was a genuine possibility. Bella's childhood friend faced this very issue after being trapped in the Italian earthquake that originally connected him to Crow's Nest last year. He would do his very best to make sure it didn't happen to Mary Lou.

The back door swung open. Mr. and Mrs. Vashen hurried in, asking after their daughter. Nick explained that there had been no change and attempted to ease their worry. His gaze darted to Mindy, who had quietly followed them back inside. Straw stuck in her hair and mud streaked her clothing. He liked that about her. She didn't mind getting her hands dirty and was not afraid of hard work. In fact, she relished it. She seemed to glow the harder she worked.

He considered how she managed as a waitress with coarse calls and demanding customers. She always had a smile. That sunny disposition of hers often showed brighter the meaner people were to her. She wouldn't be scared of discrimination. She faced it already. That made him want to protect her from it even more. Because if he asked her to walk through it with him, she would. In fact, so unselfish was she, that she didn't think she could bring anything to *his* life.

As Mr. and Mrs. Vashen crooned over their daughter, Nick stepped away, giving them a modicum of privacy. It brought him closer to Mindy. He couldn't help it. She drew him. Would a pretend relationship be enough? The thought was laughable because it would have to end at some point.

When she no longer needed his protection, where would that leave them? The entire community would turn on one or both of them for breaking the other's heart. Whoever was the darling of the town was the one they would side with. He had to make sure that person would be her.

"How is she?" Mindy pressed her shoulder into his arm, speaking quietly. "They are worried sick."

"No change." Dare he voice his deepest worry? Not in the same room as the parents. He hooked her arm to draw her outside.

"What is it?" Concern radiated from her.

He turned his gaze toward the horizon. "I worry about how hard she hit her head. But there is nothing I can do until she wakes up."

Mindy took his hand in both of hers. "God? Nick said You are the Great Healer. Can You help him treat Mary Lou?"

Nick wrapped Mindy in his arms as emotion washed over him. He felt so inadequate, so small in light of her earnest prayer.

"Was that okay?" Her voice was muffled against his chest.

He spoke with his lips against her hair. "More than."

How could he make sure that when this was over, when she was safe again, she had an abundant future? Here and now, he swore to put her first, no matter what came.

Nick stepped away from her. "Let's go for a walk." He peeked his head into the kitchen to let the Vashens know to call for him if there was any change and grabbed a couple things from his medical bag.

Despite the heat, a stroll would be welcome. Yes, he caught the glimmer in Mr. Vashen's eyes. No doubt, they, too, had heard the rumor going around that Nick and Mindy were a couple. It likely wasn't a surprise that the doctor wanted a moment with the pretty young nurse he had brought with him.

It was more than that, though. Attraction wasn't why Nick wanted to spend more time with her. Nor was it simply to keep up their ruse. She was a balm to his soul, and right now, he needed her.

# CHAPTER TEN

Not sure what to do with the thoughts in his head, Nick led Mindy toward a small pond past the Vashens's chicken coop. Heat pressed on his body, making each step a weighted one. Not even a cool breeze stirred to break up the beating sun.

"How are you holding up?" he asked her, wanting to take her hand. If the Vashens were watching from the window—which he doubted—they would expect such a move from a man courting a woman.

"I'm hurting for them." Mindy wiped a trickle of sweat from her forehead. "Is there anything else we can do or should do?"

He wove his fingers between hers. "For now, we can only wait. It will be beneficial for Mr. and Mrs. Vashen to stay with her, and we need a rest. I ... I have a couple things I want to talk with you about."

"Oh?" She glanced at him expectedly, as if he offered her a gift. He hoped she'd still think so after he shared his thoughts with her.

He led her toward a wooden bench beside the pond. Flowers grew around it, and he suspected the spot had special meaning to Mr. and Mrs. Vashen. Their home may be humble, yet he felt the love that filled it.

"This looks like Silas's work." Mindy ran her hand over the smooth top before sitting. Then she bent double, shifting her legs out of the way to see underneath the bench. "Yup. He had a symbol—an S on top of a

W—that he'd brand into the underside of any piece he created, and here it is."

She sat up quickly and swayed. Nick dropped beside her, his arm circling her shoulders. "Steady there."

"I'm fine." She pressed fingers to her temple. She'd said the same thing before, and he suspected she used the phrase frequently in order to make others comfortable.

"I'm a doctor, Mindy. You can't fool me. I know you're still regaining your strength." He slid closer, and she rested her head on his shoulder, relaxing against him with a sigh. The sound did something to his insides. This trust she placed in him.

Should he follow through on his idea if she didn't feel her best? Earlier, she'd asked how he so easily prayed. Scripture was second nature to him, but if she couldn't read, had she ever read the Bible for herself? What a painful thought. It spurred him to want to teach her to read even more. Maybe he could simply help her read by using the Bible itself.

He cleared his throat. "Would you mind if we begin our first reading lesson on a Sunday?"

She chuckled without moving her head. "It hardly seems appropriate."

"It's more appropriate than you think. I wanted to show you a couple of verses. I carry a New Testament in my doctor bag because I never know when the end is near, and when someone needs a bit of comfort." He slipped the black book from his pocket and held it before them. "It was a gift from a street evangelist I met on a corner one day, and I've carried it with me since."

She reverently rested her fingers on the cover. "Because it was a gift, you wish to offer that gift to others."

His already warm body heated more. "I'm nothing special. But yes, I have had to use it multiple times. Let's look at a couple of verses, and I can teach you to read them. Have you ... have you ever read the Bible for yourself?"

Mindy lifted her head from his shoulder. "No. The words jump around. It's not that I don't know the letters or words ... I can't figure out how to read them."

He considered her explanation. "So, it's not so much that you are not capable of reading, which I never doubted for a minute. It's more that there is something in the way of allowing you to read the way others do. Words aren't supposed to jump around, and they don't for most people."

She ducked her chin. "Why do they do this for me? Is there something wrong with me?"

He tightened his hold around her shoulders. "No, there's nothing wrong with you. We don't truly know how the brain works, how the eyes work, how the body works. We're still learning, still figuring things out. From what you're saying, I'd guess you have word blindness or dyslexia. Doctors used to believe it was a disorder of the eyes, they now consider it to be psychological." Like Mabel's condition, if his and Adaleigh's suspicions were correct.

"Dr. Thompson said I have a deficit." Mindy's words came out quiet.

"Well, the man betrayed his calling as a doctor, so whatever he said should be discounted." Nick barely restrained his offense on her behalf. "It's true that many consider the condition a mental deficiency, but with the right help, it can be—not fixed—overcome."

Her chin rose, her eyes filled with wonder. "You really think I'll be able to read some day?"

If it was the last thing he'd do. "Let's see if we can make those words sit still long enough for you to read them. I thought we could begin with a passage about Jesus healing the sick."

Fear clashed with excitement in her eyes. "Just don't judge me too harshly. I've never been able to do what you want me to do."

They'd see about that. He opened the Bible to Mark chapter two and chose verse seventeen. Then he took his writing pad from his pocket, tore off a piece of paper, tearing the single piece in half, and set the halves above and below the line. "Use your finger to go word by word. What did Jesus say in this verse?"

"I know this word because it begins with the letter T. *They.*"

"Great beginning. What's the next word?" He used his fingers to block out the rest of the sentence so she could only see the four-letter word that came next: *that.*

*They that are ...* She made it through to the fourth word before she shook her head. "Each word is so jumbled up. Do I have to memorize the look of each word? That's what I do when I create orders. I make myself notes and have my own shorthand. I can read my own language, but when it comes to reading other people's writing, I can't do it."

"I'm not expecting you to read as if you've been doing so your whole life, Mindy. You're focusing very hard, and your brain is working. We're exercising muscles you're not used to using."

Mindy gave a little scoff.

He closed the Bible over his finger. "The more you read, the easier it will get."

"Fine, whatever you say." She folded her arms. "But I have been trying to do this for years. You're not going to have a magic solution."

"Mindy, I'm not trying to have a magic solution. I'm trying to give you a tool so that you can figure out how to move forward. So you can wrangle the words as they jump around the page. From what I understand, they'll never stop jumping. Don't let that hold you back.

You can move forward. You can do this."

Mindy turned to look at him. His face was inches from hers. "You really think so?"

He swallowed. "I do."

She leaned closer, or did his arm draw her nearer? It would be so easy for him to kiss her. He wanted to kiss her. Wanted her to know how much he believed in her. Yet he held back, not wanting to offer what he couldn't give. Theirs was a fake relationship. A true one would draw her into his pain.

Mindy blinked.

Nick cleared his throat. "Shall we try this again?"

Mindy's heart hammered in her chest. Why was the doctor having such an effect on her? She really needed to have her heart checked, maybe her brain, too, because this was entirely too much. She shouldn't be feeling these things for him. But the way he expressed such confidence in her ... it gave her the courage to try anything.

She looked at the verse again and wrestled the letters into order on the page. "They that are ... whole ... have ... no ..." She pressed fingers to her temple as it began to throb.

Nick took the Bible from her. "That's enough for today."

"Can you read it to me?" She wanted to know the verse.

He tugged her close, placed a kiss against her hair. "You'll be able to read it soon enough. I know it."

A balloon filled within her chest. It must have pumped air straight into her head because before he could move, she caught his lips with hers.

It was forward, and not at all proper for her to do. Tears smarted, and she tried to scramble away, apology on her tongue. He wrapped his arms tighter around her, brought a hand up the back of her head to keep her close as his kiss whisked her away from the here and now.

A shout from the back of the house interrupted them. A positive or negative thing, she wasn't sure. She wasn't sure of much. Nick was on his feet and rushing toward the house before she'd quite gathered herself.

She'd kissed him, and then he'd taken her breath away. What must the Vashens think of them? Canoodling while their daughter lay sick. Mortification wrapped around her. This was exactly why they could never have more than a sham of a relationship. She'd lead him astray with her loose ways. Isn't that what her father said when she got the waitress job? With the way most men treated her, she believed it.

Feeling like the mud under her shoes, she hurried to the house. She entered as Nick leaned over a little Mary Lou. Mrs. Vashen sat on a chair beside the table, holding the little girl's hand, continually whispering in the child's ear.

"How is she?" Mindy asked as Mr. Vashen came to stand beside her. Maybe he hadn't seen her kiss Nick.

"Stirring, thank the Lord." Emotion clogged the man's throat.

Nick checked Mary Lou's eyes and listened to her lungs with his stethoscope. Mary Lou moaned and rolled her head.

"Shh, sweetie." Mrs. Vashen's instant comfort grew louder as her daughter writhed. Mr. Vashen crossed his arms, his jaw muscle bouncing. "Dr. Nick is here. He's gonna make sure you're feeling all better."

The little girl groaned. She was in so much pain, Mindy could feel it, see it. She pressed a hand to her side. Her still tender side. The memory of the beating that she took flashing before her.

The little girl became more violent in her movements. Mrs. Vashen's comforting words turned to tears. Nick looked over his shoulder at Mindy and Mr. Vashen. "Sir, I need you to take your wife out of the room."

The woman shook her head. "No. I won't leave."

"I'm sorry." His compassion mixed with steel. "Doctor's orders."

It propelled Mindy to action. She wrapped her arm around Mrs. Vashen's shoulders, encouraging her to stand and turning her toward her husband. "I will take care of your daughter, Mrs. Vashen. You can trust me. You know me. I promise I won't leave her side. I will keep hold of her hand. She's safe with us."

Mr. Vashen tucked his wife under his arm and led the weeping woman from the room without a word.

As good as her promise, Mindy grasped the child's hand, using her weight to hold her down. She glanced at Nick. "What do we need to do?"

Quick instructions on how to hold the little girl while Nick asked her questions. Mary Lou bucked beneath Mindy's hold. This wasn't working.

Mindy jerked back to keep Mary Lou's elbow from striking her chin. "Nick, let me ask the questions. You hold her."

Without a second hesitation, he switched places with her, holding the little girl to keep her from falling off the table.

Mindy stroked the crying girl's hair and lowered her voice to a quiet whisper. "Mary Lou, you know me. It's Mindy. I get you hot chocolate when you come to the Wharfside. It's too warm for some right now, but it sure would taste delicious."

Mary Lou opened her eyes in a quick blink.

"Hi. There you are." Mindy kept caressing her cheek. "We're going to make sure you're going to be okay, so I need you to answer a few questions for me. Can you do that?"

The little girl's cries turned into whimpers.

"Can you tell me whether your head hurts?"

Mary Lou moaned.

"Can you tell me about your eyes?" Mindy asked. "Can you open them?"

The little girl tried as tears trickled down her cheeks.

"It's too bright in here, isn't it?" She could relate. It had been too bright for her when she first awakened after the beating. "Let's try something else. Did you know those bones along your chest are called ribs? You learned about ribs in school, I'm sure."

The little girl gave a slight, slow nod.

"Yeah, you have learned about ribs in school. You like school. It's pretty fun to learn about science." Mindy knew it sounded like she was rambling, but she wanted to ease Mary Lou's fear. It's what she would have wanted in the child's place. "Ribs are what keep everything in your chest nice and safe. Let's see, does anything in there hurt?"

She gave Nick a subtle indication to test the little girl's reactions. He felt along her rib cage, testing for bruising and for any extra winces. Mary Lou didn't show any signs of extra pain in that area. Thank God. Mindy knew how painful rib injuries could be.

"Your ribs don't seem like they bother you at all." Mindy forced cheer into her voice. "Let's try your tummy now. Dr. Nick is going to see if your tummy hurts, and you tell me if it does."

As Nick palpitated Mary Lou's stomach, she didn't wince, didn't flail or thrash.

"All right," Mindy continued. "Now we're gonna move to your arms and legs."

Mary Lou swung her head. "Don't touch my leg!"

"Shh. Dr. Nick won't touch your leg. I know it's very painful right now. Did you know that Dr. Nick helped me feel better? He is a really great doctor."

Mary Lou turned her head toward Mindy's voice though she kept her eyes closed. "Did it hurt a lot?"

"My injuries hurt at first, but Nick helped me."

She sniffed. "Will he help me, too?"

Mindy smiled. "Yes, he will."

The little girl shifted to give Nick her right arm. "It's my school arm. I'm not supposed to write with my other one."

Nick's jaw ticked as he ran his fingers over the thin limb. "Your school arm is perfect."

The little girl relaxed.

"Let's look at your other arm." Nick moved around the table, bringing him close to Mindy's side. "Her head and leg are where the most injury lies."

"What does that mean?" Mary Lou whimpered. Nick sighed and shook his head. To keep Mindy from expounding?

But Mindy knew exactly what she needed to say. She leaned close to the little girl, comforting, like she would her little sister. "It means your head and leg will hurt for a little bit."

Nick made a noise in his throat. He didn't approve. But she knew it would help.

"I don't want you to be afraid, though. Dr. Nick will help you feel better in the end. Sometimes we have to go through a little pain before we can heal. You'll be in pain for a whole lot longer than if we go through a bit of pain now so that it won't hurt as much later."

The little girl gave a very slow nod. Sweet child.

"We need to wait for this swelling to go down before I can properly cast it." Nick rested his palm against the top of Mary Lou's head, saying to her, "Before I go, I need to check your head one more time."

"It hurts."

Mindy leaned close. "It takes a little while, but it will improve each day. You know what? Your mama and daddy will help you. Make sure it gets all healed, too."

Mary Lou sighed. "I'm sleepy."

"I know, sweetie. Let's get you some rest so you can keep healing, because you know that's the best way to feel better."

Nick called Mary Lou's parents back inside and gave them instructions on caring for her. He also explained that he would return tomorrow to set the bone and plaster the leg. Mindy would join him again, and—miraculously—they looked relieved.

"This is all we can offer in payment." Mrs. Vashen gave them a loaf of bread.

Nick shook his head. "Soak it in broth and give it to Mary Lou."

Mrs. Vashen teared up and hugged the loaf to her chest.

She and Nick stayed silent during the drive back to Mrs. Martins' house. What could they say? Mindy couldn't get the sight of Mrs. Vashen holding that loaf out of her head. Is that how her mother felt? Is that why her parents left Mabel in Mindy's care?

As they turned onto the street, Nick said, "There was one other thing I wanted to ask you before Mary Lou woke up."

Before their kiss.

"Would you mind if I talked to Mabel? Alone."

She opened her mouth to protest, then remembered the fear in her little sister's eyes this morning. Thought of the drawings she didn't want to acknowledge.

Nick held up a hand. "I want to ask her some questions, that's all. I have a theory I want to test."

"I don't like this, Nick." She turned to face him as he parked along the curb in front of Mrs. Martins's home. "I don't like seeing Mabel treated like a specimen. She's a little girl."

"I—"

"A little girl who is afraid of something." Mindy met Nick's gaze. "I thought she made an attempt at a word this morning. When I asked her, she ran away from me. Ran. Hid."

Nick reached for her hand. "That's what I want to ask her. I think she saw something she shouldn't have."

A shudder worked through Mindy's body. "We really are in danger, aren't we?"

"The beating you took wasn't an indication?" He pushed his spectacles up his nose. "Mindy, your father was obviously involved in something and instead of staying to work it out, he left you girls to face the trouble alone."

"You don't think I know that?" Mindy jerked the car door open. Why did men keep mistreating her? Spelding. Her father ... would Nick? How could she trust him to have her best interests in mind?

"Mindy, wait." Nick met her at the car's hood, setting his doctor's bag on top. "I'm sorry. I shouldn't have spoken ill of your father. Right or wrong, he's still your dad."

Mindy deflated. "I'm sorry I keep getting angry and running away. I wouldn't have faced those thugs if I hadn't been so upset at you and Adaleigh." She closed her eyes.

Nick tucked her under his chin, arms around her. "You're hurting, Mindy. Don't hide that from me."

She peered up at him. "What do you mean?"

"I can handle you lashing out at me, but I can't help you if you push me away."

The words sank into her soul like water to dry dirt. She put distance between them, needing to breathe. "Say that again."

He held out his hands, palms up. An invitation. "I want to help. Let me?"

"No, not that part." She shook her head. "You can handle my heartache."

"Absolutely."

"God can handle my pain, too." She whispered the words, the connection dumbfounding. "He can't help me if I push Him away."

Nick stared at her. "I hope you're not comparing me to God, Mindy. I am not perfect. You, of all people, should know that, seeing that I just apologized."

Mindy waved him off. "It's not you I'm comparing. It's what you said. I'd never thought of God that way before. I always wondered if He heard me, saw me. He does. He's here. Like you."

Nick dropped his chin.

"Mr. Matrone?" A man approached, his voice familiar. One of her attackers!

"Nick." She pressed into his back as he put himself between her and the man. He had a scruffy brown beard and calculating brown eyes. No mask today, even as he presented himself in full daylight.

"What do you want?" Nick edged toward the Martinses' door.

"I came to confirm the rumors." The man stood at ease, feet shoulder-width apart. "You and Miss Zahn are indeed a couple."

Nick's muscles bunched as he straightened his back. "We are. I ask again: what do you want?"

"Your girl has something I need." The man spoke as if this were a business arrangement. "If you care for her, then you'll help her get it for me."

"Absolutely not." Nick gave her a little shove, and she realized he'd maneuvered them so he could guard her path to the door. He dropped his voice. "Go call for help."

She didn't want to leave him, but the best way to help was to call for reinforcements.

Her attacker laughed as she darted away. "Not to worry, Matrone. If you won't help us, I know someone who will."

Mindy looked back, hand on the doorknob. The threat, leaving Nick, freezing her feet.

Nick stood firm on the walk like a valiant knight. "Leave her alone."

The man just grinned. "We were told to get you out of his way. It'll be our pleasure."

*Our.* From the right, a man crouch-ran, a knife in his hand.

"Nick!" Mindy screamed as the second man leapt at him.

# CHAPTER ELEVEN

Nick felt the presence of a man behind him as Mindy screamed. He lunged away, the man's knife catching him in the left arm. Adrenaline masked the pain, and he refrained from clamping a hand over the wound. Sticky blood on his hands would not help him right now.

He bounced on his toes, assessing the attack. Mindy stood frozen at the front door. The men were focused on him. First Man smirked, fists raised to come at him. Second Man recovered his stumble from when his knife didn't hit with the force he expected and turned, ready to try again. From behind, Nick knew a third man approached.

First Man's gaze darted over Nick's shoulder, his muscles bunching. Second Man shifted out of his way. They meant to immobilize him before knifing him. He shrugged his coat, loosening it from his shoulders. First Man gave a subtle nod. Nick bent his knees. Third Man gripped his collar, bringing the coat down to pin Nick's hands.

Predictable. Nick jerked his arms up as he straightened his knees. Hands free, he used the moment to spin the heel of his palm into Third Guy's stunned face. First Guy threw a haymaker. Nick blocked with his forearm. Second Guy entered the fray, knife in hand.

Nick snatched his coat, spun it into a rod-like shield, as Second Guy stabbed at him with the knife. Nick wrapped the coat around the man's wrist, pulling him closer. Second Man reacted with a left-handed punch aimed at Nick's face. Nick leaned into it, catching a loose fist in the jaw and hearing the sound of Second Man's breaking hand bones.

Second Man howled and dropped the knife. Nick kicked it under his car. He kept a knife hidden in his belt for use as a last resort. As of yet, he'd only pulled it out twice in his life.

First Man and Third Man came at him again. Nick struck the first with the side of his fist, sliding his forearm to push the man away. An elbow to the second man's diaphragm, then an uppercut brought him to the ground. First Man recovered, but one-on-one, Nick knew he had the upper hand. He brought his forearm up to his face as First Man threw another punch directly at Nick's nose. Nick shifted his hips, jabbed with his left, then finished with a sliding hook to the man's throat.

First Man dropped, and Nick rested his hands on his knees as he reassessed. Three injured men writhed around him. Alive, but in need of medical attention. Knives were out of reach, his doctor's bag in one piece on the hood, and ... was that a bundle of money by the car wheel? He'd look later.

Mindy stood on the porch, hands covering her mouth, eyes wide. He waved her toward the house. "Call Detective O'Connor."

Mindy nodded and disappeared inside. Nick huffed and straightened. He'd be paying for this attack by bedtime tonight. He rolled his sore shoulders.

Nick inched toward the car for his medical bag. "I'll bandage up your hand."

But Second Man backed away, shaking his head. "How did you learn to fight like that?"

First and Third Man helped one another to their feet, Third Man staring at him with wide eyes. "Who are you?"

"I've seen it." First Man spit, then leveled Nick with a glare. "Irish

Bare Knuckle Boxing. Who knew an Italian could fight like an Irishman? You'll pay for this."

"I can't let you leave." Nick leaned against the car, hiding his weakened state. "Anyway, you need medical attention."

"We'll be fine." First Man shoved Third Man toward Second Man then snatched the bundle of money by the tire. "We'll be back for you."

The look in his eye said that next time, he'd bring a gun instead of a knife. *Mamma Mia.*

But Nick wasn't in the physical place to detain them. As the danger melted away, so did his strength. He stayed on his feet until the men were out of sight. Then he dropped to his knees. His muscles screamed. His face ached, and his arm felt like fire. He pulled at the sliced fabric of his blood-soaked shirtsleeve. The wound gaped open, oozing dark red. Not life-threatening in the short-term.

"Nick!" Mindy ran out of the house. Bella and Adaleigh on her heels. Mrs. Martins stood in the doorway, keeping Mabel behind her skirts, though the little girl peeked out.

"It's not safe for you to be here. Get back inside." Nick used the car to gain his feet. Wooziness engulfed him. He'd lost more blood than he realized.

"What happened?" A shout came from down the street. A friend, hopefully, because Nick was in no shape to fight again.

"Buck, help me get him inside." Mindy tucked herself under Nick's uninjured arm, her own around his back. "Bella, get his medical bag. Adaleigh, help Mrs. Martins clear a place for me to clean his wound. I need two pots of boiling water, one cooled."

The women jumped into action at Mindy's command. Buck insisted on switching places with Mindy so he could support most of Nick's weight. Nick held his injured arm to his chest, and Mindy stayed at his side, guiding them into the house. Bella hovered close as Buck helped Nick onto the cleared kitchen table. Worry coated her eyes. She'd never seen him injured. He stretched his uninjured hand out to her. The action caused tears to cascade down her cheeks, and she hurried away.

No emotional outburst from Mindy. With unexpected efficiency, she cut away his sleeve.

"What happened?" Buck repeated his question as he helped Nick roll on his side. Mindy tucked a folded blanket underneath his shoulder to elevate it.

"We were attacked again." Steel laced her words.

"Adaleigh is cutting up bandages," Mrs. Martins said as she handed off the needle and thread, which Mindy set in the boiling water.

Nick expected Buck to ask more questions. Thankfully, he stayed quiet. Nick held his own tongue. He hated being a patient when he could be doctoring. Although seeing Mindy's confidence helped, he still wanted to tell her what poultice to make, what drink to give him to replenish the blood he lost.

Mrs. Martins set a jar of honey on the table beside Nick's head. "Help him sit up. He needs to drink this."

Buck obliged, and Mrs. Martins made Nick down the full cup of milk. Okay, so maybe these women had this doctoring thing under control. The realization caused his body to relax. While the pain radiated from his arm, he could focus on breathing through it.

"Excellent," Mindy declared as she poured boiling water into a bowl, then washed her hands. "Once this is cool enough, I need to clean the wound."

Nick couldn't help but smile. Once this was over, he'd point out Mindy's skill as a nurse. Literate or not, she was amazing.

Mindy appeared at his side with a bowl and towel in hand, and a pained expression. "I'm sorry. This is going to hurt."

"*Lo so.*" He closed his eyes, the Italian slipping out. The women would think he knew because *he* was usually the one cleaning wounds. Yes, he'd seen the type of pain cleaning a wound caused. A healing type of pain because a well-cleaned wound was less likely to be infected. However, that's not why he knew.

Mindy swished the water, and Nick forced himself to breathe. That was the lesson he learned the first time he'd been attacked for the morphine in his doctor's bag. Breathing through the pain made it easier to manage. Buck held him still, and Nick forced himself to count each breath as Mindy washed his arm.

Finally, Buck let up on him, and Mindy's cool touch rested on Nick's forehead. Her voice was quiet in his ear. "All done, Nick. I'll let it dry before we put a poultice on and bind it."

He let his head loll toward her. "Grazie."

"You lapse into Italian when you're stressed." She handed the bloody water to Mrs. Martins, who took it and the soiled rags outside. Then Mindy washed her hands before returning to his side. "Is there something I can give you to ease the pain?"

He shook his head. "I don't want it."

Buck muttered under his breath and collapsed into a chair.

Mindy grunted. Didn't approve. "Do you have other injuries I need to see to?"

Again, he shook his head. Made sure his tongue spoke English this time. "They didn't land many punches."

"One is enough." Mindy touched his cheek. Again, Buck muttered, but this time an ounce of humor colored his tone.

"A graze." He'd been punched far harder on the streets of New York City.

"Nick, how—"

The front door opened and closed. Mindy jumped. Buck leapt between the newcomer and the table, his hand going to the small of his back where Nick spotted the bulge of a gun. The man carried?

Then Samson entered the kitchen, sniffed, and trotted upstairs where Bella and Adaleigh had taken Mabel. A moment later, Detective O'Connor appeared, brushing by Buck to greet Nick. "The man of the hour. Three to one, Nick. I was expecting you to look worse."

"Three to what?" Buck raised his voice.

Nick forced a grin. "Got the jump on me, or it wouldn't be this bad."

"Of all the ..." Buck shoved his hands through his hair and paced the kitchen.

"The way you fought back," Mindy whispered. Detective O'Connor raised his bushy eyebrows.

Yeah, he should probably explain that. Maybe mention the money, too. "Help me sit up?"

Detective O'Connor grabbed his uninjured hand and elbow and leveraged him to a sitting position. Nick waited for his equilibrium to even out before sliding off the table and finding a chair.

"You need more milk." Mindy found a cup, filled it, then handed it to him. Their fingers brushed, and Nick wished he could do more than smile at her. Not that he should. Everyone here knew the truth about their fake relationship. He sipped the cool liquid.

"You were saying?" Detective O'Connor took another chair, resting his ankle on his knee.

"Maybe start at the beginning. Three men jumped you?" Buck pulled out the chair beside Nick, made Mindy sit, then took a seat across the table from them.

"It started with one, then two more. One of them had a knife. But you struck them." Mindy looked utterly confused. "You're a doctor. How could you injure them like you did? They were writhing on the ground."

"A knife?" Buck scrubbed his chin. "Impressive."

"He didn't kill them," Detective O'Connor muttered. "Not that it wouldn't have been justified as self-defense."

Mrs. Martins reentered the kitchen, stopped when she saw them around her table. "The kettle is on the back burner. Help yourselves." Then she disappeared upstairs.

"It's true. I can handle myself." Nick scratched his cheek, winced when the pain reminded him it was his bruised one. "Years ago, I saw a mafioso shot, came to his aid and saved his life. Barely. The opposing family attacked, and I ended up nearly as injured as my impromptu patient."

"Nick!" Mindy gasped.

Both Detective O'Connor and Buck leaned forward, Buck voiced their shared look. "How'd you escape?"

"Street preacher." Nick's statement was rewarded with widened eyes from the two men.

"The one who gave you the Bible," Mindy whispered.

Nick nodded. "Irishman. Former bareknuckle prizefighter. Insisted I learn to defend myself."

"That's why you have muscles." Mindy clapped a hand over her mouth, her cheeks turning bright red. "I didn't mean to say that out loud."

Detective O'Connor smirked. Buck flat out laughed.

Nick felt his own face heat. "Yeah. Though I haven't sparred much since being here. Today's events have reminded me I can't let my training lapse."

"Wise." Detective O'Connor pulled a notebook from his pocket.

"Let's go over those events."

"What kind of sparring?" Buck asked, a finger pressed to his lips.

"What do you think?" Nick bounced his brows, letting Buck fill in what that meant. Not that he wanted to hide anything from Mindy, however, prizefighting was a bloody underground sport.

"Gentlemen?" Detective O'Connor cleared his throat. "The attack."

Nick supported his injured arm against his chest as he replayed the event. Part way through the retelling, Mindy busied herself at the stove, pouring coffee, then bringing over a long strip of cloth. She wrapped it under his arm and around his neck, securing his arm in the makeshift sling. All without a word. Nick desperately wanted to know what she was thinking.

Detective O'Connor and Buck expressed plenty, mostly surprise that Nick had survived, curiosity about the bundle of bills, and determination that it not happen again. Nick had his doubts that they could stop it. Men as violent as these, who had no problem beating a woman or knifing someone, would not stop without getting what they wanted.

"I need to talk to Mabel." The declaration popped out of his mouth before he could couch it in a way Mindy would receive. *Stupido.*

The men stared at her, as if waiting for an explosion. Mindy didn't miss the flash of regret in Nick's eyes. Nor did she discount the pain she saw there. He put on a brave face even though he hurt. Pain made tact difficult. Anyway, she'd already decided that Nick needed to talk to Mabel. Or had Nick forgotten their conversation in the car before the attack? Likely, considering everything.

Mindy slowly regained her chair beside him, measuring her words. What concerned her now wasn't that Nick wanted to talk to Mabel. It was worry over what they would learn if he could get Mabel to finally speak. "Do you think she is what they want?" *Please God, not that.*

Nick turned all his attention on her. "I think she has the answers we need." How could he be so intense while recovering from being knifed? It did strange things to her middle.

"How will you get her to talk?" Detective O'Connor asked, warning clear in his words. Nick would not hurt her sister. The man needn't worry. After today, Mindy was confident she could trust Nick to do what was best for Mabel. The way he tended Mary Lou? How he listened to Mindy, and then protected her? He'd extend that to Mabel, no doubt about it.

"I don't know yet," Nick was saying, "but I'm more convinced than ever that her condition is not physical, rather psychological. She saw something that ignited fear. That fear is keeping her silent. If we can offer her safety, perhaps she'll open up."

"But she's never spoken." Mindy hugged herself. How could her baby sister be at the center of this dangerous business?

"Did she babble as a baby?" Nick asked.

"I wasn't around much." Mindy lifted one shoulder, wishing she had an answer. "She's significantly younger than me. I'm more like a second mother."

"I didn't speak until I was five." Buck crossed his ankles. "At least that's what my mother always told me."

"I've seen that plenty of times." Nick shifted in his chair. "I can think of three neighborhood children back in New York who didn't speak until four or five years of age. Perhaps just as Mabel was about to speak, she saw something traumatizing and that stopped her from ever using her voice. It would make sense."

"My poor sister." Mindy swiped at a tear that escaped down her cheek. "What could have scared her so badly?"

"I think that's what we need to find out." Nick glanced at the stairs that led to where the ladies were occupying Mabel. "How old did you say she was?"

"She just turned eight." Most of those years, Mindy had lived in Crow's Nest. So how well did she really know her sister? Guilt threatened to strangle her.

"So three years." Detective O'Connor scratched his pencil in his notebook. "That would fit the timeline I'm piecing together. That's when your father took out the loan."

"When he mortgaged the house?" Mindy asked. What had her father done? Why had he left such a mess behind?

"No, the one from the loan shark." Detective O'Connor stuck the pencil behind his ear.

"Have you figured out which shark it is?" Buck asked, and Mindy was grateful. Words scrambled in her mind the way they usually did on a page.

Detective O'Connor shook his head. "Everyone is tight-lipped."

"Have you tried going undercover?" Buck asked. *Undercover?*

Everyone stared at him.

"What?" Buck shrugged. "If you can't get answers, you put a mole in an organization. I know law enforcement does it as much as criminals do." Buck rolled his eyes. "I mean, *I* have a mole in the Conglomerate, and I can't find him."

Mindy covered her face with her hands. Loan sharks, moles, knife-wielding attackers ... what was going on?

"We need a plan of action, but, uh," Nick coughed. "I need to lie down first."

Mindy jumped up. "Of course you do!" How had she allowed this conversation to become all about her problems when Nick needed medical attention? "I'm sure Mrs. Martins has a place where you can rest."

Nick winced. "Actually, I was hoping Buck could drive me home."

"Oh." She sank into her seat. Buck and Detective O'Connor exchanged glances, then made excuses to leave—Detective O'Connor upstairs and Buck to the front door.

Nick reached across his body with his uninjured arm, couldn't reach her. She hesitated to meet him halfway. Just as he began to retract his hand, she took it.

"I should have been thinking, Nick. You lost a lot of blood. How you are even upright, I can't imagine."

His thumb grazed her knuckles. "It wouldn't be proper for you to take me home. Tomorrow, have Adaleigh bring you and Mabel to the house."

Of course, he was considering her. She should know this about him, still she struggled to trust it.

"Since we missed putting on a show for services this morning, will you let me take you out on a date? A fake date?"

"That's exactly what made you a target, Nick. No. We can't keep that up."

"I can handle myself."

"You got knifed."

"Only because I didn't expect it. Now I do. It won't happen again."

Mindy pressed her lips together.

"We cannot forget that Spelding is still a threat. We need the townspeople to see you as their darling, then they'll go out of their way to protect you."

"Everyone likes me." When she was a waitress. Maybe too much sometimes.

"Not that way. I mean genuinely looking out for you. People who won't believe rumors and insinuation."

"How is going on a date with you going to help that?"

"Because we get people to think we're a great couple while they see you at work as a nurse." Nick's jaw ticked, and Mindy braced for what he'd say next. "Then I break up with you."

"What? Why?" Why did the thought of that twist up her insides?

He took a deep breath. "Because I want them to think *I'm* the cad. They'll defend you, and—"

"No." Mindy shook her head. "No, no no. I'm not doing that. You are not a cad. You are a dependable, loyal man. I am grateful you've chosen to be my friend."

"Fine, we won't stage a break-up." Was that relief in his voice? Why? She'd put him in this impossible situation.

Oh! "Do you want to break up?" She studied him, looking for the truth. "If you want out of this obligation—"

"Ready Matrone?" Buck reappeared. "I'd prefer to get you back to the house before you pass out. You're looking a little white."

"Oh, Nick, I'm a horrible nurse." Could she be any more mortified? Nick didn't want to date her, was only doing it because she'd put it upon him and he was that type of gentleman. Here it got him injured. Yes, she'd find a way to convince him this charade needed to end before any more people—especially him—got hurt.

She helped him to his feet, tucking herself under his uninjured arm to support him. He leaned heavily on her, his arm tight around her shoulders. This was all her fault. The thought drove even deeper when he looked at Buck, as if making it to the front door was more than he could handle, even with Mindy's feeble help.

But Buck turned away instead of answering Nick's silent request. She opened her mouth to reprimand Buck when Nick's lips touched hers. A squeak bubbled up from her throat. Then Nick slid his arm from her shoulders to her waist, drawing her near, and she closed her eyes. She had no idea what they were doing kissing like this, but she liked it too much to interrupt it.

Gradually, Nick pulled away. "Tomorrow, Mindy. We will finish this conversation."

Mindy nodded, unable to speak. Buck stepped to Nick's side, and the pair walked out the front door.

She sank back into her chair. Why had Nick kissed her? They were in a pretend relationship, so there was no reason for any type of affectionate display. Perhaps he was simply grateful she bandaged his injury? Yet he talked about breaking up. Confusing, confusing man.

Tomorrow she'd find out his motives. They'd make a plan for keeping both him and Mabel safe.

# CHAPTER TWELVE

Monday, June 29

The following morning, Nick sank onto his bed, exhausted after changing the bandage on his arm. It was too deep for stitches, so instead, he soaked gauze in a hypochlorite solution, then packed that gauze into the wound before bandaging it up and carefully sliding his arm into a cotton shirt. Doing such a procedure on one's self was ... difficult. The pain made him dizzy, and his jaw ached from clenching it so tightly.

He could have waited for help, but that went against his nature. He was a doctor, and would do what was necessary. Anyway, David had left well before he woke, and he wasn't sure what time Mindy would arrive. Because the bandage needed changing, he did what needed to be done.

The empty house creaked with the humidity that encased the day. Only seven in the morning and already the upstairs was unbearably warm. It drove him from his room before he fully recovered. Dressed in trousers and shirtsleeves, his suspenders hanging at his hips, he made his way down the stairs.

No relief from the heat here. With his injured arm aching, he maneuvered about the kitchen, making breakfast with just one hand: eggs from a basket Mrs. Martins provided, and a glass of milk. Pain and the heat of the day had stolen his appetite. He'd never eaten as well as he did here. A small breakfast would suit him fine.

With sustenance strengthening him, he used the kitchen telephone to cancel his appointments for the rest of the day, except for visiting Mary Lou. Of course, he'd be available if an emergency arose. For everyone else, he gave verbal instructions and promised he'd see everyone tomorrow. Today he had two goals: rest his arm so he could return to work, and talk to Mindy.

He couldn't believe he'd kissed her yesterday. The way she talked, he could tell she thought he didn't desire to be around her. That was very much not the case. He enjoyed her company. Too much for his own good, or hers. He'd wanted her to understand that. A simple kiss was all it was supposed to be.

But no. He'd made the mistake of kissing her when his defenses were down, when pain had muddled his head. Not to mention that he'd expected her to be surprised, for her to pull away, maybe even slap him. He'd have taken that, because his actions deserved it. No matter his intentions. He shouldn't have taken liberties. Then she responded to his kiss, and he'd been lost.

At least Buck found it hilarious. The man laughed the entire way back to Mrs. Whittlebush's house. *Fake relationship, Matrone? Only pretend part about it is what you're telling yourself.*

Between Buck's observation, the warm night, and the pain, Nick hadn't really slept.

He poured himself another cup of coffee, then sat on one of the porch chairs to wait for Mindy. Mrs. Whittlebush had left the rocking chairs behind along with most of her furniture. They provided a perfect place to observe the lake. Today, the water moved in constant ripples, almost mesmerizing in its consistency.

A Ford roared up to the curb, and Buck Wilson emerged as if summoned by Nick's thoughts. The man slammed his car door harder than necessary, in Nick's opinion, then stalked toward Nick until he glowered down at him.

"Morning, Wilson." Nick sipped his coffee, knowing the unaffected tone would rile his visitor.

Buck tossed his arms wide. "What do you think you're doing? Sitting out here where someone could shoot you in the head before you saw the bullet coming."

"Honestly? I hadn't considered it." Nick assessed his thoughts on the matter, content that his mind hadn't changed from the last time he'd almost been shot. "I won't change my behavior because of a couple of thugs or a few threats. Never have."

Buck rolled his eyes and plopped into the chair on Nick's other side, looking nothing like the put-together Conglomerate Head. His hair stood up at odd ends, his suit was unbuttoned and rumpled. He even had uneven scruff that showed he hadn't shaved that morning. "Just because they came at you with a knife doesn't mean they won't try a gun next time. You're a target, Nick. Time you acted like one."

"Not the first time I've been held at knife-point. Gunpoint either, for that matter. Doubt it'll be the last." Nick sipped his coffee again. He had no fear of the thugs and what they might do to him. What they could do to Mindy, to Mabel, that made his stomach churn. His life, however, was in God's hands and he was content to leave it there. But Buck's agitation needed poking. "Anyway, I heard of some Canadian soldier surviving a gunshot wound to the head. Now, a gut shot. I know from experience, saving a gut shot man is fifty-fifty."

Buck glared at him. "How can you be so cavalier about your life?"

"My medical practice was in one of the most dangerous areas in New York City. It was a rare day when I wasn't stitching up a knife wound. An average Saturday saw a gunshot victim or two." Nick shrugged. "It's not that I became callous to the violence. It's more that I couldn't let it affect me or I'd be powerless to help people. Helping people is my job."

"But none of those injuries were yours." Buck inclined his head toward the bandage that strained the sleeve of his shirt.

"I never said that." Nick couldn't stop a chuckle as Buck's jaw loosened. "I had a reputation for helping anyone, regardless of whether they committed criminal behavior, so the number of times an armed man *escorted* me to help someone is too many to count. My medical partner didn't approve, so I couldn't treat those men at the clinic. Made for less than ideal circumstances. However, if I could save a life, that was what God has called me to do."

"I can respect that, Nick. I can." Buck leaned back in his chair. "It's Mindy I worry about. If you get killed because of this situation, she'll never forgive herself. The town might not forgive her either."

"I'm worried about that. The town, that is." Nick set his empty cup on the ground beside his chair. He wasn't quite ready to admit the fear he harbored over Mindy's safety. "I've been trying to think of a way to inspire people to side with Mindy. I'd let them turn against me, if it meant helping her."

"Like your ridiculous idea last night." Buck snorted. "I said it yesterday. The only person you're fooling is yourself."

"Maybe I am, but I respect Mindy too much to invite her into my life in a way other than as a friend." Saying the words aloud invited both grief and determination.

Buck shifted to face him. "Explain that one to me, Matrone. The way you look at her. The way you kissed her. She's not just a friend to you. Why can't it be more? She deserves a man who will treat her well. Not someone like my brother."

"You think I don't know that? Believe that?" Nick pushed to his feet and stared out over the water. "People judge me for my nationality, my skin color, my name, before they ever get to know me. Sometimes *doctor* earns me enough respect; even then, I've had people refuse to let me treat them. I could never willingly bring Mindy into that type of life."

"She lives that life, Matrone. Being a waitress, people thought her nothing more than a lady of the night."

"I know!" Nick spun. "Which is why I can't inflict that pain on her for the rest of her life."

"She can handle it, Nick." Buck stayed seated, allowing Nick to loom over him. "What are you afraid of?"

Not a question he wanted to answer. He returned to his chair. "I should ask you the same question. There are plenty of women around town, Mindy included. You flirt, yet you don't have a girl. Why?"

"We aren't talking about me." Buck shook his head. "What are you going to do when the danger ends? If you survive your stupidity, sitting out in the open with a target on your back, that is."

"First, I don't have a target on my back." Yes, he'd been considering it all night amid the swirl of everything else. "If they wanted me dead, I would have been dead. You said it yourself. Shooting me would have been much easier. Instead, they ambushed me. In front of Mindy."

Buck stood to lean his backside against the railing in front of Nick, expression scrutinizing. "You think they didn't plan to kill you?"

"Threaten. Bully. Scare. Absolutely." He rotated his injured shoulder, hoping to ease the ache. "Me fighting back made it personal, so I'm sure now they're eager to finish the job."

"Nick," Buck growled.

"Not the point." Nick held up a hand. He didn't need the reprimand. "I want to know how they knew Mindy was my girl. We were going to make our fictitious relationship a public relationship at services, but we never made it."

"Everyone knows." Buck crossed his arms. "So what are you really getting at?"

"They knew where to find us, when to find us. They went after me, not Mindy." The words of one of the thugs filtered back to him. "In fact, they specifically said they were sent to get me out of the way. They meant to scare me off. Possibly before the town got invested in me and Mindy as a couple."

"You think they wanted to make it easier to get to Mindy." Buck's eyes widened as he, likely, came to the same suspicion Nick had. "They want you out of the way so someone else can worm their way into Mindy's life."

Nick nodded. "Know anyone who would do anything to get me away from her?"

Buck groaned. "Joe."

"If Joe put the thugs up to yesterday's attack, their payback won't be until Joe gets what he wants from me. Killing me won't endear Mindy to him. He needs to scare me off—which won't happen—or make it so Mindy can't trust me—which worries me."

"As it should. What does Joe have to do with the thugs who attacked Mindy in the first place?" Buck paced as he talked. "They want something that Mindy or Mabel, or both, know. Something tied with their father. What does my brother have to do with it?"

That was the question. "I think Joe found them and planted the idea of ambushing me as a way for both them and him to get what they want."

"Namely: Mindy." Buck dropped into his chair. "That means my brother knows where to find these men."

"That shouldn't surprise you, Buck."

"It doesn't." The man sighed. "I should have seen it sooner. I've been so preoccupied with keeping him from harming Crow's Nest that I only let myself relax when he'd leave town. He probably gambles in the same places Mindy's father did."

"Have you been sleeping, like I prescribed?" Nick guessed not, but a good doctor asked.

Buck shook his head, and for a moment, he allowed Nick to see the haggard man he'd seen in his exam room the other day.

No need to pile on guilt, so he returned the conversation to what might solve all their problems. "Did O'Connor get permission to go undercover at Mindy's father's old haunts?"

Buck rested his elbows on his knees. "Sebastian refused."

"The police chief?" Nick mentally pulled up an image of the man. Short, plump, and overconfident. Now that Nick thought about it, he was surprised the chief hadn't been to see him in the clinic yet. The man had an increasing limp that coincided with a purple coloring in his face. If Nick didn't miss his guess, he'd say the chief was overindulging ...

"Pompous windbag said Mindy brought it on herself, and you—" Buck stopped, stared at him. "I'm sorry, Nick. I didn't fully believe you when you said how people dislike you on sight. It was right in front of me."

"Sebastian called me a derogatory name and said I had it coming, didn't he?" Nick wasn't surprised. It also explained why the man hadn't sought treatment for what Nick suspected was alcohol-triggered gout.

"It's not right."

"No, let's not get sidetracked." There was no point in discussing what couldn't be changed. "How can we use this connection? Can we use Joe to go undercover without official sanction?"

Buck tented his fingers and pressed the tips to his lips. He was silent for a long time, and Nick let him think. Finally, Buck tapped his fingers. "I have an idea. If we play it right, it'll solve multiple problems all at once. It hinges on one thing: when are you taking Mindy on a date?"

"A date?" Nick's heart hammered. "You mean a pretend date?"

Buck snorted. "Whatever. Take her to Sweeties today. Hot day means the ice cream parlor will be crowded, and the Swensons owe me a favor. You two walk in. I'll already be there. I'll get in your face about *stealing* Mindy from my brother. All Mrs. Swenson has to do is use the word *rescue*. Then you'll be seen as a hero."

"I don't need to be the hero. It's Mindy—"

"The townspeople already think she's flighty. Too bubbly. It's her charm, but they don't take her seriously. The look on your face is betraying your feelings."

Nick scrubbed whatever *look* Buck meant. "Go on."

"Joe will think I'm on his side. I can play that up, be the mole Sebastian won't let us have. People will believe it of me."

It was true. "How does this protect Mindy?"

"People don't like Joe. They know he went to jail. They mistrust me, even though they need the Conglomerate." Buck shrugged, yet something about the stiff way he did suggested it bothered him more than he portrayed. "You, on the other hand, have a reputation for saving damsels in distress. Everyone knows you came sweeping in here, planning to marry Cora sight unseen. Arrived again to help Marian just when she needed it."

"So they'll believe I'm helping Mindy out of the goodness of my heart." Which was the truth. Or so Nick would keep telling himself.

"Then what?"

"Then I track down who is threatening Mindy. You talk to Mabel. And when we get to the bottom of whatever is going on, you can break it off with Mindy, because your services will no longer be required. Just as you originally planned."

Nick clenched his jaw. He didn't like that ending, but what other ending could there be? "So Joe will just swoop in, then what will people say of Mindy?"

Buck glared at him. "They'll keep Joe away from their poor, sweet, hurting Mindy. Because of course someone like her fell for the man protecting her. A scoundrel they shouldn't have trusted in the first place, and they won't let another man break her heart."

Nick dropped his chin. He knew Buck was goading him. He couldn't rise to the bait. "I don't want to break her heart."

"Look, Matrone." Buck's tone hardened. "That's exactly what will happen if you don't get a handle on the feelings I saw between the two of you last night. Do not toy with her. Got it?"

"Got it." He had to get it. It was the only way. Then he'd have to leave Crow's Nest, because he couldn't let her go only to see her every day.

"Don't tell Mindy about any of this." Buck stood, signaling their conversation was over. "She can't keep a secret to save her life. Uh, I didn't mean it that way."

"But you're right." Nick massaged his injured shoulder, not bothering to hide the grimace the pain caused.

Buck studied him. "One more thing. You. Me. We're sparring every morning until this is over."

"Why would you do that?" Nick stood, needing to level the field. "In fact, why are you helping with any of this? What do you get out of it?"

"You need to be ready to defend yourself like you did yesterday, and with only one arm, you need to improve your skills." Buck waved at Nick's injury. "I can help. I box, and a few other things. And I've been working with you and Adaleigh on the clinic, so it won't be too odd for us to meet every morning to wait on the girls together. If anyone is watching."

It was a smart plan. Yet ... "You didn't answer my question."

"What do I get out of it?" Buck stuffed his hands into his pockets. "Protecting the people of Crow's Nest is my job. We'll get to the bottom of whatever trouble Mindy's father got her into. Whether we can get Joe off your back and hers? I'm less confident about that. Maybe given enough rope, O'Connor can string him up for us."

"Careful Wilson. Betraying family is a hard road."

"I know." Something flashed in Buck's eyes before he shuttered it. "You speak from experience?"

"Those are my secrets, I suppose." Not ones he wanted to discuss with Buck Wilson. The man had enough secrets to make a man doubt his integrity, and enough nobleness to think well of him. The truth, Nick suspected, lay in the murky in-between.

"Get yourself inside so I don't have to stay to protect you." Buck flashed him a smirk before donning the relaxed mask he usually wore. "I need to set things in motion. Tomorrow morning, I'll be back for our sparring match, and to continue working on the clinic. The town needs this place, Nick. They need a doctor who doesn't let his greed impede treating his patients. I know you aren't taking payment for treating Mary Lou Vashen."

Embarrassment heated Nick's neck. "How do you know so much?"

"I make it my business to know everything, Matrone."

There was more to it. "I'll let it go if you tell me one thing. How far will you go to protect the town?"

Buck met his gaze straight on, no guile, no lies. "I will go as far as I need to in order to keep the *people* of this town safe."

"Sacrificing your health? Or breaking the law?" Nick had seen men of both ilk, and they were rarely made of the same cloth.

"You of all people should know the answer to that." Buck scuffed his shoe on the porch planks. "I'm trusting that you believe in doctor-patient confidentiality."

"It's a basic tenet of my practice." Nick considered the complicated man before him. "Trust someone, Buck. Shouldering the protection of this town alone will cause you to break."

"Would that I could." Buck offered a sad smile.

"Fine. Just make sure you get some rest. Doctor's orders or that chest pain will return."

Buck saluted as he sauntered toward his car.

Nick waited for him to drive away before he followed Buck's advice and went inside to wait for Mindy. He wasn't worried about his own safety, never had been. He was concerned about Mindy's. Would they try to get to her through him again? Hurt him to manipulate her? Did she care about him enough that such a tactic would work?

He continued through the stifling kitchen and out the back door. Breath stalled in his lungs. Did he truly think that little of himself? The thought slammed into him. He halted on the back step, heaving the heavy air. Emotion clogged his throat.

How had he missed such a flaw in himself? How had he never seen it before? He'd thought he was putting others before himself, as God asked of people who followed Him. He thought he was honoring God. Never had he suspected that insidious self-depreciation had crept into his heart.

If he saw others as worthy of God's love, of medical care and compassion, then why would he think Mindy—or anyone—wouldn't view him that way? As if scales dropped from his eyes, the answer was obvious: because *he* didn't view *himself* that way. It wasn't right. It wasn't truth.

His gaze roved the apple trees that filled the property between the house and the lake, then along the barn to the large garden that lay dormant since Mrs. Whittlebush had left that winter. A warm breeze rustled the leaves, bringing the scent of manure from the farms beyond Crow's Nest. A conviction couched in a verse Papa often quoted from Ephesians, the one that drove Nick's desire to go into medicine.

*È Dio stesso che ci ha fatto così. It is God who made us this way.* Or, as the English Bible said, *we are his workmanship.*

Who was he to discount what God had made? When it came to his patients, he saw each as a valuable, handmade creation. Whether a child, an elderly widow, or a convicted criminal. Not until this moment did he realize how little he thought of himself. That needed to change.

"Padre nostro ..." He bowed his head, allowing his prayer to stay in his childhood language. "I'm sorry for undervaluing Your creation. You made me. You redeemed me. I ask that You grant me wisdom to know the best way to handle the gift of life You have given me." *And allow me to protect Mindy, and show her You value her, too.*

Nick returned inside to watch for Mindy's arrival. They'd visit Mary Lou, then Nick would take her on a date. A fake date. One that would hopefully save her without breaking her heart.

# CHAPTER THIRTEEN

Mindy slowed to a stop out of sight of Mrs. Whittlebush's house, her feet unwilling to take another step.

Adaleigh paused three feet ahead and glanced back at her. "Coming?"

Questions choked her answer. Would things be awkward between her and Nick after he kissed her yesterday? Would he discard her now that he'd gotten a kiss? Or demand more because he thought she was easy? Would he think her forward and avoid her so he didn't get dragged into her waywardness?

Ugh! She covered her face with her hands. She hadn't initiated the kiss, so why did she feel like it was her fault? Why did losing Nick's friendship over a silly kiss cause her heart to race?

She tried to take a deep breath, but the humid air strangled her. Maybe she should just turn around. Avoid Nick before he could hurt her. She knew full well how many horrible choices she made when it came to men. Nick might be one of the honorable ones, but that didn't mean he was right for her.

Or that she was right for him.

"Mindy?" Adaleigh caught her shoulders, somehow in front of her when Mindy hadn't noticed her move. "Talk to me before you hyperventilate and I need to carry you to Nick."

Carry her to Nick? No, no, no. She couldn't let that happen.

"Mindy." Adaleigh shook her. "Snap out of it."

"Maybe the pain confused him." The words tumbled out. "Made him forget that our so-called relationship is only imaginary. It was my idea, anyway. He agreed to it because he was cornered into it. I need to make sure he remembers that this arrangement will end as soon as Joe leaves me alone. It might be awkward, but—"

"Mindy, do you have feelings for Nick?" The compassion in Adaleigh's voice brought tears to Mindy's eyes.

"I can't have feelings for him. I'm a silly woman, Adaleigh. Always getting involved with the wrong men." She dashed away the tear that slipped down her cheek. "I'm selfish for wanting him to protect me."

Adaleigh hooked her arm in Mindy's, propelling her into motion. "Have you considered that Nick didn't exactly protest when you asked for help?"

"That's because he's noble." Mindy huffed. "He offered to marry Cora. Marian. Had he known you when you first got to Crow's Nest, he would have offered the same. Why not me, too?"

Adaleigh sighed. "Then you need to talk to him. Your heart matters, Mindy. If Nick protecting you with a pretend relationship is going to hurt you, then it's not effective. We need to think of a different way."

"None of it is Nick's fault," Mindy whispered. "It's mine. It was my idea, and it's my emotions I can't manage. He's been only a gentleman. I should know. I've stepped out with enough men who were not."

Adaleigh pressed her lips together, obviously trying not to say something. Mindy probably didn't want to hear it, yet she respected her friend too much not to probe.

Adaleigh sighed. "Yes, I have more I want to say, however, I'm not going to say it. This is something you need to talk to the Lord about. And Nick. You're making assumptions and I—No. I said I wasn't going there, and I'm not. Just don't protect your heart by hardening it. The sweetness that makes you vulnerable to preying men is also the gentleness that makes you an amazing friend. I'd miss that if you changed."

Mindy threw her arms around Adaleigh's neck.

"We're handing out hugs today?" Nick broke into the moment. When had they arrived at Mrs. Whittlebush's house?

Mindy ducked her head, unsure what to do, and not wanting to show him her tears.

Adaleigh came to her rescue. "Do you need one, Nick? Hugs help against pain. And Mindy is proving a helpful nurse."

Mindy shot her a glare. Some friend.

Nick laughed as he came down the sidewalk to greet them. No sling, but he held his injured arm close. "Let's compromise. Mindy, how about you drive me to see Mary Lou, then let me take you to Sweeties for a date."

Mindy tried to swallow. "A ... date?"

"I canceled all my other appointments today on account of my arm." He lifted the limb. "I think after yesterday, making an appearance as a couple would be wise. Especially since we missed services."

"Oh, right. Smart." Why did she want this to be a proper date, not a performance?

"With how warm today is, let's go to Sweeties." Nick smiled at her, genuine warmth in his eyes. It made her heart twist. He probably looked at every girl that way. "What do you say?"

"Go on, Mindy." Adaleigh bumped her shoulder, giving her a significant look. "This will be positive for you."

Mindy chewed her lip. She wanted to say yes, wanted to spend the day with Nick, but the confusion in her heart muddled her mind.

"Maybe I should ..." Adaleigh inched toward the house.

Nick stopped Adaleigh with a hand on her arm. "You think it's a good idea, don't you?"

A look passed between them, and irritation sprouted in Mindy. "What are you two conspiring about? Just because I'm simple and can't read, I'm not a child to be managed." She clapped a hand over her mouth. She hadn't meant to say that out loud.

"Hey." Nick was before her in an instant, the sun striking his glasses so she couldn't read his eyes. "I was trying to get Adaleigh to convince you to go with me. You seemed like you needed a little convincing. I thought if Adaleigh was for it, you would be, too."

She'd overreacted again. Why did she keep doing that with Nick? He evoked a powerful response in her she'd never experienced before.

"Tears." He thumbed the track they'd made on her check. He dropped his voice. "Does your hesitancy to be around me have anything to do with me kissing you yesterday?"

"Maybe. Yes. No." She jabbed her toe into the ground. "I don't know."

He eased closer, creating a world where only they existed. The glare cleared, and she saw concern in his eyes. "Mindy, do I need to apologize? Did I make you uncomfortable? Please be honest."

"Are ... are you sorry?" Her heart hammered, prepared for the rejection that usually came.

"For kissing you? No. For making you wary of me, absolutely."

"Oh, Nick." Her heart broke a little. How was she going to survive this imaginary relationship when she wanted it to be a real one? "I shouldn't have kissed you. Our relationship isn't supposed to be real. And friends don't kiss like that. I'm sorry."

"Why are you sorry?" He tipped her chin up. "You have nothing to apologize for. Mindy, I kissed you."

She searched his face, looking for any of the expressions she'd seen in other men. Dismissal, disgust, annoyance, lust. Yet she found only worry. Worry that she'd led him on? That she'd caused him to kiss her? Worry over his reputation?

His gaze darted away from her. "I see thoughts. Let's go inside so I can concentrate on them."

Before Mindy could protest, he had hooked his uninjured arm through hers and was propelling her toward the house. It was then she realized Adaleigh had left them alone.

"I forgot myself for a moment." He urged them faster. "Your safety comes first, and standing in the open like that is not safe."

"Oh." Her thoughts reeled as she let Nick lead her into the house. He shut and locked the front door, then swung her into the sewing shop Mrs. Whittlebush had created before she left. That door he left open, always caring for her, always aware.

"Now, go back to those thoughts you were having." He escorted her to a couch opposite the windows, the curtains closed, situating her on one side as he took the other. "Why are you sorry when I'm the one at fault?"

Dare she tell him? No, she couldn't. She didn't want to have this conversation with him. It was mortifying.

Nick rested his elbows on his knees, grimaced, then sat back, massaging his shoulder. She knew, no matter his discomfort, he'd sit here with her until she shut down the conversation or told him the truth.

"You really want to know?" She could hardly believe a man wanted to hear her thoughts.

"Of course I do, Mindy." He adjusted his spectacles. "You had them, so I want to know them."

"Why are you worried about ... about what happened yesterday?" She couldn't say the word *kiss*. Her lungs seized. She pushed on, suddenly wanting to know the answer. Needing to know whether Nick was the noble knight she thought him to be. "Is it ... is it because I could demand something from you because of it? Or the risk to your reputation? Or—"

"Mindy, is that really what you thought?" He shook his head. "What you think of me?"

"I ..." Mindy's words failed at the pain etched in Nick's face.

He scooted closer. "I never would have kissed you if I'd have known it would cause such thoughts. Mindy, that is not what I think at all. I kissed you to prove that I care about you. I shouldn't have used a kiss to communicate that, I know. For that, I'm sorry. But, I'm not sorry for caring about you. I have no regrets about that. As for my reputation, it's yours that matters. Do you trust me on that?"

She stared at him. "You mean that?" He was worried about *her*? Not himself?

"What can I do to prove it to you?"

"Keep being you, Nick. Keep being a man I can trust."

Nick studied her for a full minute before giving a nod. "Okay. Then let's concentrate on keeping you safe."

"That requires going to Sweeties and putting on a show?" An illusion of a date for all to see.

"Yes, ma'am. First, we'll stop by to put the cast on Mary Lou's leg, then our date." He exuded only confidence that this plan would work. Time to believe in her knight.

"All right, Nick. Let's go on this fake date and give the town something to talk about." She pasted on as bright a smile as she could manage.

"We do have one slight problem." Nick inclined his head toward the window. "I can't drive with one hand."

After their serious conversation, Mindy couldn't help but laugh.

"Then we're in a pickle because I never learned to drive at all."

Nick grinned at Mindy's revelation, grateful that her laugh broke the tension between them. "I get to teach you to read, *and* I get to teach you to drive?"

Her eyes twinkled. "You are entirely too happy about my lack, Dr. Matrone."

A laugh bounced his arm, and he winced.

"Maybe you should stay home, Nick." She circled around to check his bandage, standing close enough that he caught the whiff of sunshine in her hair.

"Nonsense. Who would teach you to drive?" Why was he flirting? She needed him to build trust, and flirting wouldn't help. He forced an amiable smile when he wanted to roll his eyes at himself. Theirs was a fabricated relationship. As in, not real.

Of course, Mindy rewarded his behavior with the sweetest smile. Innocence and joy, wrapped up in wonder. "All right. Nick. Teach me to drive."

Oh, his heart. His good-for-nothing heart. He had seen so much darkness. How could he not taint this amazing woman? Yet, he couldn't drag himself away from her. It had to be the pain stealing his self-control. *Keep telling yourself that, Matrone.*

Fortunately, Mindy seemed oblivious to his inner turmoil. She took to driving more easily than reading, laughing each time she ground the gears or braked too fast. The fifth time Nick had to brace his hand on the dash to keep from crashing into it, her good humor sank in and buoyed his spirits. He enjoyed being with Mindy, whether they were talking over coffee, attempting to drive a car, or caring for a patient. She brought joy into everything she did. It was an addicting quality that he was powerless to resist.

"Do you think you can make it all the way to the Vashens's house?" He cradled his injured arm, hopefully in a way that she wouldn't realize how much the stopping and starting hurt.

"Definitely." She threw him a toothy smile. "I'm driving, Nick. Not well, but I'm doing it."

"Yes, you are." Never had he been so proud of someone. He continued to coach her, and by the time they arrived at the Vashen farm, she eased the car into a smooth stop and set the hand brake.

"I did it." She threw her arms around Nick's neck, catching his injured arm between them. He hissed, and she jumped away. "Oh, I'm so sorry! Your arm. I forgot. Are you okay? Did I—"

"It's fine," he said through clenched teeth. He reached for her hand. "Never forget this feeling. How capable you are."

Her eyes turned watery as she nodded. A kiss seemed the perfect way to end this moment, but he couldn't lead her on. He had already blurred the line between fake and real. Their conversation this morning proved that.

"Let's go check on Mary Lou." He opened his car door, and reached for his medical bag. "I'll need your help with the plaster, especially working one-handed. It's a messy business."

Mindy met him around the front of the car. "Just tell me what you need."

*You.*

He marched ahead of her toward the house, giving leave to roll his eyes at himself. *Stupido.* He knew better, and had to get a handle on his feelings for Mindy. They wouldn't do either of them any good. The opening front door snapped him into professional mode.

Inside, Mrs. Vashen led them to the bedroom where Mary Lou lay on her parents' bed, face white against the white bedding. Nick requested a couple of bowls and boiled water, then directed Mindy on how to set up the preparations. Then he sat on the bed beside Mary Lou, asked her about her pain, her vision, and her head. All was as he expected. A bit of blurred vision. Headache with light, sound, or moving her eyes. Her broken leg ached to tears. She was a brave little girl, though, and Nick told her so.

Preparations ready, Nick guided Mindy in how to coat the gauze strips in the plaster powder. Once enough strips were ready, he dipped one strip into the water. The plaster heated as it dampened, and he lay it over Mary Lou's leg. Mindy adjusted the blankets to protect Mary Lou's modesty, then raised the little girl's leg enough to slip another gauze strip underneath. The poor girl howled in pain, her mother wept as she held her still, and her father gripped his wife's shoulders.

Without words, Mindy anticipated how the gauze needed to wrap over the injury. Her two hands took up where his one hand left off, smoothing the gauze as it molded to hold the broken femur in place. As the cast hardened, Mary Lou's cries quieted until she fell asleep on her mother's lap.

Nick rinsed the plaster dust from his uninjured hand as he glanced from one parent to the other. "She'll need lots of rest these next few days. Eventually, we'll get her crutches to use. However, this will be a long recovery."

"We'll do whatever we can." Mr. Vashen reached to shake first Nick's then Mindy's hand. "I cannot thank you both enough for helping our little girl."

"Call me if anything changes. I'll stop by again in a few days." Nick gathered his supplies, Mindy again working silently beside him.

"You haven't been a couple long, have you?" Mrs. Vashen asked as she smoothed her daughter's hair. Nick opened his mouth to answer, didn't know what to say. The woman chuckled. "I only say that because I'm surprised at how well you work together. You have the chemistry of a long-married couple."

Mindy turned bright red, and Nick felt his own cheeks heat. Mr. Vashen chuckled. "You're embarrassing them, my dear woman."

"I just like seeing such happiness in a couple. Not all relationships have that underlying connection like we do." She sighed. "I needed to see it today."

"I'm glad we could brighten a hard day, Mrs. Vashen." Mindy recovered before Nick found his words.

Mindy initiated the good-byes, then led the way to the car and slipped into the driver's seat. Nick settled on the passenger side, and Mindy navigated the roads with less and less gear grinding. Still, Nick couldn't find what to say to Mrs. Vashen's observations. He felt what she saw. Even Buck had noticed it. But his conversation with Mindy echoed in his ears. He wanted her to trust him.

So what should he do?

Mindy parked on Main Street, a block from where Sweeties was located on the Wharf. "Are you sure you want to do this? Your arm needs rest and so do you."

"I want to take you on this date." More than he wanted to admit. It had nothing to do with his plan with Buck. "I mean, pretend date. Unless you don't want to. Are you trying to get out of it? Because we don't have to."

"Stop." She smiled at him, something in her eyes that hadn't been there before. It ignited hope in his heart.

Not good. Not good at all. How was he going to keep their relationship from becoming real without breaking both their hearts and the trust she wanted to build in him?

Mindy followed Nick into Sweeties, Crow's Nest's only ice cream shop. Mr. and Mrs. Swensen opened Sweeties a few decades ago, starting out as a soda fountain and penny candy store. When the ice cream cone craze started about ten years ago, they jumped at the opportunity and became a popular spot on the Crow's Nest wharf.

While a few degrees cooler out of the sun, even inside the shop was stuffy, sticky, and uncomfortable. Mindy discreetly pulled the fabric of her skirt away from her legs. Penny candy jars lined the right side wall. On the left was the oak counter behind which the Swensens dispensed their cool treats. The thought of ice cream in such heat was a welcome relief.

Nick had never donned his usual vest and jacket before they left Mrs. Whittlebush's house earlier, making him look more like a local farmer or fisherman in his rolled-up shirtsleeves and suspenders. The cotton fabric between his shoulder blades was damp, as it was on everyone they had passed since exiting the car. Why was he so insistent on taking her on a date today? In this heat, with the wound in his arm? A pretend date, no less. If it were a real one, she could see pushing aside personal discomfort, but this? He was doing this for her, and that was it.

Gratefulness and protectiveness swelled. She wrapped her hand around his uninjured arm, bringing her cheek to his shoulder as any genuine couple might do. Only, she wasn't faking wanting to be this close to him. "We should go home. Save this for another day," she whispered. "I know your arm hurts. Let me take care of you for once."

He looked down at her, and his eyes melted like ice cream on a hot day like today. "You are the most unselfish woman I have ever met." He gently kissed her temple. Like a proper suitor might.

"So it is true." Buck appeared before them, arms crossed, looking ... angry? Mindy stared at him, confused.

"What is true?" Nick untangled his uninjured arm from Mindy's grip, and for a moment, hurt stabbed. Then he wrapped that arm around her waist, pulling her to his side, and she realized he was claiming her as his own for everyone to see. Comfort swept through her.

*It's only a show. Only fake. Not real.* If only her heart would agree. Right now, she only wanted to revel in having an upright man at her side in front of everyone.

"You stole her from my brother." Buck raised his voice, cutting through the warm feelings. Strange. Buck never made scenes like this. She eased away from Nick. He held on.

"Stole her from Joe Spelding?" Nick laughed. Why was Nick making this information so obvious? Had they set this up ahead of time?

"Protected her is more like." Mrs. Swenson interjected as she leaned over the counter. Was she in on whatever this was? "Go back to your ice cream, Mr. Wilson. Dr. Matrone, what can I get you and your girl?"

"This isn't over, Matrone." Buck brushed by them, just shy of hitting Nick's injured shoulder. If he'd really been upset, Buck would have aimed directly for the injury, wouldn't he?

She watched Buck leave the shop, a disgruntled churning replacing the warmth from a moment ago.

# CHAPTER FOURTEEN

"What ..." Mindy's mind raced.

"Mindy?" Nick pulled her attention back to him and smiled at her as if he hadn't just had a mini argument with the head of the Conglomerate. "Chocolate cone?"

She nodded, too disquieted to speak. Murmurs spread through the room. Scowls directed at the door where Buck had exited. Approval at Nick. Sympathy at ... her? Mindy met gaze after gaze. Disquiet turned to wonder, then blended with gratefulness. That brief exchange had somehow changed the popular opinion of her. It hadn't even lasted a minute, which showed how fickle people could be.

She shouldn't be surprised, not really. Recently, she'd orchestrated similar ways of spreading truthful rumors as a ... wait a minute.

"Orchestrated." The word slipped out as Nick finished giving Mrs. Swenson their order. Buck knew the truth, approved of them pretending to date, and thought his brother the criminal he was. Understanding dawned. That conversation was entirely staged. Everyone had bought it, including her. Is that why Nick insisted on taking her on a date despite the pain in his arm? Her gallant knight.

Nick leaned close to her ear. "I'll explain. Just sell the date a while longer."

*Sell the date.* This was just a show and had nothing to do with how Nick felt about her. Gullible woman.

Mindy blinked back the prickles of tears as she accepted her cone. Why did she wish this was a real date? Silly, foolish girl, believing for a moment she and Nick could have anything real between them. Talking of trust, and yet Nick hadn't told her about this facade. Or had he and she ignored it?

Nick handed her his cone so he could pay for them both, then took it back, his fingers brushing hers. She hated the attraction she felt at the movement. Self-loathing dragged her down. It was nothing she didn't deserve after she began this lie without his permission. It was just like her to fall for the wrong man. Only this time, he was an honorable man who put her safety before his own wellbeing. She couldn't be mad at him for that. He must have a reason for not telling her about the set-up ahead of time.

"Ready?" Nick escorted her to a back corner, where they could sit side-by-side and talk quietly without being overheard. They had barely sat down before Nick jumped into an explanation. The exchange was Buck's idea and meant to do exactly what it had done. Now the locals would side with Mindy and Nick, not Joe. And Buck could handle the negativity sent his way. In fact, it gave Buck an in-road to discover what trouble her father had found.

Through blurry eyes, Mindy watched a trail of melted ice cream drip down her fingers, then turned her gaze up at Nick. How could she have doubted him? He was a hero. He and Buck. Fighting a battle for her when they had nothing to gain and everything to lose.

"Why the tears?" He reached for her, cone in his uninjured hand. He grimaced as he switched the cone to his other hand. "Stupid injured arm. Mindy, don't cry. It's going to be okay."

"I know. I know." She lay her head on his uninjured shoulder. "Even with an injury. With this all being a ruse. Still, you put my safety, Mabel's safety, before everything. No one has done that for me before. I ..."

Words failed her. Worse, love blossomed. Falling indeed. She couldn't deny the emotion. No, not emotion exactly. It was deeper. The kind of *something* she saw between David and Adaleigh. Of considering the other before themselves. Of sacrificing for one another. Not infatuation, or attraction, though David, in particular, looked at Adaleigh with such mooneyes, it made Mindy laugh. But that emotion was built on a foundation of rock. Brick by brick, stone by stone, the same foundation was being laid in her heart for this man beside her.

Oh, her heart was in trouble. *She* was in trouble. Now what would happen when this all ended? What would she do when Nick no longer needed to pretend to court her? While she might be physically safe then, her heart would be anything but.

"What's wrong, *Dolcezza*?" Worry deepened his voice. "*Per favore*, please tell me."

Mindy ducked her head, couldn't stop the smile, so she showed her face. "You speak Italian when you're nervous or worried. It's adorable." Oh mercy, she was lovesick. Her cheeks blazed.

"Adorable, huh?" Nick bumped her. "But it made you smile, so all is good. We are good?"

Before Mindy could respond, and a kiss had been what she had in mind, Sweeties's front door burst open and one of the younger fishermen plowed inside. "Dr. Matrone! Captain Mann collapsed at the Wharfside."

Nick muttered more Italian as he jumped up and tossed his cone in a trash bin. "Mindy, get my medical bag from the car and meet me there."

"Yes, sir." Mindy also tossed the rest of her cone, disappointment flooding her. Though the interruption had saved her from embarrassing herself.

Nick caught her fingers. "We haven't finished this conversation."

But they had. She wouldn't force him into more of a relationship than the counterfeit one she got him into. She made her lips form a bright smile. "Go, Dr. Matrone. I'll be right behind you."

Nick studied her for a moment, then pressed a kiss to her cheek and darted out the door. She watched him leave Sweeties with a sigh.

"You've got it bad." Mrs. Swensen chuckled beside her. "Next time he brings you in for a date, ice cream is on the house."

Mindy ignored the older woman's observation, wishing she wasn't so transparent. "Thank you, Mrs. Swensen." Then she hurried into the heat to help the man with whom her heart insisted she fall in love.

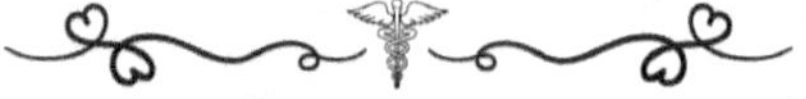

With his left biceps throbbing in time with his raised heart rate, Nick slowed his jog as he entered the outdoor seating area of the Wharfside and took in the scene. A group of people clumped together in the center of the outdoor seating area. He pushed through them to see Mann on his stomach, while David knelt on the retired fishing captain's legs and pressed his back to force air into his lungs.

Nick dropped beside his friend, keeping his injured arm tucked close to his body. "What happened?" He took Mann's wrist to check for a pulse, struggling to find one.

"He collapsed," David huffed, obviously having been performing resuscitations for long enough to be as winded as Nick. "Grabbed his chest as he walked in off the wharf. Fell here."

Heart, most likely. Not uncommon for someone of his girth in this heat. "Let's turn him on his back and raise his hands over his head."

Nick motioned for David to move. The man needed a break, or his efforts would be futile. Nick also preferred performing resuscitation while the patient lay on his back rather than his front. It was an older method Nick considered at least as effective as the current cardiopulmonary resuscitation method David had employed.

The crowd murmured around him. Did they not approve of his doctoring decisions? Tough.

"You—" he pointed to another fisherman—"hands here on his chest and push with each of your exhales."

David sank to his haunches, chest rapidly rising and falling, worry etching lines in his face. "What can I do?

"Clear the area, would you?" He didn't need an audience, let alone a disapproving one.

"Nick!" Mindy's voice reached him, however, he couldn't see her past the people gathered. "Excuse me, excuse—ouch!"

Nick glared at David, who was already jumping to his feet. With an enviable commanding presence, David sent the crowd inside to "let Dr. Matrone save a life." No pressure there. Mann's pulse was thin and erratic.

"So many people." Mindy knelt beside him, her blonde ponytail brushing his shoulder. "Here's your bag. Tell me what you need."

Nick took it from her, found the ammonia. Couldn't grip the bottle to open it. She snatched it from him. He handed her the cloth he kept for the purpose. "Apply it to this and put it by his nose."

Mindy did as directed. Already the softest breeze reached him without the crowd being in the way. It was warm and fishy, but a breeze nonetheless.

Nick filled a syringe with a heart stimulant, epinephrine, and injected it near the vagus nerve in Mann's throat. Then he put the used syringe back into his bag, and took up Mann's wrist, counting his pulse, which grew stronger as the moments ticked by. Mindy held the cloth to Mann's face, though her gaze roved from Mann to Nick to the man performing resuscitations, and then to David as he returned to kneel beside them.

"Anything?" David asked, crossing his arms over one bended knee.

Suddenly, Mann heaved a huge breath and coughed violently. Mindy jumped back. The other fisherman scrambled away. Nick went to roll Mann onto his side, one-handed, to keep the man from choking. Immediately, David's hands were beside his own. Cheers and claps spread through the crowd, bringing them back to Nick's awareness. They had encroached again.

"He needs a hospital. David, did anyone call for the ambulance?" The clinic wasn't enough for the severity of this attack, even if it had been fully operational.

Mindy pushed to her feet. "I can—"

"No." The word shot from Nick before he could temper his intense reaction to her offer. "Let David go."

"Okay." Mindy switched places with David, bringing her to Nick's side to help hold Mann on his side. The man groaned, pain twisting his pudgy features. "What now?"

Right. She thought he wanted her here to help him. In all honesty, he simply didn't want her to face her old boss alone, and his need to focus on his patient didn't allow an explanation of a less emergent matter.

"Raise his arms over his head again. It will help bring air into his lungs." Sweat trickled down Nick's back. The sun beat on his neck. Slowly, as his adrenaline faded, the pain in his left arm grew from smoldering to flames. He pinned his gaze on his bag, hoping he hid the wave of nausea that rolled through him.

Then Mindy was beside him again.

"Breathe, Nick." Her words were so quiet, he could barely hear them over his increasing pulse. "Take Mann's wrist. Count his pulse."

Nick obeyed, and by the time the ambulance appeared, he'd gotten his reaction to his pain under control again. He and Mindy stood side-by-side as the white-clad medics hoisted Mann onto the stretcher, then into the ambulance.

"Thank you." He wove their fingers together, needing to keep her close. "You were brilliant today."

"You are in too much pain." She didn't tug away, neither did she move closer to him. Did she think him forward for taking her hand? It had nothing to do with their ruse. She didn't know that. Didn't need to know either.

The ambulance drove away, and the onlookers dispersed. A few congratulated him on saving Mann's life. A few muttered surprise at his competence. Others didn't hide their disapproval of his resuscitation methods. A doctor could never please everyone, but as long as he knew he did the best he could for the patient, he didn't let it bother him. Or he used to let it roll off his back. Now ... the words jabbed like barbed hooks.

"You look done in." Mindy looked up at him, and he forced his gaze away to avoid forgetting himself. "I prescribe immediate rest, Dr. Matrone."

"A solid plan." David stepped to Mindy's other side, wiped his forehead with his sleeve, then replaced his flat cap. "Take Mindy home, and Grandma will fix you up with something to eat. And Matrone, get that wound looked at. You're in pain."

"That obvious?" Nick rotated his shoulder with a grimace. Yeah, it hurt. Was it because he overused it or because it was becoming infected? He'd have to look at it.

Mindy made a noise in her throat, then waved the keys. "David, my good man, would you be a dear and bring the car around?" she said, attempting a posh accent.

David laughed. Nick snorted.

"What?" Mindy grinned. "A little humor after an intense moment. I've always found that helpful. You both are smiling now."

"I—" Nick slammed his mouth shut. *I love you* had been on the tip of his tongue. Wow, was he ever overtaxed, overtired, and in too much pain, if that was his reaction to her teasing!

David cocked an eyebrow. Mindy kept on talking. "It's strange being here and not needing to get back to work. It's the first time I've been back since I lost my job."

"It's not the same without you." David rocked on his heels. "I miss seeing you as I leave the shanty every afternoon. But the job you have with Nick is well suited to you. You work well together. What you both did to save the captain..."

"She's a great nurse." Nick cast an approving smile down at Mindy, whose cheeks had turned a lovely shade of pink. He carefully shrugged his left shoulder. "She's an amazing left hand."

David laughed again, as Nick intended. Mindy rolled her eyes, then sighed. "Speaking of your arm, let's get you off your feet."

Nick liked the idea, though he needed to check his wound before he could rest.

David tossed the keys in his hand. "I'll bring the car close. Maybe step inside to get out of the sun. You're turning pink." David winked at Mindy, then left them alone.

Mindy dislodged her hand from Nick's and poked at her face. "Fair skin and sun do not blend. You do not have that problem, do you?"

"No." Nick caught her chin to get a clearer look at her skin, which was indeed reddening. Not because of a blush. "But I have an ointment that will help. When we return…"

A wavy, older voice reached his ear, pausing his words. Mrs. Bindle. He searched her out. Her wrinkle-lined face was unnaturally pale as she spun in a slow circle just outside the door. "Why am I here? Why did I come here? Where is here?"

"Mrs. Bindle." Nick stepped toward her, instincts shouting. Heat was a killer. The very young and the elderly were most vulnerable. Mrs. Bindle fit the latter description.

She swayed.

Nick jumped to her side, his uninjured arm snaking around her waist. The older woman's body was damp from sweat, yet her skin was cold and clammy. "Mindy, I need cool, wet cloths. As many as you can gather. Hurry!"

He helped Mrs. Bindle into the dim interior of the cafe, praying they could save her life.

"What do you think you're doing?" Willie Clifford blocked Mindy's path to the kitchen. "This is an eating establishment, and you are no longer employed here."

"A customer requires medical attention." Mindy pushed past him. She'd noted Nick's urgency. Whatever was ailing Mrs. Bindle required cool cloths immediately.

"Not so fast." Clifford grabbed Mindy's arm in a crushing grip.

"What's this about?" Chief Sebastian wiped his mouth with a napkin, then rose from a nearby table, his paunch stretching the fabric of his uniform. Sweat dampened his clothes. "Were you responsible for the hubbub taking place outside?"

"She's trespassing." Clifford tossed her aside like an old rag.

Mindy caught her balance and raised her chin. "Dr. Matrone requested cool clothes to save a woman's life."

"Then ask a waitress and move along." Sebastian returned to his chair. The man was a pompous fool who loved his own authority. Since he became chief of police, he'd let no one forget it, especially anyone friendly with the Martins family. He raised a graying eyebrow. "Or I will arrest you."

"Nurse Zahn!" Nick's voice boomed through the cafe, bringing it to a dead silence. "The cold cloths at once, or a woman will die."

Her knight. Mrs. Bindle's knight, too. Without waiting for a reaction from either Sebastian or Clifford, Mindy dashed into the kitchen. Clifford's laugh followed her.

"Nurse?" Sebastian's condescension made her wince. "Matrone, what did she offer you to get that job?"

Mindy grabbed a bucket and pumped water into it, as if the brusque action could beat back the tears. No one came to her defense. Not a word followed the chief's insinuation. One heartbeat, two … each one breaking her on the inside.

"Gentlemen." Nick's voice sliced through the moment. Frosty. Angry. Yet unnervingly calm. Mindy's hand shook as she lifted the filled bucket of water and grabbed a handful of nearby towels.

"You're going to defend your woman? Or is it *mistress*?" Sebastian goaded. "I forget what your type calls them."

Pain cut for a different reason. She marched out of the kitchen. "Leave him alone. He's saving lives. Can't you see that?"

Clifford spit on the ground. "I should have known someone like him would take up with a woman like you."

"That's enough." Buck Wilson pushed through the gawking crowd. Then he turned to Nick. "We might have our differences, but saving lives take precedence. David filled me in and is right behind me. What else do you need us to do?"

"Keep the area clear for Mrs. Bindle." Nick took the bucket from Mindy. "And get us more cold water. And a cup."

*Us.*

She followed Nick to where he had set Mrs. Bindle in a chair, her feet up on another. The corner was stuffy, though out of the sun. The older woman's face was pale and pasty, her breathing seemed erratic. However, it was the confused look in her eyes that concerned Mindy the most. Propriety aside, Mindy unbuttoned the top clasp of Mrs. Bindle's blouse and as she reached to dunk a cloth in the cool water, she found a wrung out one pressed into her hand. Nick. He gave her a nod to continue. She wrapped it around the back of Mrs. Bindle's neck.

David stepped in to prepare more wrung out cloths as Nick took up Mrs. Bindle's wrist, monitoring her pulse. Mindy removed the older lady's hat as her head lolled to one side and placed a wet cloth in its place. Buck dropped off a cup, and Nick helped her sip it. Mindy rolled up her sleeves and rested damp cloths there. Mrs. Bindle muttered about seagulls eating her bread, and her eyes kept rolling back.

Mindy took another cloth from David and dabbed it against Mrs. Bindle's forehead. "Doesn't seem to be a change."

"There is." Nick set down the cup and lifted the cloth from her right arm. "Watch. When I press on her skin, it bounces back. Dehydrated skin doesn't do that. Her pulse is also slowing. You're doing well."

Mindy smiled, the compliment sinking in deep.

"I'm right here, you know," David muttered. "And you say I have mooneyes?"

"You do." Mindy covered her embarrassment. "Have since those first days when Adaleigh arrived."

Nick chuckled and helped Mrs. Bindle drink another sip of water.

"Dr. Nick?" The older woman blinked. "Where am I?"

"Hi, Mrs. Bindle." Nick gently bumped Mindy to the side so he could move front and center. "The heat got to you, I'm afraid. My nurse, Miss Zahn, and I needed to cool your internal temperature before you experienced a medical crisis."

"I am undressed in public." Her hand fluttered to her throat and the damp cloth fell. Mindy snagged it.

"We were careful to keep you covered, Mrs. Bindle." Mindy used her hip to slide Nick back out of the way. "May I help right your garments while David brings you another glass of water?"

"Yes, thank you." The woman's gaze darted around. Mindy made quick work of buttoning that top button of Mrs. Bindle's blouse and securing the long sleeves, then she exchanged the cloth over Mrs. Bindle's head for her hat.

"All put back together." Mindy smiled at her the way she would have as a waitress. Not too chipper, yet full of confidence that she could handle what the customer—or in this case, patient—needed. "Here is David with water."

Mindy took the glass from her friend, who left again with the bucket and cloths. She supported the glass as Mrs. Bindle attempted to raise it to her lips. Mindy felt Nick watching her. Did he think she overstepped? He would say something if he did and so far he'd offered only praise.

"Thank you, dear one." Mrs. Bindle relaxed. "Did I hear Dr. Nick call you his nurse?"

"Yes, ma'am." Mindy braced for the accusation. Mrs. Bindle was known for her firm opinions and traditional expectations.

"Good." Mrs. Bindle patted Mindy's hand. "He is a wonderful doctor and an excellent man. Takes care of an old lady like me. Dr. Thompson never listened. Dr. Nick does. Working for him is preferable to being a waitress, don't you agree?"

"Yes, ma'am." She would have said those words either way, but the truth of them caused a sigh to slip out with them. Mrs. Bindle winked. Winked!

"Matrone," Buck interrupted. "We've got two more complaining of nausea and another not looking well."

Nick rubbed his neck with a wince. His arm had already been hurting him and now he wouldn't be able to rest it. "It's this heat. Will Clifford let us set up an emergency medical station here? Or do we need to move—"

"He'll set one up here." Buck spun away, no doubt to force compliance.

"That one is a complicated man." Mrs. Bindle wagged her finger at Buck's retreating form. "Now, what will you do with me?"

"I'd like you to sit and drink the rest of this water." Nick took the glass from Mindy and slid it on the table beside her. "When it's gone, I'll have a waitress bring you another one. I need to go see to the others."

"Take this sweet girl with you, Dr. Nick." Mrs. Bindle gave Mindy a little shove. "I'd put a ring on her finger, if I were you."

Mindy's neck and cheeks, no, her whole body heated. Nick just laughed. "I'll take that under advisement, Mrs. Bindle."

"Good. Now go on."

"You heard the lady." Nick handed his bag to Mindy, and for a moment, his doctor's facade slipped to reveal his fatigue and pain. Her heart responded with a *ker-thump*. He needed her. Then the capable doctor emerged again. "Let's get to work."

# Chapter Fifteen

Within twenty minutes, Nick had an emergency medical station set up within the cafe.

Buck and Adaleigh, whom David called in to help them, took over directing people through a sort of triage, leaving Nick and Mindy to care for the more severe situations. David passed out water and coordinated with Clifford—thankfully, the man left them well enough alone except to gather the money patients paid for medical services, of which Nick suspected Clifford kept a cut. Of course, Sebastian also stayed to "keep an eye" on them while being no help whatsoever. Fortunately, when Mrs. Martins appeared with Bella and Mabel in tow, also in answer to David's summons, they jumped into helping. Even Mabel, who stuck close to Bella's side.

As noon came and went, and the afternoon heat grew, more and more people came to the Wharfside with heat-related complaints. At one point, Adaleigh left for David's fishing shanty to check the weather report. The temperature had officially reached 100 degrees, with no cool down expected tomorrow.

Nick took the news stoically, as a doctor should, but inside, he wilted. Back in the tenements of New York, he'd lost too many to the stifling summer weather. He didn't want to lose anyone today. However, his arm felt like fire, and chills raced through him. Could he will himself not to succumb to either infection or the heat?

"We have enough hands to manage for a few minutes." Mindy tugged his uninjured arm. Still he attempted to resist. His patients needed him. As if Mindy read his mind, she pulled harder. "If someone in a dire emergency comes in, we'll tell you. For now, you need to sit down, or you'll be no good to anyone."

She was right. He let her take him into a back room, likely Clifford's office, and set him in a chair in a corner. He leaned his head against the wall. Exhaustion, heat, and pain drained him. "Mindy?"

No answer. He raised his head and realized she'd left him alone. He didn't want to be alone. However, now that he'd sat down, he didn't have the gumption to rise again.

Then, like the sun reappearing from behind a cloud, Mindy swept into the room and shoved a glass of milk into his hand. "Drink. I'll change your bandage."

He was too grateful for her presence to protest. While she fetched water and prepared the tweezers and bandages, he finished the milk and carefully freed his arm from his shirt, leaving the fabric bunched on that side of his neck. It covered half his torso that way, and maintained some semblance of propriety. The last thing he wanted was to cause Mindy discomfort.

Her gaze drifted to his revealed skin, then darted away, her cheeks pinking. Nick couldn't help looking down to see what she saw. With muscle tone from years of sparring, perhaps he looked appealing, but his skin was still dark ... swarthy ... since he sparred without a shirt when the weather cooperated to do so outside.

Mindy peeled the bandage away, yanking Nick from his thoughts.

"I'm surprised." Mindy sat back in her chair. "I expected an infection with the way you look right now."

"It's not infected?" So did he. He moved his arm so he could see the gash. She was right. It wasn't red or inflamed, and no pus leaked out.

"I'll repack it with fresh iodine on the gauze." She pointed to the empty glass of milk. "More, Dr. Matrone?"

"Later." The relief at not seeing signs of infection caused a smile to emerge. "Iodine, huh, Nurse Zahn?"

Her cheeks reddened as he hoped. "This bottle, right?" She held up the correct tincture.

"You know that, how?" Would she see what he saw?

Confusion dimmed her eyes. "Because it says it right here on the bottle."

He let loose a full grin. "Says it? The bottle spoke to you."

"No, silly, I read—" Her eyes widened.

There it was, the look he wanted. "You read it, Mindy. All on your own. You knew its purpose. I am so proud of you."

Her eyes sparkled, her lips quivered.

Doctoring with one hand in heat such as this, with his pain increasing, Mindy had shone as a bright spot throughout the day. Being his extra hand, anticipating what he needed, as if they'd been working together for years. Seeing her succeed like this, admiration and gratefulness mixed within his heart and his head screamed a warning that he was in danger of repeating yesterday's lapse. That emotion would take over, and he'd kiss her, right in front of everyone.

Dangerous, dangerous, dangerous. He was weak right now, and he knew it. How was this sheltering her? Protecting her?

She pulled the packing from his wound, and he gasped in pain. Served him right.

"Perfect, you are both here." Greg Alistar entered the room and, without so much as a by-your-leave, pulled a chair to face them. Neither did he mask the sneer at Nick's state of half-undress. Of all the times and places for the man to show up.

"What do you want?" Nick ground out the words, praying his eyes didn't water as Mindy pressed the treated gauze back into the wound.

"The inside scoop." He withdrew a notebook and pencil. "The two of you have been making names for yourselves, and it has been pointed out to me that I have yet to hear your side of the story regarding your so-called attack. Now is your opportunity to set the record straight."

Mindy paused her work, and Nick glanced at her. He read her expression easily, partly because it echoed his own thoughts. No way was Alistar here to set anything right. He never had before, which meant he had another angle and any words they used—even their silence—could be used against them. It had been that way for their friends. So why was Alistar pretending to play nice?

"Let's start with you, Dr. Matrone." Alistar even said his name properly, which set Nick even more on edge. He flinched as Mindy continued to pack his wound and concentrated on breathing, on relaxing his muscles. But his teeth refused to unclench.

"Mr. Alistar, can't you see we are busy?" Mindy spoke lightly as she tortured Nick. "This is neither the time nor the place."

"She's right, Greg." Buck appeared, finally, and leaned against the doorframe, arms crossed. "I'll be their spokesman."

Greg laughed. "I heard you and Matrone got into it at Sweeties today." He was back to saying Nick's name wrong. Good?

"A man has to stand up for his brother." Buck didn't blink. Oh, the man was an accomplished actor. No one would guess the ruse he and Nick cooked up. Unless Nick was the one being conned.

"All done packing it." Mindy ran her fingers down his aching arm. The gesture soothed, and he wished everyone would go away. No heat.

No patients. No annoying men looking for … whatever they were looking for. He just wanted to have Mindy to himself, to enjoy a summer day without danger or gossip or prejudice.

"All done means ready to talk." Alistar turned his shoulder to shut out Buck.

"Hardly." Mindy prepared the wrap that would protect the wound. "Once I finish seeing to Nick's arm, there are more patients to tend."

"Patients." Scorn dripped from the word. Then a predatory gleam lit his eyes. "You mean the men you're servicing? Does that include the doctor here?"

Nick leapt at him. Only the pain hadn't cleared from his head and he lost his balance. Alistar shoved him back, and Nick missed the chair, landing on the floor with a crash. Mindy cried out. What anyone else did, Nick didn't know. Humiliation weighed him down, and pain made his head spin.

"Up you go." Buck hauled Nick back into the chair. Where was Mindy?

"Just sit." His beautiful angel pressed her cool hand to his forehead, causing the fog to clear. "Are you hurt?"

"Hurt?" Alistar laughed, the sound grating through Nick.

"Alistar, leave them alone." Buck stood between them, feet braced shoulder-width apart. Protecting them.

"I'm confused, Wilson." Alistar tapped his notebook with the pencil. "You defend them, yet you don't approve of Nick stealing your brother's girl. Which is it?"

"I want my brother's girl to have a clean reputation, and you're besmirching it." Buck growled. "I don't care what you do to Matrone, leave Mindy out of it. Understand?"

"Fine." Alistar shoved past Buck to loom over Nick. "I heard you were run out of your practice in New York. Some sort of criminal behavior. You've brought that here."

"It wasn't criminal," Nick ground out.

"Leave him alone." Mindy tried to get between them. Nick snagged her hand to pull her to the side.

"Yet you were run out of town." Again the gleam lit Alistar's eye. "Take the wrong man's girl?"

"What's he talking about?" Buck demanded, even as he took a step back so he was behind Alistar, and mouthed: *Get yourself out of here.*

The realization that Buck played both sides settled Nick. He'd treated mob bosses and prizefighters. Crooked police officers and those determined to see justice done. He could manage one annoying reporter.

Tugging down his shirt, knowing he'd still need his wound bandaged, Nick rose. "Mr. Alistar, if you would have made an appointment with me, been willing to interview me during regular business hours, I would have told you the truth. But ambushing me here while Nurse Zahn cares for my injury is neither professional nor welcome. More patients have come in since my wound needed tending, so I must return to my job. Lives depend on it. Or, would you like rumor to spread that you are responsible for keeping the people of Crow's Nest from medical care?"

Alistar's mouth bobbed like a fish.

"And you, Mr. Wilson." Nick had to sell this to keep their ruse intact. "Putting your personal feelings above the town you are supposedly trying to help. Shame on you."

"Nick." Mindy hugged his uninjured arm.

"He's right." Buck stuffed his hands in his pockets and rocked on his heels. "Sorry, Matrone. I'll escort Alistar out."

"I want my interview." Alistar pointed at Nick. "Give me a story or I'll print what I know."

Nick gave a nod. "Wednesday morning at the clinic."

As Buck escorted Alistar away, Nick sank to his chair, exhaustion claiming him.

"Nick. You need to go home." Mindy pulled her chair close, motioning him to free his arm again, which he did and she began bandaging the wound. "You are in no state to help anyone like this. What do you think you were doing, making an appointment with Alistar? Chastising Buck? Are you mad? Even if—"

Nick pressed a finger to her lips to get her to stop talking. "Trust me. Can you do that?"

"Of course." But Mindy shook her head. "Why won't you tell me?"

"Because this isn't the time or place." He grazed his thumb over her cheek, then leaned away from her. "I'm a doctor, the only doctor in town. It is my responsibility to see to my patients."

"What good will you do them if you collapse?" Mindy tied off the bandage and crossed her arms. "Who takes care of you?"

The words struck, whether she intended them to or not. The loneliness he'd been battling since his medical partner turned his community against him could be summed up in that one question. Who could he lean on when he had spent his last effort? Who could he turn to when he needed help?

"God takes care of me." The answer his mother would have expected popped out, however, he'd been praying and it seemed God had yet to answer. Except that He'd brought Mindy. A woman who deserved someone better than the likes of Nick.

"He cannot make sure you eat or rest or heal." She cleaned up her workspace, discarding the old bandages with efficient movements. "God brings people to us for that. He brought you to protect me. Maybe he's brought me to protect you, too."

Emotion clogged Nick's throat, so he did the only other thing he could think of. He stood, stopping her in her tracks, and placed a lingering kiss on her cheek. Then he exited the room to see to his patients.

Mindy followed Nick, entirely too unsettled, yet more determined to make sure Nick took care of himself. He needed a nurse, and she'd be exactly that.

Refusing to take *no* for an answer, she made him settle in one spot, and insisted on David bringing patients to Nick, rather than Nick going to patients. David complied more easily than Nick, but her friend also had a twinkle in his eye that made her heart pound.

"Leave it alone, David," she hissed at him before letting him return to the triage section of the cafe so she could get back to Nick's side.

"Leave what alone, Nurse Zahn?" His attempt at innocence failed miserably when his lips turned up at the corners.

"I didn't tease you about Adaleigh." Mindy crossed her arms. "I helped you."

He laughed outright, there in the middle of the cafe where every eye turned on them.

"Would you hush up?" Mindy hated her ridiculously pale skin that turned red at the slightest embarrassment.

"You like him, Mindy." Thankfully, David had lowered his voice.

"So?" That wasn't what she wanted to say, yet something in David's tone made her defensive. "You don't approve?"

David grasped Mindy's shoulders. "I can't help being protective of you, Mindy. Him calling on you ..." was supposed to be all a ruse. He didn't say it aloud, but she knew that's what he meant.

Mindy tried to pull away, not wanting to hear what David would say next. Would he scold her for letting her heart run away when surely Nick was merely playacting? David held her firm, his gaze locked on hers. She squirmed. He didn't let up. It was as if he mined for answers she refused to give.

"Martins." Nick grabbed David's wrist. "Are you bringing patients to me or keeping my girl from helping me?"

David twisted his arm out of Nick's hold, then leaned close to Mindy's ear. "I approve."

Mindy gaped at David's back as he returned to his post. He approved of Nick? Or approved of her liking him? Or both?

"What was that about?" Nick asked as he escorted her back to the corner where she'd stationed him.

"Not here." Mindy wouldn't discuss their relationship with so many ears, plus she needed to think first. Now wasn't the time for that either.

Bella escorted a patient over, giving a quick description of his symptoms as Nick took charge. Mindy stepped away, snagging Bella's elbow. Nick wasn't the only one she worried about today.

"How is Mabel?" Mindy searched out her little sister. She stood beside Mrs. Martins wringing out cool cloths that the woman placed on one of the older fishermen.

"She is molto *bene*." Bella grinned. "I adore her, Mindy. Truly."

Oh, that did her heart good. No one had ever said that about Mabel before. At least not that Mindy had heard. Those who were not critical were concerned. Bella acted as if nothing were wrong with Mabel, that her lack of speech was ... normal. Was it? Was Mindy being no better than those who wished to keep Mabel tucked away from society?

"Nurse Zahn?" Nick interrupted her disconcerting questions. "I need your help over here."

"Coming." She smiled at him, then turned back to Bella. "Would you bring Nick a glass of milk? We need to keep him strong."

"Sí, sí." Bella winked.

Oh dear. Yet that sense of approval and welcoming that Bella cast toward Mabel wrapped around Mindy as well. What would it be like to have Bella as a sister-in-law?

Whoa! The heat was getting to her. Mindy whirled to help Nick, shoving such a thought aside.

Within minutes, she was wrapped up in nursing care. She'd never seen so many people succumb to the heat as they had today. The old timers couldn't remember the temperature ever getting over 100 degrees. Ever. They all commented on it.

"There was that June in 1910." One of the older fishermen said later that afternoon as Mindy counted his pulse and Nick used his stethoscope to listen to the man's labored breathing. "And 1911. Got close to one hundred that year. What Martins said, that the official temperature was 101 ... That true?"

"According to both the Weather Bureau and the U.S. Commission of Fish and Fisheries." Mindy handed the older man a cup of water. "Adaleigh filled me in."

"Smart girl, that one." The fisherman coughed, ending on a wheeze. "She'd know."

Nick wiped his forehead with his cuff. "Never been this hot before? It's not even July or August yet. No wonder so many cannot handle this type of heat. Doesn't bode well."

He said that last bit as a mutter under his breath, but Mindy caught it. Agreed.

"Seems you are having an asthmatic attack." Nick looked at Mindy.

"Have a waitress make him a cup of strong black tea."

"Hate that stuff," the fisherman groused.

"But it will help you." Mindy tucked her arm around the older man to help him to his feet.

With a little cajoling, she got him settled and drinking the brew. Within a couple of sips, his cough lessened, and Mindy returned to Nick's side. She rested a hand on his uninjured shoulder as Adaleigh brought over an older woman with pasty skin. Nick straightened under her touch, as if strengthened by it. In turn, it infused her with determination. She was helping him, and even if it broke her heart, she'd keep it up. He needed someone who cared about him.

"Nick!" Patrick Martins ran into the Wharfside, panic written all over his face. People parted as he rushed to Nick. "It's Samuel. Come quick. He's breathing hard and is barely waking up. He won't eat and Meri is exhausted."

No! Mindy's heart twisted. Nick had said heat targeted the very old and the very young. But Samuel? Poor baby. Poor Meri.

Patrick jabbed hands through his hair. He hadn't even bothered to put on a hat, let alone snap up his suspenders. "Please help us."

"Go." Mindy pressed a hand to Nick's back, moving him toward the door, forcing the handles of his medical bag into his uninjured hand. Patients watched them with conflicting expressions. Their doctor was leaving. To save an innocent baby. "We've got it covered here. Your patients are in good hands."

She'd see to that.

Nick's steps stalled as he glanced toward David's worried gaze, then to Mrs. Martins. They trusted him to save Meri's little boy. A baby's life would rest in his hand. His one hand. Should she go along? She propelled him forward even as she followed him out into the oppressive sunlight.

"Nick." Patrick had already cleared the outdoor seating. "Hurry up, please."

"Go, Patrick." Mindy waved him on, noting Nick's slow steps. "Nick is just giving me last-minute instructions."

Patrick didn't waste a minute. Nick, however, didn't move.

"What's wrong?" Mindy stepped close so it forced him to look at her. Worry shimmered in his brown eyes. "I'm ..."

"What, Nick? Tell me."

He rotated his shoulder. "What if I can't save him?"

"Nick." He wouldn't if he stayed rooted to this spot. It wasn't like him. What happened?

"Seeing the look in Patrick's eyes. I've saved, and lost, babies. Yet knowing the Martinses like I do ... I've never flinched like this. Not when a mafioso held a gun to my head while I treated a family member. Or when my partner betrayed my trust by spreading rumors about my loyalties. Or even when I sold my practice and moved to a whole new town away from everything I knew. What if I lose Samuel?"

"Then you will have done everything within your power to save him." Mindy pressed a palm to his chest. "Do you hear me? God will give you the wisdom, but it is in His hands when we take our last breath. You are a doctor and a fine one, but you are not God. Let Him carry that responsibility. You use the gift He's given you."

Nick's muscles relaxed, and a tear leaked down his cheek. "Thank you."

Unsure what to say, and needing to get him to Samuel as quickly as possible, she urged him toward the glassy lake. "Patrick and Meri have a telephone in Silas's old workshop. If you need me, call Mrs. Collins at The Barn. She'll come get me."

"Okay. If you need me here?"

"We've got it." She reached up and pressed a gentle kiss to his cheek. "Go, Dr. Matrone. Save their little boy. I believe in you."

His shoulders squared. "Thank you, il mia dolcezza." Then he jogged after Patrick, leaving her wishing she knew what he'd just called her.

# CHAPTER SIXTEEN

*Tuesday, June 30*

Mindy stumbled down the steps of Mrs. Martins' home, drawn by the smell of coffee. With the setting sun, the impromptu medical center at the Wharfside had been disbanded. Mindy suspected they'd need another one today. After a fitful night with too many thoughts, she couldn't think of anything more welcome than coffee. Even the muggy morning couldn't deter her.

Except Nick's smile when he spotted her. He stood beside the stove, sipping from a mug. Face haggard and more lined than she'd ever seen. Shoulders slumped. Hair in disarray. Injured arm held tightly to his chest. Yet, when he saw her, his eyes brightened behind his spectacles and he smiled over his cup.

"Where is Mrs. Martins?" she asked, hyperaware that they were the only two in the kitchen so early in the morning. Mabel still slept upstairs, Bella was a late riser, and David would be fishing, which meant Adaleigh was at the shanty. "What about Baby Samuel? Did Meri finally fall asleep?"

"Mrs. Martins went to the grocer's." Nick set down his cup, reached for another, and poured steaming coffee into it. "Patrick insisted on keeping watch over Samuel last night, so Meri finally relaxed enough to sleep. They're all upstairs still."

When Nick discovered both mother and baby were suffering dehydration, he insisted on bringing them to the Martinses' house where there were plenty of willing hands to help the young family. Adaleigh gave up her attic room for them, and Mrs. Martins went full mother hen.

"How are you feeling this morning?" She took the mug from him, nodded toward his injury. "How is your arm?

He offered a ghost of a smile that did nothing to hide the pain. "It hurts. I overdid it yesterday, but that couldn't be helped."

Mindy sipped her coffee to keep the rebuttal from slipping from her lips.

"About yesterday ..." Nick ran his thumb along the rim of his mug. "I don't usually seize up when a baby is in danger."

Mindy considered him. Should she wave off his discomfort? Encourage him again? Or probe deeper? Where was Adaleigh, with her skills at pulling secrets from a person?

"But thank you for helping me." He shifted his feet. "You have been a bright spot to me."

The warmth of his compliment gave her the courage to ask, "Why did it scare you?"

He sought her gaze, questions in his brown eyes. His throat bobbed. Then he whispered, "What if I failed?"

Mindy set her mug on the table. "What if you did?"

"The Martinses, they've taken me in." He slid his mug onto the countertop. "To repay them by losing the baby?"

"You think they'd turn on you?" Mindy didn't believe that for a moment. "It's not like them. You know that."

Nick's black brows bounced. "Yeah."

"Surely you've lost neighbors you've treated before?" Is that what this was about?

He gave a humorless laugh. "Of course I have. However, neighbors can still turn on a person."

"Nick." She wanted to hug him. His tender heart had been severely wounded, and it made her want to tend to it. To him. Maybe she could. "Have you changed your bandage this morning?"

"What?" The change in topic took him by surprise.

"Your wound needs cleaning." She frowned, thinking of last night. When David had escorted her to the Martinses' after closing up the emergency clinic, Nick had been fully occupied with doctoring Meri and Samuel. Bella made her eat supper, and then Mindy had insisted on continuing her role as Nick's nurse. Until Nick had sent her to get some sleep. "Did you even change the bandage last night?"

A red tinge crept up his neck. "I did, but I don't think I packed it well myself, which is why it needed the fresh dressing midday yesterday, too."

"Let me help you, Nick." Mindy stopped his rambling. "Do you want to do that now? Before the others wake up?"

He nodded, embarrassment flashing in his eyes. He didn't want others to see how much it hurt?

While Nick lowered himself into a chair at the kitchen table, Mindy fetched his bag from near the front door. She studied him as she returned down the hall. The stiff set of his back. The drumming of his fingers on the table. He knew what pain was coming and knew he had to face it.

She set the bag on the table, drew a chair near him. "Are you sure there is no other way to treat your wound?"

"This method heals it from the inside out. Otherwise, it risks infection and abscess." He freed his arm from his shirt as he had the day before.

She'd never seen a man without a shirt, and what little she could see of Nick's chest made her understand how he could fight so well. It was all muscle. As a lady, she shouldn't be looking. She dragged her gaze back to his.

"I wish you didn't have to be conscious for it."

He captured her hand with his uninjured one. "I know. However, changing the dressing twice a day doesn't allow for that. Some day, maybe they'll develop a local anesthetic other than coca. I've seen that go poorly too many times to use it. Are you sure you can do this?"

"Can? Yes." Of course she hated inflicting the pain on him, but like she told Mary Lou, a little pain now would save a lot of pain later. They'd both have to buck up and get through this so Nick could heal. "Want to … I don't want to hurt you."

He released her fingers, only to cup her cheek. "I thank you for that."

Her heart pounded as a crazy idea took flight. Should she act on it? With the way his darkened gaze had latched onto hers, maybe? Maybe … she leaned forward. His blinking rapidly increased. Then she tossed caution to the wind and kissed him on the lips. A fast kiss that left her more shaken than she should be when about to dress a wound.

"From what Adaleigh told me last night, today should be another hot one." She peeled the wrap away from his biceps to keep from looking at him. "If yesterday was any indication, we'll be busy."

Nick cleared his throat. "Adaleigh left early with David to monitor the weather. David's fisherman's instincts were firing this morning. Something about the weather that he didn't take the time to explain."

"That doesn't bode well for the rest of the week." The wound now visible, she took a moment to examine it. The skin around the gauze was pink and puckered. "How do you know it's healing?"

"See the pink? That's a healing color. As opposed to red and inflamed.

That's a sign of infection."

"So pink is good." *Excellent.* She washed her hands at the sink, then poured boiling water into a clean bowl that she brought to the table. Then she washed her hands again. "We'll keep it that way. Ready?"

"You don't have to be chipper for me, Mindy. I know this is going to hurt, and that's okay."

"It doesn't mean I can't help take your mind off of it." She selected the tweezers, ready to carefully extract the gauze. Some may think it squeamish work, Mindy found it fascinating. If only it didn't hurt Nick. "Do you want to check on Mary Lou today?"

"I think we could skip today, unless her parents need me to check on her." Nick closed his eyes as she worked the gauze from his arm, his words coming faster. "I'll call them on the telephone later, see how she's doing. I also want to check in on Mrs. Bindle. I should call the hospital to see how Mann is doing."

"Take a breath, Nick." She set aside the old gauze. "All done for now."

He exhaled. "That's not even the worst part."

"Why pack your wound, not stitch it?" Mindy asked as she washed out the deep gash. The body really was a magnificent creation. It made her want to learn more.

Nick rotated his shoulder, as if forcing the muscles to relax. "Packing is an old system of healing a wound that is open and deep like this one. If we stitched it up, it could fester underneath the closed top surface. So the thought is to allow it to heal from the inside out. Since the discovery of iodine as an anti-infection treatment, it's made this type of wound care even more effective."

Finished with the cleaning step, Mindy tossed the old wrappings and washed her hands again. "You are a braver soul than I. I don't think I could manage having such a wound treated day after day like this."

Nick turned, watching her as she prepared for the hardest part of dressing his wound. "Don't worry for me, Mindy. I've been stitched up too many times, so I know how to manage."

"Stitched up too many times?" Mindy returned to her chair, prepared the gauze with the iodine. "Is that what you were talking about with the street preacher? That prizefighter who gave you the Bible and taught you how to do that fighting thing you did when you got this wound?"

"Bare knuckle boxing?"

Mindy nodded. She braced herself, then began inserting the gauze. Nick's jaw and fists clenched. She needed to keep him talking. "Being a doctor in New York was that dangerous?"

"I worked in the poorest sections and was the doctor people called to treat those society shunned. Those too poor to pay, injured criminals, ladies of the night who'd been beaten or were with child. Treating those patients took me into dangerous areas, or put me in the path of dangerous people. I have more scars and more stories than I know what to do with. However, I firmly believe that, no matter a person's actions, they are loved by God and deserve expert medical care. If only that they might live another day to experience the love and mercy He shows."

Mindy blinked to clear her vision. Such conviction touched her deeply. "Then why did you leave?" Did it have anything to do with the fear that had paralyzed him yesterday?

Nick emitted a humorless laugh. Was he ready to tell Mindy the truth? Reveal the real reason they couldn't be more than friends? Even though he'd kissed her. He nearly had again when she asked why he'd frozen before treating Samuel. Mortification swept through him at the memory.

"I don't, I don't mean to pry." Red washed over her cheeks, and she fumbled the tweezers, jabbing him in the sensitive inner wound. A gasp escaped him. "Oh, Nick, I'm sorry."

"It's okay." It was his fault for causing her to lose focus. "You want to know?"

"It's just, I have a feeling that Greg Alistar is going to find a story. Whether it's a true story or not." Mindy's fingers shook against his bicep.

"Hey." He reached across with his uninjured hand to touch her arm. "I don't care about Alistar. Do you really want to know why I left New York?"

Perhaps he expected curiosity, however, the look in her expressive eyes startled him. She didn't just want to know, or need to know, she longed to know. He suspected she sensed it was a deep part of his story and learning it would help her learn about him. Did he want to open up to her like she desired?

She gave him a smile that said she didn't expect him to share, then returned to inserting the gauze. He barely held in a hiss of pain. The distraction of telling his story would be welcome. And, if he was being honest, he did want to tell Mindy his story. Because she had helped him overcome his fear yesterday. He wanted her to understand where he'd come from, why she mattered to him. Even if it was the same reason he couldn't ask her on a date for real.

"You know how men like Alistar and Clifford and Spelding always refer to me negatively because of my nationality? That's the case in a lot of places. I'm used to it and, since I worked among other Italians, I didn't need to worry too much about it."

"Doesn't make it right," Mindy muttered.

True. "My medical practice partner, who I thought I could trust, harbored ill will against the Italians. I learned he only worked with me because he thought he could steal the practice. What did the swarthy Italian know about anything? How was an immigrant like me supposed to hang on to the practice anyway? Obviously, there was criminal behavior going on." The bitterness that had taken root since his partner's true nature revealed itself, seeping into his words, oozing like an infected sore. "He figured I'd probably eventually end up dead. At least that's what he told me before we parted ways."

"Oh, Nick." Mindy set down the tweezers to cover the wound. Her wound packing skills were becoming more efficient.

"The worst part of it was, before I knew I couldn't trust him, I shared my thoughts on Italy's current struggles. The plight of my people. They're under the thumb of the Blackshirts and Mussolini's people. It's why Bella left Italy after Nonna died. Even her dearest friend lives in fear of them, unable to immigrate to America because of the immigration laws. But the look my partner gave me was such a mixture of disdain and fear." Nick shuddered at the memory of it. "I didn't understand it at the time, because I thought I was speaking up for my people. I thought I was speaking against the atrocities that were happening. Instead, he not only spread my private thoughts, he provided commentary: that because I disagreed with the Fascists, that made me a Communist. With the fear of the Russians after the First World War, even my own people turned against me."

Mindy's fingers grazed his arm as she wrapped the bandage around his biceps. Comforting, understanding. It caused the rest of his pain to leach out.

"My neighbors were so afraid to be seen with me, to even be associated with me as a fellow Italian, that they stopped coming to see me as a doctor until the only people willing to allow me to treat them were criminals.

So when Mrs. Whittlebush telegraphed that Marian needed my help, I sold my half of the practice and moved here." He shrugged and Mindy's hands fell away, the bandage securely in place. "Bella wanted adventure, and my family was tainted by association, so I brought her with me. My parents refused to leave, and I worry about what they will face because of me. I hope my absence will free them from the trouble."

"I'm so sorry, Nick." Compassion soaked her words.

Nick hardened himself against it as he met her gaze. "That, Mindy, is why you and I can only be friends. I cannot cause you more pain. You deal with enough people thinking less of you because of being a waitress, because of your personality. A personality that I—" Goodness, the word *love* almost slipped out of his mouth! "A personality that I *admire* very much. I cannot, in good conscience, invite more trouble or bring more pain your way."

Mindy cleaned up in silence. Nick adjusted his shirt and watched her as if they stood together on the side of Brooklyn Bridge. Would she push him over the edge, into the dark water below? It's what he wanted, for her to push him away. Footsteps sounded upstairs, signaling that company would join them soon. Their conversation would be over.

After a minute, Mindy returned, sitting before him, weaving her fingers between his. "Don't you think it's up to me to decide whether I want to be involved with someone who people think is a Communist?"

Nick chuckled, and yet the fear of finding out the answer made it more of a strangled sound. "If I gave you that choice, what would you say?"

Mindy had the audacity to wink. "I think you need to ask me before I just give away the answer."

"Mindy." This was serious.

She shook her head to silence him. "Just ask yourself the question: if the tables were turned, what would you say to me?"

A knock at the front door ended the conversation. The footsteps he heard upstairs flew down the steps, revealing Patrick in rumpled shirt, trousers, and hair. "It's Buck Wilson. I saw him walk up. I'll send him on his way."

"Let him in, Patrick." Nick stood. "He might have news I need."

News that could free Mindy from a relationship, whether real or imagined, with someone like him.

Mindy retreated as Nick greeted Buck, her emotions in too much turmoil to be more hospitable than required to pour the coffee. More footsteps on the stairs, a pair of them, and Mabel and Bella appeared. Bella skipped up to her brother and planted a kiss on his cheek regardless of the men watching her. Mabel, however, froze at the base of the stairs.

"We're sparring today." Buck slapped Nick's uninjured shoulder. "We need to talk. I spent last evening at an ... establishment. This heat has tempers high."

"Was it the people we want?" Nick followed Buck to the kitchen area. Patrick eyed them from where he stood, and Bella watched with curiosity.

"No, but they knew of them." Buck smiled at Mindy when she handed him a full mug. "Seems your father went far afield for his business dealings."

A strangled squawk came from the other side of the room, and they all spun. Mabel's eyes had grown as wide as silver dollars, her face as white as a cloud. Then she ran, darting past Bella, ducking under Patrick's legs, and dashing out the front door.

Calling some sort of Italian phrase over her shoulder, Bella ran after Mabel. Guilt assaulted Mindy. *She* should be chasing her sister. Instead, Nick guided her to a chair and Buck blocked her way.

"She knows something," Buck observed, as if not stating the obvious.

"You think?" Mindy shot the words at him. They pinged off him like raindrops.

"Did I bring my wife and baby into something dangerous?" Patrick folded his arms as he approached the table. "We've had enough of that to last a lifetime."

"You're right." Mindy was on her feet again, regardless of the men who hemmed her in. "I'll take Mabel and we'll—"

"Stay at Mrs. Whittlebush's house." Nick finished for her.

"Her reputation?" Buck glared at Nick.

Nick squared his shoulders. "If it comes to it, I'll marry her."

Mindy buried her face in her hands. This was a nightmare. She thought they had something special between them, but that type of feeling only led to one place. He didn't want to marry her, yet his nobleness wouldn't allow her to suffer. Her knight was sacrificing his happiness for her. She should feel safe, cared for. Instead, her heart cracked open. Would she ever be loved, truly loved, simply for being herself?

*Does God even love you?*

"Mindy. *Cuore mio.* Please look at me." Nick touched her shoulder, standing like a warm wall behind her. "I'm a fool, I know. I'm sorry."

"Where were Bella and Mabel going at such speeds?" Mrs. Martins broke the moment. Mindy spun to see the older lady standing in the hall entrance, looking at each of them, a full bag of groceries tucked in the crook of her arm. "What is going on here?"

Between Buck and Patrick, they explained as they helped her with the groceries, but Nick kept Mindy tucked into a corner, his presence turning her insides to pudding. What was going on between them? Why did she have to want it to be more?

A moment later, Bella stuck her head in through the back door. "Niccolo." Her accent thickened as she addressed her brother, spouting off Italian words faster than Mindy could make sense of them, had she even understood them.

"Sí, sí." Nick nodded, motioned Bella back outside, then returned his attention to Mindy. He cupped her shoulders, his eyes full of petition behind his spectacles. "Bella caught up to Mabel, convinced her to talk to me. Mabel does not want to come inside. Too many people."

Too many people she couldn't trust, he meant. Including her own sister.

"Don't you worry about us." Mrs. Martins cut in, whether welcome or not. Mindy leaned toward not. Her heart hurt too much. "I'm making cookies. Patrick, go check on Meri and Samuel. Buck, use my telephone to call Adaleigh. She's at the shanty while David is out on the boat. Tell her she's staying here with Patrick and Meri while I chaperone everyone else at the Whittlebush house."

Nick dashed his thumb across Mindy's cheek, then exited the house. Mindy hesitated. Others had taken command of the situation, made decisions without her, though those decisions directly affected her. It made her ill at ease. No one gave her a task either. As Buck and Mrs. Martins finalized plans and Buck asked for the operator, Mindy made her own choice. Mabel was her sister and as much as Nick wanted to talk to her alone, and Bella made it sound as if Mabel didn't want Mindy to join them, Mindy needed to know why the poor girl was scared to death.

Quietly, she slipped out the front door and crept around the house, stopping at the corner where she had watched the Matrone siblings talk the other day. Bella sat in the far rocking chair with Mabel on her lap, angled so Mindy could see their faces. Nick sat in the chair beside them, his back to her. Jealousy had Mindy crossing her arms against the pain in her chest. Mabel rested her head against Bella's shoulder. Mabel had done nothing like that with Mindy since she came to stay with her. What did Bella have that Mindy did not?

# CHAPTER SEVENTEEN

Mindy rested her head against the corner of the house as she watched Nick speak with Mabel and Bella. He leaned forward, his one elbow on his knee. "I'm glad you asked to talk to me, Mabel. I'm guessing something scared you." His voice rumbled, sure and strong. Mindy could picture the earnest concern on his face.

Mabel nodded her head against Bella's chest.

"You know what's really hard when you're scared?" Nick continued. "It's hard to know what people you can trust. Especially when you know something that could hurt people you love."

Again Mabel nodded, and Mindy's aching heart twisted.

"When I was a little boy, I saw my neighbor hurt somebody." Nick shifted in his chair, making Mindy wonder what he'd actually seen. "The man caught me watching and told me that if I ever said anything, he would hurt my mom."

Mindy covered her mouth to hold in a gasp. Both Mabel and Bella had eyes as large as soup bowls.

"A couple of days later, the man moved away. I still said nothing, not even to my parents, because I was afraid he'd find out I talked. But, Mabel, about six months later, I learned that my parents had known about it all along. They had heard what happened and called the police. They were the reason the man moved away, because the police took him to jail. So I was safe long before I knew that truth."

Mindy pressed fingers to her lips. What had Nick seen in his life? The suffering, the fear. Yet, to be so selfless as to offer marriage just to protect someone he didn't love. He might not love Mindy, and that thought caused a deep ache inside, but all she could see was a hero reaching out to a scared little girl.

"Let's see if I can take a guess here, Mabel." Nick's voice oozed kindness. "Did you hear something or perhaps see something, and the person who did the bad thing warned you that if you told anybody, they would hurt you? Or maybe hurt Mindy or your mamma. Is that true?"

Mabel didn't move her head. Which could only mean her sister wouldn't acknowledge something happened, but she didn't deny it either. *Oh, sweet Mabel. Why didn't you tell me?*

"I know how scary that is, Mabel," Nick continued in the same calm tone while Mindy's pulse pounded in her neck. "I'm also guessing you're afraid you'll slip, and say what he didn't want you to say, so you chose not to say anything at all. Is that correct?"

Mabel nodded.

Mindy wrapped an arm around her chest. Her sweet baby sister. So scared she couldn't speak. Nick and Adaleigh had been right.

"You're a brave girl, Mabel." Nick's voice rumbled. "It's scary to have a big strong man yell at you. Did this happen a couple of weeks ago, or was it a couple of months ago? Or maybe even a couple of years ago?"

Mabel blinked.

"Years ago, wasn't it?"

She nodded again.

"It feels like it happened yesterday. I know." Nick leaned back in his chair, the picture of easy conversation. How did he do that? "That means you were a little girl, probably playing where you weren't supposed to."

Mabel's face turned red.

"Like in the barn. Maybe in the hayloft, where you didn't think anybody would see you."

Her eyes widened.

"I guessed because that's what I would have done if I lived in the country. When it happened to me, I was playing where I shouldn't have been, too. I wasn't in a hayloft because I lived in the city. However, if I was in the country, that's where I would have been. Then you probably made a noise, a squeak, or something. Then that man heard, and he told you never to speak a word of it."

Mabel nodded as if Nick had laid the answer to the world's problems at her feet.

Perhaps he did. It seemed he'd unlocked Mabel's secrets without making her say a word. Still, Mindy wanted Nick to ask the identity of the man who threatened her sister. What did he do to cause such fear? Was their father involved? Though how Mabel would ever answer, considering she couldn't speak, Mindy didn't know. As it was, Nick was operating with simple yes and no questions.

Yet he was getting somewhere, so she held her tongue. Let Nick work his magic while she tried to keep her heart from breaking into a thousand tiny shards.

Nick kept his face neutral as he watched Mabel's expressions. Since she did not use words, he needed to read her in every other way possible. Her eye movement, her hands, the tilt of her head. He sensed her fear, understood it from his own experience, and wanted to ease that discomfort as much as possible.

Despite the rising temperatures—not that it had cooled down overnight—and his uncomfortably dampening shirt, he kept his posture relaxed and his focus on Mabel. Though he did sense Mindy over his shoulder and, at one point, glanced back only to see her shift to keep out of sight. He didn't think Mabel knew she was there, which was probably helpful.

Bella, bless her heart, kept quiet, which was a miracle in and of itself. She, too, kept her attention on the little girl in her arms, holding her securely. Providing the physical comfort Mabel needed as Nick probed the little girl's wound.

As a doctor, he'd learned how to separate himself from the pain he caused. Debriding a wound was excruciating, but losing a limb due to infection because he'd been too soft was much, much worse. In those moments, he was never more grateful for a nurse—not a family member, who was usually asking why he had to hurt their loved one—but an outsider who could calmly comfort a patient while he worked. Bella served as his nurse during this emotional debriding, allowing him to do what was best for Mabel, while making sure she also felt as safe as possible.

Question was, where to go from here? How could he find out more about these people who hurt Mabel, especially if the beginning trauma that made her mute was years ago? In his professional speculation, he guessed that whatever had happened, happened right as she was beginning to speak. Perhaps age four or five. However, his instinct also told him that had simply been the beginning. How to ask the questions he really wanted to know without hurting both Mabel and Mindy?

Putting it off wouldn't make it easier. He adjusted his posture to ease the ache in his arm. "Mabel, can you tell me whether you saw this man again, the one who made you so afraid? Have you seen him since that first day?"

The girl's eyes widened. Fear made her chin tremble. Bella bit her lip, and he knew she was trying her hardest not to react. She didn't like the fear she felt coursing through Mabel, and she tightened her hold on her in a tight hug around the little girl's waist.

Mabel's lack of response told him more than words. "It's okay, Mabel. I know you've seen him again. Did you see him right before your parents brought you to Mindy?"

The poor little girl froze like a wild animal who knew danger circled overhead.

Nick hated this, yet kept pushing, knowing the answers she kept locked in her mind could free her. "Mabel, did your father talk to this man who threatened you?"

More frozen silence.

"Did your father ask you not to say anything?" This was the question that worried him the most.

She shook her head. Relief that her father had not been some of the cause of her fear washed over him. Yet her father had done nothing to stop it. Or had he?

Banking on her tells and her willingness to deny what wasn't true, Nick asked, "Did your father bring you to Mindy to keep you safe?"

Mabel cocked her head. Not quite a yes or no.

He'd try another angle. "Was it your mother's idea or your father's idea to leave you here with Mindy?"

Confusion danced across her little face.

Nick realized his mistake. He had to keep to yes or no questions, so he rephrased. "What I meant to say is: was it your mother's idea to send you to Mindy?"

Mabel shook her head. Nick and Bella exchanged a glance. If Mrs. Zahn did not like this arrangement, did she not think it was too dangerous to send Mabel? Or had she thought Mabel would be safer with her?

Bella pressed her cheek to Mabel's hair. "Did your mamma and papa fight about it?"

This time Mabel nodded, and a tear slipped down her pale cheek.

Nick's insides ached. "It was your father's idea to give you to Mindy, wasn't it? He wanted to keep you safe, keep you away from the mean man."

More tears coursed down Mabel's cheeks. Behind him, he heard Mindy shifting, sniffling. He wanted to go to her, beckon her, anything to comfort her, but couldn't disrupt this moment of revelation. The trauma Mabel went through was becoming more clear to him. He'd seen it, experienced it, and hated that she had, too.

He lifted his spectacles to massage the bridge of his nose. "Mabel, did the bad man say he was gonna hurt your daddy if your daddy didn't do what he wanted?"

Again, Mabel nodded.

Nick blinked against the tears stinging his own eyes. He couldn't imagine having a daughter in danger, especially if it was his own fault. "Did your daddy say no?"

Mabel's head bobbed up and down as tiny sobs shook her body. Bella rocked her, tears in her eyes. Mindy silently appeared at his side—his injured arm side—and crouched where his body blocked her from Mabel's view. He wanted to take her hand, wipe away the emotion mottling her cheeks.

Instead, he continued his questions. "Mabel, sweetie, did your daddy get very upset and tell that man not to touch his family?"

Mabel nodded, burying her face in Bella's chest. Bella wrapped her arms around the little girl.

"But the bad man said he would hurt your family if he didn't do as he said, and that is why your father sent you to Mindy. He thought they would chase after him, and that if you were not near him, you would be safe. That is what you heard your parents fighting about, isn't it?"

All three females wept. He twisted, drew Mindy around where he could reach her with his uninjured side. If propriety didn't hold him back, he would have tugged her to his lap. Instead, she knelt, her head on his knee, and he caressed her hair as she sobbed.

"Sometimes our parents make difficult decisions, even when they don't want to, in order to keep us safe." Nick met Bella's gaze, knew they were both thinking of their own stories. "Sometimes it works out as they plan, and sometimes it doesn't."

Mabel hiccupped. Mindy shuddered under his touch.

"My parents left Bella in Italy when they came to America." He swallowed down the emotion and the vivid memory of that day. He hadn't wanted to leave his little sister, but he was a child and had no choice. "Our parents couldn't afford to bring the whole family, so they had to choose. They believed it was better for Bella to stay with our nonna than it was for me because I was a boy old enough to work, which I did when we reached New York. It was the hardest decision my parents ever made. Many a night, I woke to hear them fighting or crying about their choice. It broke our family apart. Bella and I didn't see each other for years."

Bella squeezed her eyes closed. They'd written often, sharing the grief from across an ocean.

Mindy lifted her chin to look between him and Bella. "Why did they do it? Why did they have to choose?"

"Because it was the best chance for us to survive." He thumbed away one of her tears. "The hard times we were facing in Italy, the dangers, the lack of food. We would have starved. In the end, breaking our family apart saved us. I think that's why your parents made the same decision."

"You think so?" A sliver of hope ignited in her eyes.

Nick nodded, glanced at Mabel. "Unfortunately, the bad man thinks he can still find out where your parents are through you both. That's probably what they want to know, why they want to get to Mabel. They think she can tell them where your parents are."

Mabel raised her head from Bella's chest, watching Nick closely.

He met her gaze. "They think your daddy is hiding and if they can threaten you and make you afraid, then you will tell them. Do you know where your daddy and mamma are, Mabel?"

An odd expression crossed Mabel's face, and Nick could whack himself as he realized what he'd just asked.

"Oh Mabel, I'm sorry. You do know, don't you? I just asked you the same question that those bad men want to ask you." He shook his head. "You don't have to tell me. I don't need to know where your parents are. Knowing that you do, I will protect you. You are the prize that bad man wants. Well, you know what? I won't let them touch you. Mindy won't let them touch you. None of us will. We want to keep you safe, Mabel. While your mamma and papa thought it would be safer for you to be away from them, that's not how Mindy or Bella or I, or any of us, are going to treat you. We're going to keep you safe by keeping you close. Do you understand?"

Mindy was speechless. So many thoughts and emotions careened through her, yet the one that rose to the surface was admiration for Nick Matrone. Yes, if she had any doubt she was falling in love with him, these last minutes erased it. This man was the noblest of men, and she loved him for it. Loved him for his gentle care of her sister. Wished she could go back in time to save him, and Bella, from the heartache of growing up apart.

"Now, Mabel, do you think you can help us?" Nick's attention might be on her sister, but his thumb rubbed circles on Mindy's collarbone. The motion was both comforting and distracting. "We want to get the bad man so Detective O'Connor can put him in jail. Remember how I said that my parents helped put the man who was mean to me in jail? Do you think you can help me put your bad man in jail, too?"

Mindy watched her sister. The thoughts Mabel worked through as she considered Nick's question played across her face. Fear, trust, concern, hope.

It was a lot to ask of a child, but this conversation had shown Mindy that Mabel wasn't as in need of coddling as she thought. Nick had pushed and probed, and yet Mabel hadn't run away. She was stronger than Mindy realized. It made Mindy proud. As did the expression Mabel gave as her eyes cleared with decision. Determination grew with the set of her mouth, the lowering of her chin, the narrowing of her eyes, then suddenly Mabel jumped up and dashed inside.

"But—" Mindy made to go after her. Nick held her still. She looked at him. "I didn't think she'd run anymore."

"She is not running." Bella peered inside. "She's going upstairs. I think ... I gave her a drawing pad, which she will not show me. She keeps it under her pillow at night. She has been drawing furiously lately. I think she is getting it."

"A drawing pad?" Mindy considered the past few weeks, the drawings her sister had made for her.

"Did you know she likes to draw?" Nick's question held no judgment, yet Mindy felt the weight of her lack of knowledge.

Her shoulders rounded. "I'm a horrible sister."

"No." Bella swiped at her eyes, clearing the tearstains from her cheeks. "Mabel adores you."

"How do you know?" Why did Mindy feel like a parched wanderer needing the answer?

"Because she watches you with love in her eyes." Bella adjusted her position in the rocker. "Just because she uses no words does not mean she does not communicate. She loves you."

Before Mindy could absorb Bella's words, Mabel returned, the drawing pad, indeed, held tightly against her chest. Her steps faltered, and her gaze jumped from person to person, settling on Mindy, then glancing back at the house. If she looked at Mindy with love as Bella suggested, then why was there worry in her eyes now?

Nick eased out of his chair. "It's all right, Mabel. Mindy wants to keep you safe, and I know you want to keep her safe. Can you trust me to do that? To keep your sister safe?"

Mindy watched as her sister's worry melted. Mabel nodded, and instead of sitting on Bella's lap, she leaned against Nick's other knee once he returned to his chair. She didn't relinquish her drawing pad, however. She looked toward the house.

"Do you want to go inside?" Mindy asked. She should leave this to

Nick. He'd worked a miracle so far, but she wanted to connect with her sister. Then something clicked in her mind. "You first ran away when you saw Mr. Wilson? Buck. Is he who you're scared of?"

Color drained from Mabel's face as she shook her head.

"Not Buck?" Nick rested his hand on Mabel's shoulder. "Was it someone close to him?"

Mindy swallowed. "His brother Joe?" No, please no.

Mabel shook her head, and a relieved breath rushed from Mindy. It wasn't Joe. Of course, if there was criminal behavior within a twenty-mile radius, Joe would find it. Perhaps there was still a connection, a connection that was locked inside Mabel's little head. Why had that bad man stolen her words? It wasn't fair. Mabel was a child!

"Did you hear the bad man talk about the Conglomerate?" Nick asked, bringing Mindy back to the moment.

Mabel's gaze darted around. Nick had guessed correctly.

"It's okay." Nick captured Mabel's chin, his dark skin so opposite Mabel's pasty pallor, and turned her gaze toward him. "Buck is going to help keep you safe. Okay?"

Mabel scratched her nose. She wasn't so sure about that, neither was Mindy. Something about Buck set Mabel on edge. Mindy was learning her little sister was more perceptive than anyone guessed. What didn't she trust about Buck Wilson?

Nick tapped Mabel's nose. "All right. One thing at a time. What do you want to show me in that notebook of yours?"

Mabel set the drawing pad on Nick's knees and opened the cover. Mindy barely held in a gasp at the quality of the sketches. Her little sister had a talent! Page after page, she'd drawn of people. Mother, Father, Mindy. Other people Mindy recognized, like David, the local pastor, their neighbor, all against the backdrop of the farm. Because their parents never took Mabel away from it. Until they left her with Mindy.

"What am I looking at here?" Nick asked as he turned the page and stopped at a sketch set inside the barn. Father and another man faced each other. Father had an angry expression, the other man had his back to Mabel. Then she spotted something that made her itch.

"Mabel, sweetie?" Mindy's voice trembled. She pointed to the far corner of the picture. "What is this?"

Mabel snatched the drawing pad back, shaking her head.

"It's okay." How could Nick stay so calm? Did he not realize what she'd seen? "Why don't you and Bella go check on Baby Samuel for me? Ask his mamma if she needs anything, then tell Mrs. Martins. Can you do that?"

Mabel brightened. Nick and Bella exchanged a silent conversation in that way they excelled at. Then Bella led Mabel inside, and Buck emerged with a plate of cookies.

"Your grandmother is a force to be reckoned with." Buck shoved the plate at them. "She made me help make these. I don't think I've ever spent that much time in a kitchen. Wait. What's with the look on your faces? What did you learn from Mabel?"

Mrs. Martins bustled out with a tray of glasses and a pitcher of milk. "I'll leave this here for you. The girls and I will keep Meri company until Adaleigh relieves us. Then we'll move Mindy and Mabel to the Whittlebush house."

The older woman left without waiting for a reply. Buck stuck his thumb over his shoulder. "See what I mean? Now, spill. What did you learn?"

Mindy took a cookie, needing something in her hand. "It's about—"

"You still up to sparring with me?" Nick interrupted.

*What? Now?*

"Yeah." Buck took a bite of cookie. "Eat a cookie so we're even."

Nick laughed and snatched one as he pushed from his chair.

Mindy stepped in his way. "What about Mabel? The pic ..."

Nick squeezed her hand, quieting her. "Can you trust me?"

Could she? She had before, but now?

Buck watched them, so Mindy nodded.

Why didn't Nick want her to tell Buck about what she saw in the picture? Did he not trust Buck as much as he said he did?

Buck suggested she go inside out of the heat, and Nick agreed. Mindy went to the back door as the men moved to the middle of the yard, then hesitated. Should she stay against their wishes or go check on Mabel? No, these two needed watching. She settled back into the chair to keep an eye on them. Mabel was in good hands, safe inside.

Anyway, she'd never watched two men spar, whatever that meant, and her curiosity rose. Until the two stripped down to their trousers and cotton shirts, the sleeves of which they rolled to their elbows. Embarrassment warmed her more than the rising temperature. She grabbed a cookie and stayed put. There was more to learn, from Nick, Mabel, and Buck. She'd let everyone have their moment to recover from Mabel's intense revelation, but she intended to find the answers before anyone left the house.

No matter what Mrs. Martins, or anyone else, dictated.

# CHAPTER EIGHTEEN

Setting his feet in the grassy area between the house and Mrs. Martins' garden, Nick raised his uninjured hand in a boxer's position, keeping his left close to his chest. Buck raised both arms. Could Nick use his injured arm? If the knife hadn't sliced through his bicep, maybe. However, it would take the adrenaline of real danger to overcome the pain.

Buck circled him, sending a weak side jab to get Nick moving.

For now, Nick needed to work out how to defend himself—and Mindy—without using his damaged arm. He studied Buck's traditional boxer's stance. A sport that went back centuries, it was considered the legitimate form of fighting, as opposed to the bare-knuckle variety. Probably because boxing wasn't as bloody. On the streets, it was, as Herbert Spencer said in response to Mr. Darwin, the survival of the fittest. Nick was anything except the fittest right now.

Buck jabbed with his left. Nick blocked it easily with his right. Buck parried in a swift roundhouse punch directly toward Nick's injured shoulder. Nick spun out of the way before Buck's fist connected with his bandaged arm.

"Matrone, get your feet in the game." Buck stayed on his toes, returning to the traditional boxer's stance.

Nick rolled his eyes. "I know that."

Buck grinned. Yeah, he knew Nick knew such boxing basics and was goading Nick into taking this seriously. All right, then. Nick leaned into his rear foot, weight set on the balls of feet. Buck drew closer. Nick sent a quick jab toward Buck's nose, retreated to his back foot. Buck dodged. Nick followed up with two jabs. Intensity glinted in Buck's eyes. Buck threw a series of punches, driving Nick toward Mrs. Martins' garden. At the last moment, Nick pivoted. Two punches toward Buck's face, then a sideways jab that caught Buck behind the ear.

"Nice one." Buck stretched his neck, then advanced again.

Round the yard they went. The sun beat down. Sweat dripped down Nick's face. His shirt clung to his back, Buck's equally wet. His muscles ached, making him wish he hadn't missed so many days of sparring. Buck proved of equal skill to his own, and Nick was wearing down. Should he call it? Practice more a different day?

Suddenly, Buck twisted on one foot, darting the other out in a kick that caught Nick right in the lower stomach. As Nick stumbled backwards, Buck followed with a punch to Nick's face. It caught him in the chin and sent him to the ground.

"Nick!" Mindy shouted.

"He's fine." Buck held out a hand.

Nick grasped it, and Buck hauled him to his feet. "You need to teach me that move, Wilson."

Mindy pushed between them, shoving Buck away. "What were you two thinking? Buck, you could have hurt him."

"It's okay, Mindy." Nick rubbed his stomach, which hurt more than the bruise he'd probably have on his jaw. "There was something different in that kick than what I've seen. Where'd you learn it?"

"Had a job with the railroad." Buck dragged his sleeve over his sweaty face. "Made friends with a few Chinese laborers. I taught them English, they taught me their *kung fu*. Every culture has their fighting techniques. From what I can tell, you've mainly learned the Irish form, mixed with a bit of Greek boxing."

Mindy gaped at Buck. "How do you know all that?"

Buck shrugged. "I've gotten around, needed to learn to defend myself."

Nick didn't miss the man's shuttered expression. Buck Wilson wasn't the wealthy businessman he portrayed. Nick worked in an area of New York that required it. Buck? Now that he thought about it, did anyone know anything about him from before he came to Crow's Nest and took over the Conglomerate? "Let's go again. First, what part of the foot did you hit me with? The ball or the heel?"

Mindy huffed. "Fine, you boys beat each other up. But I'm not tending to any broken parts." She marched back to her rocking chair.

"Feisty," Buck laughed.

"Watch it, Wilson." Nick glared at him.

"Oh, please. You two are dancing around the fact you like one another. She doesn't want to see her man get hurt. What woman does?"

Nick opened his mouth. What could he say when Buck was exactly right?

"See? Now let's make sure you can defend yourself. And your girl."

"What were they doing?" Bella exited the house half an hour later, her eyes suspiciously red, and Mabel clutching her hand. "Nick and Buck came into the house soaking wet."

"Sparring." Mindy muttered, heat rising as she thought about how their cotton shirts stuck to their chests. Both men had significant muscle tone. They also stank, which helped curb her reaction. At the time. "They're cleaning up now, thankfully."

"You were out here the entire time?" Bella shook her head. "I do not know how you stayed. I watched Nick spar once, and never wanted to watch again. I flinched at every punch."

"Yeah." Mindy had, too, but she couldn't not stay. She needed to be available in case Nick got hurt or re-injured his arm, which he apparently didn't do because he assured her he was fine. Even though Buck sent him to the ground thrice. Yes, Mindy counted. What did *that* say about her? Mindy sighed, then turned her attention to Bella. "Are you okay?"

Bella pointed to her chest, her eyes turning glassy. Mabel tugged a paper from Bella's pocket, and before Bella could snatch it from her, Mabel gave it to Mindy.

"I don't need to read it." Mindy folded the paper. "Want to tell me about it?"

Bella sank into a chair. "It is from la mia amica. My friend Margherita. She is home in Italia. It is not good there." She shook her head.

"You're scared for her." Mindy's heart broke at the tears that slipped down Bella's cheeks. Mabel hugged her new friend.

"She must leave our home, but so few Italianos are allowed into America. It is doubtful. She is not ... she has ..."

Was this the same friend whose broken leg had not healed properly? The one Nick mentioned?

Bella shook her head. "It is unlikely she will be granted entrance, but she cannot stay. It is too dangerous for her."

"I'm so sorry, Bella."

Bella forced a smile, then nudged Mabel and stood. "Go by your sister, sì?"

The conversation was over. Mindy returned the letter, and Mabel glanced up at Bella, as if asking permission. Mindy's heart twisted. She kept her smile in place, though, determined to repair whatever had gone wrong between them. Bella gave another nod, and Mabel slid onto Mindy's knee.

"Are you okay after Nick's questions?" Mindy brushed her hand over Mabel's blonde hair. How could she regain the trust that had eroded since Mabel came to live with her? The little girl squeezed her arms around her drawing pad, worry tugging her mouth into a frown. "Dear Mabel, why didn't I see how scared you were? Why didn't you let me help? I love you. You're my sister. I would do anything for you. You know that, right?"

Mabel's head bobbed almost viciously. If Mabel knew that, then why did she seem to mistrust her? Mabel set the drawing pad on the table with the cookies and milk, pointed to herself, then Mindy, then crossed her arms over her chest.

"You love me?" Mindy nearly choked on the words. Again the almost violent nod. A realization struck. It wasn't mistrust at all. "Oh, Mabel, you didn't tell me to keep me safe?"

Mabel's eyes brimmed with tears as she nodded again.

"Sweetie!" Mindy opened her arms and Mabel flew into them. Mindy hugged her tight. While still too thin, the little girl had more bulk on her than when she had arrived. Were their parents in such trouble financially that they couldn't feed Mabel? What about the money Mindy sent home? What if her father had gotten a hold of it and used it in his gambling? She squeezed her sister tighter, tucking her face in Mabel's neck.

"Everything okay?" Nick's quiet question broke the moment. Mabel didn't move from Mindy's arms as Mindy met his questioning gaze. His hair was damp, and his shirt was now a clean tan cotton. He massaged his shoulder.

"How is your arm?" Mindy asked. "Don't tell me fine like you did before. I let you because you needed to wash up."

"She means you were *puzzolente*." Bella waved a hand in front of her nose.

Nick glared at his sister. She smirked, then curtsied, only for the door to bump her backside.

"Pardon me." Buck reddened as he emerged from the house. He also had cleaned up, and now wore an impeccable gray suit, looking much more like the Conglomerate boss he was.

Bella stuttered, and Nick's glare darkened.

Buck's gaze bounced from person to person, then settled on Mabel's drawing pad. "Whose is this?" He picked it up. Mabel raised her head from Mindy's shoulder, fear in her eyes.

Bella reached for the pad. "Why does it matter?"

Buck dodged Bella's attempt to grab it, and Nick moved to look over Buck's shoulder. "Why? What do you see?"

Mindy glanced at Bella's disgruntled expression, then back at the men. Did Buck see what Mindy had wanted to ask about before the men sparred?

"Who are these men?" Buck tapped the picture. Mabel emitted a tiny gasp that would have been a squeak. Why didn't she want Buck to see the picture?

"The girls' father." Nick pointed. "And that's the man who threatened Mabel."

Mabel trembled in Mindy's arms. Mindy tightened her hold and whispered comforting words. What had she drawn that worried her so? Was it what Mindy had seen stashed in the barn's corner? Should she mention it or wait to see whether Buck noticed it?

"I've seen him before. He's a businessman over in Hawk's River." Buck's jaw hardened. "Joe met with him last night."

Joe? Mindy shuddered, and Mabel climbed fully into Mindy's lap. Bella backed toward the house, slipping inside.

"And?" Nick demanded, crossing his arms.

"And ..." Buck hesitated, his gaze darting this way and that. An action so unlike his usual confident self it set Mindy on edge.

"What, Wilson?" Nick squared off. "If it's something we need to know to keep the girls safe, tell me."

"I know." Buck looked at the picture again. A moment, two, ticked by, then his shoulders relaxed. As if he'd come to a decision. What kind of decision did he have to make? Whether to tell the truth? "He's a suspected counterfeiter."

"Counterfeiting?" Nick hissed.

Mabel's breath came in short bursts, and Mindy found it hard to find her own. Her sister had drawn stacks of money in the corner. Did that mean it was fake? If so, this situation was worse than Mindy feared.

Nick glanced at Mindy, his jaw firming, then looked back at Buck. "Why haven't you turned him in?"

"Because there's no proof, only rumor." Buck slapped the pad on the table, making Mindy and Mabel jump. "When Joe met with him last night, it was the first lead I had to find out the truth."

"Lead?" The word slipped from Mindy's lips. Buck knew more than he'd told them. Maybe more than he'd told Detective O'Connor. Why were they trusting this man?

Nick squeezed the bridge of his nose, pushing his glasses to his forehead. "What are you talking about, Wilson?"

"Not only do I think Joe is the one who set you up," Buck said, pointing at Nick's shoulder, "but I think he's making a play for the Conglomerate."

Nausea had Mindy pressing fingers to her mouth to keep from gagging. Was Joe the mole? The one who had caused all this trouble from the beginning?

"I think he saw an in, thanks to your father." Buck tapped the drawing pad again. "Somehow, your father got mixed up with Emisher. When Joe realized the connection, he exploited it."

Just like the sleazy man. Oh, why had she agreed to step out with him last year?

"Then we need to bring in O'Connor." Nick paced to the corner of the house and back. "Can we use Joe to bring the threat to Mindy and Mabel to an end?"

When Buck hesitated, Mindy asked, "Do you not want this to end, Buck? Are you working with this Emisher, too?"

Buck dropped his chin, looking so much unlike himself that Mindy felt a dash of compassion for him. She hardened her heart. This was her sister at risk.

Nick stopped beside Buck. "Turning in a sibling is hard, whether estranged or not. All four of us would do anything for our siblings."

It was true ... she, Mabel, Buck, Nick ... Just because Joe was on the wrong side of the law didn't make Buck's desire to protect him any less.

"It's more complicated than that, but yes, I hoped I could make a difference in Joe." Buck scuffed the toe of his shoe on the ground. "Give me a day to think about this?"

"Buck." Nick warned.

Buck met his gaze. "I promise not to do anything that would put your girls in harm's way. You have my word, Matrone."

*His girls?*

Nick gave a nod. He was claiming them? "Nick?"

He knelt beside them, his uninjured hand on Mabel's shoulder. "When I promised to protect you, I meant both of you. I still do. Beau, employer, friend. It doesn't matter what others see it as. I care about you both and aim to fulfill my promise."

Mindy's heart beat wildly in her chest.

Mabel, however, simply nodded and removed Nick's hand from her shoulder. She rested it, upturned on Mindy's knee, then placed Mindy's hand in Nick's. Mindy's gaze tangled with his. Nick squeezed.

Mabel patted their joined hands, then her little mouth opened, and she said one earth-shattering word: "Love?"

Nick stared at Mindy's hand. The single whisper reverberated through him like the clang of metal. Mabel had spoken. Finally. What had overcome her fear? Her desire for him, Nick Matrone, to protect—no, *love*—her sister.

"Mabel, we can't ..." Mindy's breathless words seeped from her.

"I'm honored, Mabel." Nick couldn't let Mindy chastise Mabel for her presumption. Because it wasn't that. Not from where he stood. Mabel saw more than he allowed himself to see. "I'm honored that you would trust me with your sister."

Mabel locked eyes with him. Trust shining in their depths. Then she slipped from Mindy's lap and wrapped her arms around his shoulders. His arm screamed, yet he shifted to hug her.

Buck had the look of a cat who ate a canary. He had the audacity to wink before disappearing inside. The man reminded him too much of the reverend prizefighter who gave him his pocket Bible and taught him to fight. The criminal turned saint, and friend. Was that who Buck was destined to be? Nick's friend? The man had secrets, but of all the men he'd met in Crow's Nest, whom he would consider a friend—David, Silas, Gilbert—it was Buck who challenged him most.

"Come with me, Paperotta." Bella leaned out the back door, beckoning her inside. "We will pack so we can stay with il mio fratello."

Mabel skipped away, leaving her drawing pad where Buck had slapped it onto the table.

Mindy tugged her hand free and stood. "Now what do we do?" She was worked up, and there were too many causes for him to guess at the reason for her disquiet. He'd tackle what he could.

"I trust Buck to look into this." And he did. He picked up the pad. "For now, let's move you and Mabel to the Whittlebush house. I need to get to town, deposit the money from yesterday's emergency clinic—I don't like having that much cash lying around, especially with the danger close—and then we'll know whether the heat causes a repeat."

Mindy's frown said that wasn't what she wanted to know at all, however he wasn't ready to address Mabel's word yet. Too much churned through his mind. Namely, if he and Mindy were to move their relationship to a real one, the way his emotions said they should, and the way Mabel hoped they would, then he needed to be confident that it was exactly what God wanted for him. For them.

He searched the picture that Buck had noticed. "I wouldn't have suspected counterfeiting. However, paired with the gambling and the economic trouble, it makes sense. Plenty of counterfeiting going on back in New York City. I've treated many patients while listening to the clacking of a counterfeit press."

"Had you let me point out what I saw before sparring with Buck, you might have." The edge in her tone had him raising his chin. "Look in the corner of the picture."

Nick spotted it at once. He closed his eyes. "I'm sorry, Mindy."

"We also need to talk about what Mabel said. The fact that Mabel spoke. The word she used, the way she joined our hands, and—"

"Hey." Nick set the drawing pad aside to draw Mindy close. He shouldn't, not with so much unresolved between them, but he couldn't allow the panic edging her voice to go unsoothed. "One thing at a time."

She looked up at him. "She spoke and her first concern was me."

He tilted his head. "Why does that surprise you?"

She ducked her chin, and he nudged it back up. The vulnerability in her expression cut into him. He was no better than Joe Spelding. Toying with her heart before he knew he could act on it. He pulled away, anger at himself and shame at the pain he would cause her spinning together.

"I'm sorry, Mindy." He massaged his neck. Couldn't face her. "I shouldn't have agreed to a fake relationship. I should have found another way. It wasn't fair to you." *Here I thought I was a man of honor, sacrificing myself for a damsel in distress. Ha. All I'm destined to do is hurt her.*

"You didn't hurt me." Mindy's quiet statement had him spinning around, heat coursing through him.

"I said that last part out loud?"

She nodded. "You were—you *are*—my knight in shining armor. I've always thought so."

"But Mabel's word. Our decision to stay only friends." He searched her expression, hoping for ... what? That things had changed and he could invite her into his complicated reputation?

"You wouldn't be so worried if you didn't care about me." Mindy rubbed her arms. "You didn't flinch when you realized Cora would be protected by Silas or Marian was protected by Gilbert. And you made sure those men were worthy of the women they cared about while you easily drifted into being their friend. Nothing more."

He shuffled his feet. "I couldn't do that with you."

"I know. I couldn't do that with you either." The vulnerability again. "It's why I didn't like it when you didn't listen to me and chose to spar with Buck instead. I know it was selfish of me, but there it is."

"I can't hurt you, Mindy. It would kill me."

"You think pushing me away is the answer?" She eased forward, his senses spinning like a broken compass. "I just don't understand why I'm the one you want to protect."

He cupped her cheek, his head screaming at him to stop. "Because you are strong and look out for everyone except yourself. Even now, your frustration subsided as soon as you realized I needed reassurance. I ..." *love that about you.* The truth of that statement sunk in deep, had him closing his eyes and lowering his chin. He loved Mindy.

Mindy's hand snaked up to behind his neck. "This is forward of me, but ..." She pressed her lips to his, and in a moment he was drowning. Common sense flew away on sparrow wings. He loved this woman. Would do anything for her, even break his own heart for her happiness.

A clearing throat interrupted.

"Sorry, Matrone." Buck didn't sound sorry at all. "Adaleigh telephoned. A distress call came in from one of the fishing boats. Heat again. We have about forty-five minutes before they arrive at the wharf."

"I'm going with you." Mindy's firm jaw said she wouldn't be budged.

"Wise plan. Stay close to Nick." Buck shut the door behind him, keeping whatever he was about to say from being heard inside the house. "I explained the situation to Patrick, and as much as he doesn't want Meri and Samuel in danger, he understands what it means to keep a child safe. He'll look after Mabel and Bella."

"You'll find this counterfeit person?" Mindy spoke with confidence. "Take them to Detective O'Connor?"

"Yes, ma'am." Buck squared his shoulders, but the haggard lines Nick had noticed when Buck came to him about his lack of sleep looked engraved on his face.

"Give me a minute, Wilson." Nick wrapped his uninjured arm around Mindy's waist, capturing her full attention. "No pretend relationship. I don't want counterfeit. I want you."

Mindy's jaw dropped.

"You are the most honest person I know. You wear your emotions for all to see. What some might call naivete, I see as sincerity. I've had enough of double-speak, of people who say they care turning on me. You couldn't do that if you tried. I've seen that from the first moment we met. You are sunshine and hope. And I ... I love you."

He didn't give her a chance to respond, didn't want her to, so he kissed her again. Knowing full well his little speech had changed everything between them. Whether that was good or bad, whether he was ruining her life because of it, being selfish to claim her—he had no idea. He just knew he had to tell her the truth and manage the destruction he caused later.

Buck clapped him on the shoulder. "A magnificent display, Matrone. But the clock is ticking."

Nick left one more kiss on Mindy's lips, then led the way inside.

# CHAPTER NINETEEN

Mindy sat in the backseat of Buck's car. With half an hour before the boat with the ill fisherman would dock, Nick and Buck were deep in conversation about the best way to set up another emergency center, as it looked like the heat would continue at record temperatures for a second day in a row.

Before leaving the Martins home, Nick gave Bella instructions on calling yesterday's patients, particularly Mary Lou's parents. If any of them needed him to pay a house call, Bella would telephone David's fishing shanty and leave a message with Adaleigh. Mindy had left Mabel under Patrick's protection. Meri assured Mindy that Mabel was the perfect help with baby Samuel. Mindy hoped she spoke the truth, but it didn't make leaving her sister any easier.

Mindy tuned back into Nick and Buck's conversation. Apparently, Nick didn't like keeping too much cash on hand—something about having been mugged too many times, Lord have mercy—so their plan was to drop Nick at the bank to deposit the previous day's income while Buck gathered supplies at Conglomerate Headquarters. Then they would meet at the clinic to retrieve anything else needed before carting it to David's shanty. Though Buck planned to try convincing Willie Clifford to allow them to set up at the Wharfside again.

What they didn't address was what Mindy was supposed to do

between now and when the fisherman needed her nursing skills. It didn't help that her mind and emotions were still in such turmoil. She needed them to tell her where they wanted her. Decisiveness evaded her. So much had happened that morning.

Mabel spoke.

Nick declared he loved her.

He kissed her.

Did that mean she and Nick could have a future together? Her main doubt, that no man could love a woman like her, had been washed away. From her perspective, nothing stood in their way. Except Nick himself. Would he follow through on his declaration? Or would he martyr their relationship with his good intentions before it even began?

He was correct that seeing him sabotage himself had drawn her out of the panic that had her spiraling. He needed someone to protect him as much as she did. She would be that person for him. If anyone dared put down the man who was her knight, she would put an end to such things. Nick deserved to be considered a hero. Because he was one.

Okay. So maybe she could be decisive.

They pulled up to the bank, and Nick glanced back at her. "Stay in the car, Mindy. It's the safest place for you."

"Who will protect you?" She looked significantly at his wounded arm, but meant so much more.

"He can handle himself, Mindy," Buck said over his shoulder.

"Well, I'm not letting him out of my sight." She scrambled out of the car before either could stop her.

Nick met her on the curb, grabbed the top of the car door before she could close it. "I like this side of you."

Mindy stammered.

Buck leaned across the passenger seat. "Stop making mooneyes at each other and get off the street. I'll be five minutes. Can you stay out of trouble that long?"

"It's a bank. We'll be fine." Nick slammed both car doors and held out his elbow. "Shall we?"

Mindy wrapped her arm around his, and he escorted her into the building. Their steps echoed on the marble floor, the sound bouncing against the tall ceiling from which a gold-plated chandelier hung. It wasn't a large space, yet the bank owner had splurged on making it ornate.

Nick approached one of the two teller stations. "Good morning." He smiled at the teller, Mr. Risher, a middle-aged man who had lost his foot in a fishing accident a decade ago. Mindy shuddered at the memory.

Mr. Risher adjusted himself on his stool. "Deposit or withdrawal today, Dr. Matrone?" He didn't say Nick's name correctly, something Mindy was realizing happened more often than not. It bothered her.

Nick didn't appear to notice. He took the envelope of cash from the inside pocket of his coat and slid it under the brass bars separating them from Mr. Risher. "Deposit, please. How's the knee? Is the new crutch helping?"

"Yeah, yeah." Mr. Risher grunted. He counted out the bills, slowed as he reached the lower denominations, then paused and started again. Mindy inched closer to Nick, a feeling of unease growing in her belly. Finally, Mr. Risher stood. "One minute, Dr. Matrone."

"What's going on?" Mindy whispered as Mr. Risher used his crutch to walk to the back room where the bank manager's office and the safe were located.

"I don't know." Nick wrapped his uninjured arm around Mindy's waist, tucking her into his side. "I've never had trouble with a deposit before."

"Dr. Matrone!" The bank manager, Mr. Conrad, followed Mr. Risher out of the back room, the bills now in his hand. He wore a simple black suit with a gold watch chain. "You usually deposit on Fridays. What brings you in today?"

"The emergency clinic yesterday." Nick shifted his feet. "It is not wise to have that much money so close to the medicine I carry."

"Smart." Mr. Conrad flashed a large smile that filled his round face, but didn't reach his eyes. "Feels like it will be another warm one today."

"Yes." Nick's fingers dug into Mindy's side, awakening pain from her attack that had subsided weeks ago. "Is there a problem with the deposit?"

"Why would you think that?" Mr. Conrad narrowed his gaze. "Is there a problem with it?"

Mindy wove her fingers between Nick's, disengaging them from her side, and reminding him she was here for him. "We need to get to the wharf, Mr. Conrad. A fisherman is coming in with a medical issue."

"Of course." Mr. Conrad smiled at her. "You're his nurse now, correct? Why don't you go set up, and Dr. Matrone will be along shortly?"

"No, she stays with me." Nick backed away from the counter, pulling Mindy with him. "In fact, we'll both come back later."

"I can't let you do that, Mr. Matt-ron." The booming voice came from the front door. Chief Sebastian, with his pistol aimed at Nick. In an instant, Nick had placed himself between the chief and Mindy. "Nick Matt-ron, you are under arrest for passing counterfeit bills."

"What?" Mindy stalked around Nick as his chin dropped to his chest. Oh, no way would she allow this. Nick had nothing to do with counterfeit bills, that was her father. "What are you talking about?"

Chief Sebastian gave her a look of condescending pity as he kept his pistol trained on Nick. "Your man here is a criminal. Did you know about the operation?"

"She has nothing to do with this," Nick growled.

Mindy's heart pounded. Why had she gotten Nick into her mess? He didn't deserve this. "Nick has nothing to do with counterfeiting. You can't even say his name right."

Pity turned to annoyance. "Step aside, Miss Zahn, or I'll arrest you, too."

"Mindy." Nick wanted her to follow the chief's direction. Not happening.

She planted her fists on her hips and raised her chin. "I—"

"Chief Sebastian, what's going on here?" Buck entered the bank, taking in the scene in an instant. A niggle of worry rose in Mindy. Had he set them up? "Why are you pointing a weapon at these two citizens?"

"Criminals. Not citizens." Sebastian motioned with the muzzle of his pistol for Mindy to step aside. She refused. "Matt-ron here tried to deposit counterfeit bills."

"That can't ..." Buck's words trailed off, and he set his jaw. Okay, so he didn't know, but he had pieced together the same connection she had. Somehow, her father's counterfeit connection had captured Nick in its grasp. Mindy tried to catch his eye, silently pleading with him to do *something*! Buck sighed. "Sebastian, put the gun down and let me see the bills."

"What do you know about counterfeit bills?" Sebastian lowered the pistol and glared at Buck.

Buck stuffed his hands into his pockets, that infernal lackadaisical posture igniting Mindy's ire. "I'm head of the Conglomerate. I know lots of things. Let me confirm the bills are counterfeit so I know how to proceed."

"Know how to proceed?" Sebastian demanded, pistol ready at his side. Buck shrugged. "Whether to provide a lawyer."

Nick grunted behind her. Mindy blinked against the tears stinging her eyes. "You mean if the bills are counterfeit, you wouldn't help him? You ..." Sparred with him just this morning. Identified a counterfeiter in Mabel's picture. Had they trusted the wrong person?

"Here, Buck." Mr. Conrad passed two bills to Buck, pointing to the first. "This is one of the bills he tried to deposit."

Buck took one look, and his face fell. "I'm sorry, Nick. It's counterfeit."

"I trusted you!" Nick growled, stepping forward. Mindy tried to catch his arm, not wanting him to get into more trouble. Sebastian's pistol aim stopped Nick in his tracks.

"Turn around, Matt-ron." Sebastian waited for Nick to obey, then wrapped metal cuffs around Nick's wrists. Mindy could only watch, her heart breaking. *God, why aren't You helping? Why won't you listen? Nick doesn't deserve this.*

"Well, well, what is this?" Joe Spelding entered the bank. Of all the rotten timing. *God, why?* Then she spotted Joe's smirk. He had something to do with this.

"Mindy, you need to leave. Now." Nick spoke quietly from beside her. Like a mouse caught in a trap, she couldn't move. "It's not safe."

"Aw, isn't this so sweet?" Joe advanced on them. Mindy could feel Nick's anger radiating from him. "You have a thing for criminals, Mindy?"

"Joe, leave it alone," Buck said from his position, blocking the door. "Let Sebastian do his job."

"I intend to, brother." Joe stepped to Mindy's side, and she shuddered. "I'll take over protecting this one."

"Don't you touch her." Nick strained against Sebastian's grip. It freed both a tear and Mindy's feet. She twisted to stand in front of Nick, placed a hand against his heart.

"Nick, stop." She stared into his handsome brown eyes. "I love you, too."

Then she kissed him. In front of everyone. This was her man. No pretend relationship. No counterfeiting. Nothing would stand in her way of declaring to the world that she believed in her hero and would stand beside her knight no matter what lay ahead.

Nick savored Mindy's kiss, knowing how selfish it was of him, and too broken inside to fight off the longing. He knew he shouldn't have allowed their feelings to deepen, shouldn't have told her he loved her. He wasn't the right man for her. Not after being cast out of his old community, and here the chief of police in his new town couldn't even arrest him by the proper name. Now she was linking herself to a man accused of counterfeiting. It would destroy her reputation.

He pulled away from her, ignoring the smirking and snide comments muttered by Sebastian and Spelding. He had eyes only for Mindy. Hers brimmed with tears, her cheeks and nose rosy with emotion. "You are beautiful."

"Let's go, lover boy." Sebastian shoved him forward.

"Wait." Mindy stopped them, turned to Joe. "Did you do this?"

"Why would you think that?" Joe advanced on her. Nick clenched his teeth to keep from jerking from Sebastian's grip. "When I heard he was getting arrested, I was worried for you. Of course, I was gonna make sure you were okay. What else would I do? I'm your boyfriend."

"No, you are not." Mindy stamped her foot. When would the man listen?

Joe snorted. "Why would a pretty girl like you aspire to be around someone like him?"

Nick hardened himself against the barb, yet it sunk into his tender underbelly. Someone like him, indeed.

"Someone like Nick?'" Mindy raised her chin, facing down Joe without an ounce of fear in her marvelous eyes. "Because I love him."

Joe laughed even harder. Nick couldn't take his eyes from Mindy. This woman who defended him. He wasn't worthy of her, and yet she loved him anyway. Why had God blessed someone like him with someone like her? He sure didn't deserve such blessing. It was selfish to hang on to it too tightly.

"All right, that's enough." Buck moved aside from the door. "Sebastian, take Nick to jail. Nick, make sure you get a lawyer and do not say a word."

"You're on his side now?" Joe glared at his brother.

"I'm against anyone being railroaded." Buck rocked on his toes. "Nick is one of my Conglomerate people. It is my responsibility to make sure that fairness is handled, no matter my personal feelings on the matter."

As if that made it all okay. Obligation didn't equal respect. Nick thought he and Buck shared that, but maybe he'd been mistaken. Maybe Buck set him up. Or maybe Buck just used him. It didn't fit with his experiences with Buck. Then again, he was being arrested for a crime he didn't commit.

Joe scoffed. "Then you go with Nick. I'll take care of Mindy."

"No." Nick spat the word, unable to keep silent against his better judgment. "She can stay in the waiting area at the jail."

Buck shook his head again, and Nick knew he saw reason where Nick did not. "I'm taking her home, Nick. Me, Joe. Not you. You wait this out. Until she says it's okay for you to come around again."

Would Joe abide by his brother's declaration? Nick doubted it. The man already had a smug smile on his punchable face. Nick squeezed his eyes shut. He was a doctor, not one to condone violence. However, Joe made him want to fight.

"We finished here?" Sebastian's sarcasm pulled Nick from his thoughts. "I'd like to get my prisoner to jail."

Prisoner. Like Communist. Words that labeled him, then turned others against him. He was a pariah. If he got out of this mess, he would have no choice but to leave Crow's Nest. They'd probably send him away with pitchforks, like his community back in New York had done. Nick took one last glance at Mindy, her blonde ponytail askew, and steeled himself for what lay ahead. He couldn't break up with her now, here. Not with Joe looking on with such a haughty expression. Nick knew he would need to eventually set her free from himself. Once she was safe. Then he would leave.

"I'll send a deputy to collect the counterfeit bills," Sebastian said to the bank manager, pausing at the doors. It placed Nick next to Buck, who ducked his chin, allowing Nick to spot the tick in his jaw. Buck hadn't done this. He was playing the game so he could help. As if God whispered it to his very soul, Nick knew he could trust Buck with Mindy's safety.

"Take care of her," he whispered. Buck raised his gaze, gave a subtle nod. Nick relaxed. Whatever happened to him, Mindy would be okay.

"Let's go, Matt-ron." Sebastian pushed him into the sunlight. The heat wrapped around him. Cloying and oppressive. The fisherman. He would be docked by now, looking for medical attention, and here the town doctor was being arrested for counterfeiting.

Nick dug in his heels before the door closed behind them. "Nurse Zahn, the fisherman. You know what to do."

"Don't worry, Dr. Matrone." Mindy's voice slipped through the door just as it closed, tremulous, yet confident.

"Gullible woman." Sebastian hauled Nick toward his police car. Not gullible. Strong.

As much as he hated to do so, he had no choice except to leave the fisherman, and any other residents that could succumb to the heat, in her inexperienced hands. Another day like yesterday and people could die. Children could die. Because he was being falsely accused. Could Mindy handle what she'd likely face today? Of course she could. He'd seen her capability from the first moments he met her. He didn't just offer her the nursing position because he had an affinity for her. She was good at it. She'd be fine. Buck, David, and Adaleigh would be beside her. Would they protect her as well as Nick could?

*Padre nostro, I leave Mindy in Your hands.*

Before Sebastian shoved Nick into the open police car, Greg Alistar, of all people, hailed the chief from a block away. Of course, Chief Sebastian waited for the newspaperman. Nick closed his eyes and bowed his head. It was happening all over again. False claims. Assumptions. Even if he didn't go to prison for something he didn't do, by the time Alistar was finished with the article he'd write, Nick would be cast out of Crow's Nest for sure.

Sebastian answered all Alistar's questions, painting Nick in a criminal light. Convicted before being tried. Nick had no choice except to stand there and take it on the chin. Anything he said would be misconstrued. Any action he took would be forcibly stopped. He could only hope Buck would get him out of this mess. Obviously, the counterfeiters knew they needed to get Nick out of the way, and when violence hadn't done the job, they set him up to go to jail. He couldn't protect Mindy this way.

Finally, Sebastian stuffed him in the back of the patrol cruiser. Heat had baked the car, making the air stifling. It threatened to steal the air from his lungs.

No. He wouldn't panic. It wouldn't do him any good. He brought up a mental image of Mindy, her smile, the brightness of her eyes. Even the memory of her soothed him. He might be a doctor, but she was the healer. God had given her an incredible gift, and Nick was grateful he could be a recipient of her favor.

Sebastian set the car in motion, and Nick watched the buildings of Main Street roll by. Only a couple of blocks to the jail. Then Sebastian was leading him inside.

Nick had never been arrested before, however, he'd heard plenty of stories from the criminals he treated. After a few minutes of paperwork, Sebastian led him down a flight of stairs to a dark hall with four cells, two on each side, separated by iron bars. The cell Sebastian released Nick into was nothing like the tales he'd been told. First, he was alone. Not another soul shared either his cell or any of the other three.

Second, it was eerily quiet. As Sebastian's footsteps and whistle faded away, Nick sat on the lone cot to observe his surroundings. A single window, not more than a foot wide and six inches tall, near the top of the back wall, showed the bright blue sky overhead. The cells must be half below ground, considering the stairs they'd gone down to get here, and the cool damp temperature. A welcome change after the heat outside. However, it would sink into his bones before long.

Nick leaned against the back wall, his head resting against the cream brick so common in this area of Wisconsin. He'd only known red brick, so it had stood out to him on his first trip here. A spider caught his eye as it built its web in the upper right corner of his cell. No telling how long he'd be here, which gave him ample time to wrestle through the tangled knot in his chest.

Betrayal. Loss. Pain. Humiliation.

As a doctor, he could set emotion aside during an emergency—the previous day's episode with baby Samuel aside—but why do that now? He could let it all wash over him. He'd been cast aside. Taken out of the equation. Made worthless.

That's what hurt the most.

He wanted to make a difference. Save people. Treat people. Here he was, falsely imprisoned and unable to treat an ill fisherman.

*Macché.* No use lying to himself. Not here. Truth was, it bothered him he wasn't the one to protect Mindy.

"I have a hero problem." He raised his spectacles to rub his face. "*Padre Nostro,* what kind of prideful man am I? So full of my own importance that I think I'm the only one who can protect Mindy properly? Yet, I have failed at that because here I sit."

*Here I sit.*

Oh.

His street preacher friend once said that sometimes the Lord's conviction was so obvious, it was like being hit over the head by a steel beam. Instead of pitying himself for being taken out of the fight, he could use this time to get his heart right before God. Like the minute break between boxing rounds.

That way, when God let him back into the fray, Nick would be ready in every way that mattered.

Maybe he'd even be ready to see where a relationship with Mindy could take them.

# CHAPTER TWENTY

Mindy watched Nick being led away, then turned to Buck who was giving instructions to the bank manager. "I need to get to the wharf."

The boat with the ill fisherman would dock any minute, if it hadn't already. Without a doctor, a nurse would have to be the next best thing. That was her. She'd take Nick's mantle. Tend his patients. Until he returned. Proven innocent. Buck raised a finger, then returned to the conversation. Maybe Mindy would just go without him.

"Now, why would a pretty girl like you need to do that?" Joe inched closer, his finger catching her ponytail. "You shouldn't get your hands dirty with sick people."

Mindy yanked away. "I'm a nurse, Mr. Spelding. Just because Nick was taken away in cuffs doesn't mean I don't love him. Now leave me alone."

Joe loomed over her. "You don't mean that. You went out with me first."

"She does mean it, Joe." Buck stuck his arm between them, effectively forcing Joe to back up and blocking his view of her. "I tried to help you, brother, but the heart isn't logical. And forcing Mindy to do something she doesn't want won't endear you to her."

Mindy huffed. The heart isn't logical. Please. She made a choice to love Nick. It had nothing to do with wishy-washy feelings. If it did, why would she stick up for a man arrested for counterfeiting? She believed in Nick. Joe was a sleazy man who gave her the willies.

"I'll make sure he pays for that." Joe looked around Buck's shoulder to pin her with an icy glare. "Once he's gone, you will choose me. I'll be the only man who will accept damaged goods like you."

Mindy wrapped her fingers in the fabric that stretched across Buck's back. What lengths would Joe go to make her date him? There had to be more going on. No one could be that desperate for one girl. Could they?

"That's enough, Joe." Buck pushed them past his brother, leading her toward the outdoors. "Threats don't look good on you."

"Well, that's where you're mistaken, *brother*," Joe hissed. "I'll be back for her, or it's your life that will be forfeit."

Mindy barely held in a squeak. Buck didn't respond. Instead, he pushed them into the bright sunlight and led Mindy toward his car. "You're coming with me. I made a promise to Nick to keep you safe. The fisherman will just have to survive without medical help. I'm sure Adaleigh will do just fine."

"No." Mindy wrenched away from him. Several blocks up the street, she spotted Nick being led into the jailhouse. She wanted to run to him, but he'd given her a task. She squared off against Buck. "I'm a nurse. Nick faced worse to see his patients in New York. The least I can do is see to his patients here until he returns. This is my fault anyway."

"It's not, Mindy, but I see your point." He opened his passenger side car door. "In you go."

One hand on the car door, he placed the other on her head as he helped her sit. She looked up at him. "We also need to tell Detective O'Connor. He'll find the truth."

Buck didn't answer. He closed the door, circled the car, then drove away. North. Away from the Wharfside, where the fisherman was being taken.

"Where are we going?" Mindy demanded. Why were they leaving town?

"Somewhere you'll be safe." Buck fisted the steering wheel. "I told you. I made a promise to Matrone, and I aim to see it through."

"Buck, you let me out of this car." Dare she jump out while it was still moving? She put her hand on the latch. "I'm getting out now."

"Mindy." Buck slammed on the brakes. The car rocked as it came to a screeching halt on the outer limits of town.

She twisted in her seat to face him. "I'm a nurse now, Buck. That means I have a responsibility. Take me to the dock."

Buck studied her for a full minute before he finally gave in.

"Where's Nick?" David met them outside his fishing shanty. "Boat is five minutes out. They hit a rough patch of waves and had to slow down."

Mindy adjusted her grip on Nick's medical bag. "He was arrested for counterfeiting." She'd never forget the way Chief Sebastian handcuffed him.

"What?" David demanded. "Counterfeiting? Where? How?"

"Let's set up, and I'll explain." Buck led them to the shanty, where Adaleigh joined them in the back room. As the four of them laid out the supplies, the cloths, the water buckets, and anything else Mindy thought they would need, Mindy and Buck shared everything that happened that morning. From Mabel's revelation to Nick's arrest.

As David went to check whether the boat had docked yet, Mindy knelt beside Buck, where he was dunking cloths into cool water. "What do you know about the counterfeit bills, Buck? You recognized them rather quickly."

"Keep your voice down," Buck growled, glancing over at Adaleigh, who sat at the radio, listening to the latest weather report. "It's not a coincidence that counterfeit bills ended up in Nick's hands. Somehow, they were included in the payment Nick received yesterday. It was too hectic to pin down who it could be. There are several possibilities."

"Like Joe?" Mindy crossed her arms.

"Like Joe." Buck sat on his heels. "He wasn't in the Conglomerate office when I stopped there, so how did he know to visit the bank at the exact time Nick was being arrested?"

"You think he knew?" It would make sense.

Buck nodded. "Did you see Greg Alistar on the sidewalk as we got in my car?"

Mindy shook her head. She'd been too distracted by everything else.

"What about Willie Clifford?" David reentered the room, drawing their attention. How long had he been listening? "He supposedly took care of the money brought in during the clinic yesterday. Did he know any of them were counterfeit?"

Adaleigh replaced the radio receiver. "Do you think that's why Gilbert Cox couldn't find anything wrong with the Conglomerate books?"

Buck straightened. "Money laundering. They're using the Conglomerate to launder money. Why didn't I see that?" He shoved both wet hands through his hair, causing it to stand on end before he smoothed it down again.

"Uh, what's money laundering?" Mindy asked, rising to her feet.

Buck joined her, dusting dirt from his suit pants. "When you pay in counterfeit money and get real money back. It washes it. Which is why the term *laundry* is used. We need to tell O'Conner."

"We will." David thumbed toward the water. "The *Sea Woman II* is coming in. I'll call Patrick to alert him to the latest, then have my uncle meet us here. Buck, stay with Mindy. Bring Jones into the shanty when they dock."

A solid plan. Yet as Buck led the way outside, Mindy couldn't help asking him, "How do you know so much about counterfeiting? What the bills look like, and how to wash or launder or whatever it's called." Unease settled in the pit of her stomach.

Buck glanced at her, their feet matching rhythm on the wooden planks of the wharf. "I can't tell you, Mindy."

"Why?"

The sounds of the lake filled the moment of silence. Chains clanking. Seagulls cawing. Fishermen shouting as they docked their boats.

Buck sighed. "Because you're too honest, Mindy. Yes, I have information that could help. I just don't know what to do with it. However, we're going to tell O'Connor about what Mabel saw. We're going make sure that you and Mabel stay safe. We're going to find a way to get Nick free from these false charges."

Mindy grabbed his arm, stopping them in the middle of the wharf. "Thank you, Buck."

The men from the *Sea Woman II* hailed them, and Mindy hurried forward, Buck at her side. Just before they reached the boat, Buck leaned close to her ear and whispered, "You and Nick are right for each other. Neither of you needs to martyr yourself, okay? Trust me."

Buck's tone suggested he spoke from experience, but there was no time to delve into it. The fisherman, Jones, was indeed suffering from the heat. She directed them to bring the man into the shanty and set to work on saving him. After working with Nick yesterday, she recognized the signs of heat stress. The clammy skin, increased pulse, lethargy. They needed to bring Jones's temperature down before it caused permanent damage.

The initial flurry over, David left to help the fishermen of *Sea Woman II*, seeing that they were one man down, and Adaleigh cataloged the catches brought into the shanty by other boats. This was the busiest time of day. Mindy pushed away the activity to focus on her patient. If only Buck's statement would stop roving around her mind. Maybe asking would stop it from nagging her.

As Buck knelt beside her with a freshly filled bucket of water, she broached the subject. "Did you martyr yourself for a girl once?"

Buck jerked, spilling water over his knees. "Why would you ask me something like that?"

"I'm just thinking about you and Adaleigh." Mindy changed the cloth around Jones's neck. The man was still half-delirious. "Did you ever have a thing for her? It seemed like you did. Now you two are working together."

Buck took the warm cloth from her. "Looking out for your best friend, are you?"

"Absolutely." She mopped Jones's forehead.

"She's safe, Mindy. I like her, of course, always have. But she and David have something that she and I never would have had."

Mindy cast him a glance. "So you considered asking her out?"

Buck ducked his head in an odd show of modesty. "Of course I considered it. What man wouldn't? She's a pretty lady. You're a pretty lady. But neither of you are my type of woman."

She raised an eyebrow. "What is your type of woman? Someone more like Adaleigh than me, I'd guess."

"Don't take it personally, Mindy." He handed her another cloth. "I had a girl once. Yeah, she was like you. Strong. Determined. Willing to stand up to her man, tell me the truth, even if I didn't want to hear it."

The longing in his voice had her whispering, "What happened?"

"I made the biggest mistake of my life." He gave a humorless chuckle.

"Why?"

"It's complicated, Mindy."

"Complicated, complicated. What do you think my situation is?" Mindy snatched another cloth from him. Jones stirred, mumbled incoherent words. Though worry crept in, Mindy couldn't let that derail her attempts at treating her patient. She needed to stay calm, so when Buck didn't reply, she asked, "Where does she live?"

"Chicago."

"What does she do? Is she married now? Do you talk to her at all?"

"Really, Mindy?" Buck rose, taking the bucket of water. "She's a journalist."

Mindy stared up at him. "Like Greg Alistar?"

"She's the opposite of Alistar." He said it so vehemently, he obviously still had feelings for this woman. He stormed away to retrieve more water. Mindy expected him to change the subject when he returned. Instead, he said, "Her goal in life is to ferret out the truth. She can find it, too. She goes to places that I don't recommend. So headstrong."

Mindy scratched her cheek. "If she was going to prison, would you do anything you could to get her out?"

Buck grabbed the back of his neck. "I did. Already have. Yes, I've done exactly that."

Mindy set to work changing out the warm cloths once again. The heat didn't allow them to stay cool for long. "Then what do you think I will do to make sure Nick gets out of jail?"

Buck gave a slow nod. "Alright. Alright. We'll do what we can."

Jones shifted in his chair, the glaze in his eyes clearing. She grinned. She'd done it, helped him. Of course, the man had more recovery to go, but she'd helped him. And success felt wonderful.

If short-lived.

A moment later, David jogged into the back room with news of several more people suffering from the heat. In no time, Mindy was set up at the Wharfside, just like the day before. There was no time to continue her conversation with Buck or to speak with Detective O'Connor when he arrived. She noticed Buck didn't speak to him either because the man didn't leave her side.

As he sent yet another patient to Adaleigh to drink more water, Mindy planted her hands on her hips and turned to Buck. "You have information you need to share with Detective O'Connor. Not just what Mabel said. You know something about the counterfeiting that's going on. You need to tell him what you know."

Buck blinked, obviously stunned.

"You can leave my side for five minutes to have a conversation with him. This is for Nick. I understand you won't tell me. Then tell him. You know you can trust him." The heat must have been getting to her, too, because she blurted out, "You'd do it for your girl."

Buck waved over another patient. "I don't love Nick like I loved Caroline."

"Caroline?" Mindy had a name, and she'd use it. "Would Caroline tell Detective O'Connor?"

"You play dirty, Mindy Zahn." Buck studied her for a moment. "Which makes you more like Caroline than you think."

"And?" She didn't care about that. She wanted Buck to fight for Nick.

"Nick has been a friend when no one else has." He watched David helping one of the older widows toward them. "Even men like David, Silas, Gilbert, have held suspicions about me. How can you truly be friends with someone when you doubt them?"

"And Nick hasn't doubted you?" She took a fresh cloth, ready for when David and the patient reached them.

"If he has, he hasn't let on. He's treated me like a human being, without judgment." Buck bumped her shoulder, like a friend would. "You're right. I need to extend the same kindness to him. Consider it done."

"Thanks, Buck." She smiled at him, so he'd know her sincerity. "That's what I needed to hear."

He gave her a nod, and they returned to work.

As the sun sank, casting his jail cell into darkness, Nick settled on the uncomfortable cot. Back against the cold brick. Knees up. He crossed his arms, resting them on the top of his knees so he could lay his forehead on his wrists.

His wound ached, pulsing with each beat of his heart. No one had visited him. No one had provided a way for him to change his bandage. He was alone. Deserted. The positivity he'd battled for earlier slipped under the wave of despair that washed over him.

He tried to pull up a mental image of Mindy. Her smile, her cheerfulness. He didn't expect her to visit him. It wasn't safe. Still, it stung that she hadn't. The tension caused a throb in his temples.

Nick fought to regain his hope from earlier. Like a sparring match, he parried and punched. The night wore on, fatigue weakening his spirit. Despair grew stronger, backing him into an emotional corner.

Then, in the wee hours of the morning, his mamma's voice echoed in his memory. It was of a time when, as a child, he'd been sick with a high, dangerous fever. His mamma knelt beside his bed and prayed all night.

Following his mamma's example, the words of the Lord's Prayer whispered from his lips ...

> Padre nostro che sei in cielo sia santificato il tuo nome.
> Venga il tuo Regno. Sia fatta la tua volontàqui in terra come in cielo.
> Dacci anche oggi il cibo necessarioe perdona i nostri peccati come noi abbiamo perdonatoquelli che ci hanno fatto dei torti.
> Fa' che non cediamo alla tentazione ma liberaci dal male.

Deliver us from evil.

The phrase struck him. Could he say he'd been falsely imprisoned by evil men? It seemed dramatic. Yet, Nick yearned for deliverance. Hours into this ordeal, and he floundered. Jesus hadn't just spent hours in a jail cell, falsely accused. He was killed in a gruesome death. He understood how Nick felt, and so much more.

Instead of wrestling, Nick surrendered. He gave his current situation, Mindy and Mabel's safety, his own feelings of inadequacy, over to God. Perhaps he even fell asleep. Because when the sound of footsteps had him opening his eyes, dawn's faint light filtered through the tiny window near the ceiling.

"Nick?"

Mindy!

Nick attempted to leap up from the cot, but his cold muscles stiffened. He shuffled to the bars that separated him from the woman he loved. "It is wonderful to see you."

Mindy smiled at him, that gorgeous, heart-stopping smile that had captured him from the first moment. Then she held up a key. "The night guard was one of my biggest tippers when I worked at the Wharfside. He snuck me in to change your bandage."

He realized she carried his medical bag, too. "Did you arrive with an escort?" Or chaperone. They couldn't be alone down here or it would risk her reputation.

"We have fifteen minutes." Mindy stuck the key into the lock. "I prepared the bandages and tweezers ahead of time. I figure as long as I don't touch the wound, I should be able to keep it clean."

"You are remarkable." Nick sat on the cot and freed his arm from his shirt. He faced away as Mindy worked, her closeness getting to him, until the pain stole his attention. "It never hurts less."

"I'm sorry, Nick." She wrapped fresh bandages around the gauze-packed wound. "I couldn't figure out how not to use my hands with this bandage, but I think it'll be okay. The fabric touching your wound is properly clean."

Nick returned his sore arm to his sleeve, then leaned forward and kissed Mindy's forehead. "Thank you."

"You're doing okay down here?" Mindy looked around. "I should have brought a blanket. I didn't expect it to be cold considering how hot it is outside."

"How was the fisherman?" Nick asked.

"Fine now. You taught me well." She squeezed his fingers. "We're going to get you out of this. Buck talked to Detective O'Connor last night. I'm not sure what all they said, but both are determined to get these charges dropped."

"You are safe?" Nick searched her expression. "The night guard will walk you home?"

"Between Buck and the Martins clan, they have me and Mabel under lock and key. If I didn't know how Adaleigh snuck out that one time to have coffee with me, I wouldn't have made it here. Mabel is covering for me."

"Mindy." Nick squeezed the bridge of his nose.

"I had to see you, Nick." She laid a kiss on his cheek. "I need to go before Chief Sebastian catches me here."

Nick snagged her hand. "I love you."

Mindy beamed. "I know."

"No fictitious relationship." He held her gaze. "Real this time."

"Aw, isn't this sweet?" A harsh voice cut into their moment.

Nick placed himself between its owner and Mindy. "Who are you?"

Out of the hall shadows emerged a man Nick had only seen one other time. In Mabel's drawing, arguing with the girls' father.

"Emisher." Nick silently sent up a prayer for help.

Mindy pressed into his back, giving and taking comfort. "Where's the night guard?"

"Sleeping." For a moment, a haggard expression creased Emisher's face. It was gone as fast as it appeared. "I need a doctor. You're coming with me."

"Why?" Nick demanded, though he suspected. He'd been through this before. Many times.

"My son was shot last night." Emisher jerked open the cell door. "You're going to save him."

Mindy gasped. Nick straightened. "Only if you leave the Zahn family alone." It was an empty threat. He was a doctor. No way would he allow someone to suffer when he could help it. But if he could save Mindy and Mabel while he was at it, he'd try.

"A child for a child." Emisher motioned for his goons to enter the cell. "My son for her sister. You save my boy, and my people will never touch her."

"Deal." Nick reached for his bag. It was something he could work with. "I'll come with you."

"And your nurse." A glint flashed in Emisher's eye. "She's a tough one, my boys say. I'll have her beat again if you don't comply."

Mindy squeaked, sliding as close to Nick as she could. Nick took a moment to control his anger. He would not allow the man to goad him. "You won't need to make me comply, Emisher. If a child's life is at stake, I will do everything in my power to save him."

"You better." Emisher motioned for the men to take them captive. "Or you'll watch me kill your woman. Do we have a deal?"

# CHAPTER TWENTY-ONE

Mindy was led into the dim interior of a room off a lower-level speakeasy. The place was quiet, it being just after sunrise. The smell of stale alcohol burned her nose and roiled her stomach. As her eyes adjusted, she realized a young man, no more than sixteen, lay on a table, blood-soaked bandages around his middle.

A gut-shot.

Behind her, Nick was shoved toward the boy.

"Fix him," Emisher growled, then stood against the wall, arms folded. The thug holding her arm released her and joined the other two in blocking their only escape.

Never in her wildest imaginings, could Mindy have pictured herself in such a situation. She did not know how to conduct herself. Mindy looked to Nick for direction.

Nick's jaw clenched, then his shoulders went back. "I need my nurse to assist at the boy's bedside. I also need boiled water. Lots of it. And clean rags. Now!"

The room exploded into action as Emisher sent his three thugs to fetch what Nick demanded. Mindy sidled toward Nick, where he stood at the boy's side.

Nick handed Mindy his medical bag and rolled up his sleeves. "I don't need to tell you the odds on this one. I'll know more once I see where the bullet penetrated."

Mindy nodded, set the bag beside the boy's head, and rolled up her own sleeves. If they didn't save Emisher's son, what would that mean for Mabel? "We have to save him," she whispered.

Nick bumped her shoulder with his uninjured one, the gesture assuring her he would do his very best. Then he circled the table and bent over the boy. One of Emisher's thugs—the one who had beat Mindy those weeks ago—plunked a pot of boiling water on the table beside the boy's hip with a grunt. Nick didn't acknowledge him as he held out his hand to Mindy. He didn't need to say a word. She knew what he needed and placed in his palm the bar of soap he kept in his medical bag. Using the boiled water, he scrubbed halfway up his forearms, dampening his cuffed sleeves, then handed the soap back to Mindy.

She washed up, mentally resigning her dress to the rubbish pile once they were saved. Because they had to get out of this alive. Mabel needed her. Saving this boy meant saving Mabel. Failure was not an option.

Finished, she traded that pot of water for the one brought by another thug. In this one, she washed Nick's tools. A pincer tweezer, a scalpel, and several clamps. Meanwhile, Nick peeled away the bandages to reveal a hole in the boy's side, about four inches from his navel. It oozed dark red blood. Mindy pressed her lips together, the coppery smell cloying in the stuffy room. Nick rolled the boy on his side toward Mindy, and his features hardened still more.

"It's not through and through?" Mindy finished laying out the tools on a portion of the table she cleaned with water and soap, then dug out the chloroform for what she expected to be a delicate surgery. Had the bullet struck even an inch or two further from the center, the wound would be only a deep graze. Dangerous, yet with a better chance at survival.

"Fortunately, the wound is low enough in the abdomen. I don't think it will have nicked any major organs." Nick rolled the boy onto his back. Nodded for Mindy to administer the chloroform. The boy was already unconscious, however they couldn't have him waking at the wrong time. "My worry is the intestines, which have their own issues. I won't know until I get in there."

"God, guide Nick's hands." The prayer slipped out, and Mindy stared at Nick, an odd swirling in her middle. "That felt so natural. It's never been that way before."

Nick smiled at her, then raised his voice. "Where's more water, people? If you want me to save this kid, then move faster." That got Emisher shouting orders again, and Nick winked.

"You put him to work." Mindy whispered, leaning over the table.

"Didn't you feel him staring at us? He was brooding, and I needed to take the pressure off." Nick selected the scalpel. "If his men share some responsibility for the outcome, it will help us. I hope."

"You mean if it goes poorly?" Mindy readied a clamp and pincher tweezer, ready for whatever Nick would need.

Nick bobbed his eyebrows. Then began the surgery.

With only the necessary words between them, Mindy assisted Nick as he first dug out the bullet, then attempted to stop the internal bleeding with clamps and cloths until he could stitch up the internal lacerations. How much time ticked by, Mindy didn't know. Except her back ached from bending over the table. She monitored the boy—Bobby, she learned, was his name—and each breath he took was a relief.

From the doorway of the room, the thugs stood guard. Emisher paced. It was difficult to picture a counterfeiting criminal who could order a woman beaten and still be a devoted father, worried over his son. It affected her view of her own father. Mindy hadn't realized how much she blamed him for leaving, for putting her and Mabel in danger. Even fathers make mistakes. Grave, horrible, criminal mistakes. Their children caught in the cross-fire. It evidently didn't mean those fathers didn't care about their children.

Nick heaved a sigh. "There. I think I got all the bleeders."

"He'll be okay?" Emisher cautiously approached. His drawn expression tugged on Mindy's compassion. She steeled herself against it. Just because he cared didn't mean he still hadn't done wicked things.

"I can't say." Nick washed his bloody hands. "But he has a fighting chance if we can keep him from infection."

"You haven't closed the wound." Emisher pointed toward his son's stomach.

"That's next." Nick waved Mindy to the water bowl. "We need to wash up so we close him up clean. Where's the fresh water?"

Mindy stifled a smirk. She knew now Nick was purposefully being the demanding doctor, flexing his authority in front of these counterfeiting criminals. It wasn't him at all, but she recalled his stories of having treated others while in similar situations. He knew how to manage them, to get himself—and her—out alive. She trusted him completely and marveled at how his commands seemed to keep the room at ease as well.

Finally, Nick had closed up Bobby's wound and issued instructions on how to, hopefully, battle an infection.

"It's not guaranteed," Nick said as he washed his tools in a freshly boiled pot of water. "We gave him a fighting chance. That's the best we can offer."

Emisher's throat bobbed. "Thank you for saving my son. The younger Zahn girl is absolved from her father's misconduct." Relief nearly had Mindy's knees buckling.

Nick raised his brows. "Thank you. And Mindy?"

Emisher's mouth flattened. "I saw how much she helped you, and if I wasn't a man of my word, I would absolve her as well. But I made a deal, and I always stand by my deals. It's why your father will still pay, Miss Zahn. Once I find him. A deal is a deal."

Her relief evaporated, and her tongue stuck to the roof of her mouth. What did all that mean?

"What deal have you made for Mindy?" Nick asked what Mindy couldn't form the words to say.

Emisher thumbed toward the door, and Joe Spelding entered the room with a horrible grin. Mindy shrank behind Nick.

"Come now, doll," Joe advanced. "I would hate to ask more of Emisher. This deal works well for all of us. Your doctor saved your sister. You are coming with me to save him."

"No." Nick palmed one of his tools that lay drying on a towel. A scalpel. Could her knight save her with a surgeon's blade instead of a sword?

Joe threw a punch, which Nick blocked with ease. Mindy slipped around the table, putting it between her and the men. The thugs blocked the door. Emisher crossed his arms, watching.

Jab. Jab. She recognized the moves as ones Nick and Buck had parried earlier.

"Mindy, run!" Nick dodged a blow, bumping into the table.

She threw herself over the unconscious Bobby to keep him from rolling as Joe and Nick hit the table again. The boy didn't deserve to be caught in the middle again. She was his nurse.

"Enough!" Emisher shouted. The thug who beat her grabbed Nick by the arms, held him while Joe punched Nick's stomach. Emisher watched with a frigid gaze.

Tears gathered in her eyes. She couldn't take the brutality. This was the payment Nick received for saving a boy? "Stop! Just stop already!"

The room froze.

"I'll go, just let Nick go."

"Mindy, no," Nick breathed, but the grimace on his face renewed her resolve. She couldn't let him suffer.

She looked from Nick to Emisher to Joe. "Nick is a hero. He saved this boy's life. I won't let you harm him on account of me."

"Emisher, what's the meaning of this?" another voice shouted from the hallway. "I demand a cut of the proceeds, do you hear me?"

Everyone turned to the doorway as Buck Wilson sauntered through, waving a handful of bills.

The distraction was exactly what Joe needed to catch Mindy by surprise. He snaked his arm around her waist and hauled her against his chest. She squeaked, drawing Nick's attention. Anger darkened his features.

"I'm not cutting you in, Wilson." Emisher spat on the rough wood floor. "Men, detain these two while Joe takes the little lady away. She protected my son, we'll deal with these two men where she doesn't have to watch."

*No!* The word was strangled by Joe's arm tightening around her abdomen. He swung her off her feet and Nick charged into motion. A thug attempted to tackle him. Buck stopped the man with an uppercut. By the time Joe dragged Mindy to the door, Nick and Buck stood back-to-back, fending off all three thugs. Emisher waved them down the hall as he hollered for reinforcements.

Mindy couldn't let that happen. She struggled against Joe's hold. *God, I need an idea. Some way to get free. Please.*

Then, like a whisper, an idea came to her. God had given her a gift. A sunny personality and beautiful features. It drew unwelcome attention, so she had always thought it was a curse. Now, she would wield it like a weapon.

"Joe, stop. Please. You're hurting me." She kept her tone even, not panicked or angry, like she wanted it to be. Years as a waitress had honed that skill.

"You're coming with me." Joe didn't even slow down. The steps were mere feet away. Footsteps thumped down them. Four thugs barreled past, forcing Joe to stop.

*Thank you, Lord. Protect Nick and Buck.* Mindy needed to act now.

"It's not that I don't want to go with you." The lie tasted like dirt on her tongue. "You're walking too fast. And now that we're away from Nick, I can speak honestly."

"Oh?"

Her smile grew as Joe stared at her. She'd hooked him. Time to reel him in, as if she were one of David's fishermen and Joe a fish. But how could she detain Joe so she could rescue Nick? Ah! She had just the thing, and it made her smile even larger.

She took Joe's hands, keeping his attention on her despite the noises coming from down the hall. Then she reached up and tugged the ribbon holding her ponytail in place. Her hair fell around her shoulders. Joe's jaw dropped open. With deft fingers, she wrapped the ribbon around Joe's wrists, his distraction allowing her to secure the knot before he blinked and schooled that ridiculous expression.

Movement beyond Joe's shoulder caught her eye. Could it be? Her grin widened, and she turned back to Joe. "There's something you need to know, Mr. Spelding. I have the dearest friends. They have my back. They support me. I know I can rely on them more than anyone else in the world. I also believe God gave me the opportunity to get away from you. Now I never want to see you again."

Anger twisted Joe's mouth. He glanced at his hands. "Why you conniving little—"

Mindy curled her fingers into a fist and drove it into Joe's nose. Pain exploded through her hand, but it was worth it to be able to say, "I'm giving you to Detective O'Connor so I can save my Nick."

Friday, July 3

Fortifying himself with a prayer, Nick knocked at the Martinses' front door. It had been three days since he'd seen Mindy, and he missed her.

Steps sounded inside the house. Nick's respiratory rate increased, causing an ache through his torso. Over the past three days, he had not only answered more questions than he could comprehend about the counterfeiting ring, and then been acquitted, he'd spent those days sequestered in a hospital room. For protection, Detective O'Connor claimed. Nick only partially believed him. Unfortunately, Nick had the benefit of being a medical professional and knew he was at risk for infection and complications from the fight.

Nick rubbed his sweaty palms on his pant legs, then adjusted his repaired spectacles. The door opened and Mrs. Martins greeted him with a knowing smile.

"Is Mindy here?" he asked.

"I'll send her out." Mrs. Martins reached for his arm and gently squeezed. "I'm glad you're alright, Nick. You gave us a fright."

"Thank you, *signora*." Nick nodded, too nervous to do anything except stick to the politest response.

Mrs. Martins winked at him, then hurried down the hall. Nick couldn't help noticing she appeared more energetic these days. Having a great-grandson would do that to a person, he'd guess.

In another moment, Mabel dashed down the hall, a paper fluttering in her hand. She skidded to a stop at his feet and shoved the paper at him.

"*Grazie.*" He smiled at her.

She grinned back, then ran back into the house. Okay, then. Nick took one glance at the paper, and his nerves vibrated. It was a picture of him and Mindy—his dark hair and spectacles, Mindy's thin frame and blonde ponytail—standing side-by-side, holding hands. What hit him most was the wedding veil Mindy wore. Mabel had just given her blessing for him to marry her sister.

He let out a slow breath. Would Mindy want to spend the rest of her life with someone like him? She'd nearly broken her hand in defense of him, and still wore a bandage, according to David. Then again, since the counterfeiting ring was shut down, Nick was lauded a hero in town. Even Chief Sebastian was quoted in the *Gazette*, in an article written by none other than Greg Alistar, stating how honored he was that Nick was the new town doctor. The entire situation had saved Nick's reputation in the eyes of the people of Crow's Nest. Would they turn on him one day like his own community did? He couldn't borrow trouble. Would Mindy see it that way?

He caught sight of her as she turned into the hallway. Hair down, not in her usual ponytail, and wearing a gorgeous blue sleeveless dress that made her shine. Wow, she was beautiful. He offered a ridiculous wave, and she gave him a shy smile. Was she as nervous as he?

"Hi, Nick." Her gaze ran over him. "I thought you were discharged from the hospital this morning."

"I was." He could have asked the detective to bring him here instead of the Whittlebush house, but he'd wanted to wash up first. "Would you allow me to take you for a stroll?"

"Are you sure you should?" Worry creased her forehead.

No, however, he couldn't wait another day. "Absolutely." He held out his elbow.

Together they walked toward Lake Michigan, off which a cool breeze blew. The heat had finally broken, and, while it was still warm, the reprieve was much appreciated.

"Have you heard from your parents yet?" he asked, the silence strangely uncomfortable. He never felt that way with her.

"Not yet. Mabel said another word this morning." She looked up at him, eyes sparkling. "She said, *bella*."

"As in my sister?" Nick chuckled and shook his head. "Why doesn't that surprise me?"

"I don't think so. She said it to me. And pointed at me." Mindy's cheeks turned pink. "It means *beautiful*, doesn't it?"

Nick nodded, words trapped in his throat.

"I was trying this dress on, and hadn't tied up my hair yet." She shrugged. "When Mabel said that to me, I didn't have the heart to change."

The picture he'd folded and placed in his coat pocket crinkled. "Did she know I was being discharged today?"

"Yes."

"Did she learn before or after you tried on the dress?"

"Before. Why?"

They reached the edge of the cliff. Fifteen feet below, the blue water lapped the rocks. "Did she suggest you try on the dress?"

"Nick, yes, but what does this have to do with ..." She trailed off as

Nick removed the picture from his pocket and handed it to her. Her cheeks turned a brilliant shade of pink. "This ... I ..."

"It's adorable." This was it, his opening to ask her out for an actual date. It's all he'd been able to think about as he lay in the hospital bed the last few days. Seeing her threatened, working beside her in an emergency, feeling the relief at finding her unharmed. It all led him to be sure of one thing: he loved Mindy Zahn and felt the Lord's permission to pursue it. If she was willing. Having Mabel's blessing confirmed it.

"Nick." Mindy hugged the paper to her chest. "This is childish wishing. Now that the danger is over, I release you from having to be my fake beau."

"What?" Nick's heart jumped into his throat. She didn't want to be attached to him? He squeezed his eyes shut.

"You've been my knight in shining armor. You've kept me and Mabel safe. It nearly cost you your life." Her voice choked, and his eyes popped open.

He squinted at her. "If we ended our pretend relationship, would it make you feel sad or relieved?"

She stared out to where the water met the horizon. "It doesn't matter how I feel. This is the right thing to do."

His lips twitched as certainty flooded him, eliminating his nerves. "I would feel sad."

"What?" Her gaze shot to his.

"Devastated, really. I'd understand, of course, and let you go. However, my heart would be irreparably damaged." He snaked his injured arm around her waist, grateful the pain had lessened since the hospital had treated it to prevent infection. "Knowing how you'd feel matters to me because I love you."

"Nick." She placed a palm against his chest, and he held in a wince as she pressed against one of his sore ribs. "You don't need to pretend anymore."

"I'm not pretending. I would be heartbroken if I could not call on you anymore. There's nothing I want more than to ask you out. Not as a pretend date, not as a ruse, but as a real old-fashioned, courting opportunity." He loved the feel of her in his arms. The breeze ruffled a strand of hair in front of her face, and he hooked it behind her ear. "But I won't ask you if it's not something you want. I know I'm not the ideal man. I wear glasses, I'm darker-skinned, I work long hours ..."

"You're the best man I know, Nick. That's why I don't understand. It's me, not you." Mindy stiffened in his arms. "Nothing has changed. I mean, some things have. I'm now semi-literate. A nurse instead of a waitress. But, I'm still just me."

He bent to look her in the eye. "I love you."

She melted then, like chocolate on a hot day. "You still love me? After everything?"

He nodded. "Do you feel the same way?" His heart pounded triple time as he waited for her answer.

It took her a breath to gather her words. "I do, Nick. I love you, too." Then she bounced up on her toes and kissed him.

He held her close, gratefulness seeping into his kiss. This amazing woman chose him? *Grazie, il mio Padre.* The prayer sang from his heart.

After a moment, he pulled back to rest his forehead on hers. "Someday I will ask you to marry me. Not now. We need time. I know I have your sister's permission, and one day, we can stay together forever. In the meantime, will you allow me the honor to call on you?"

Mindy's eyes turned into liquid pools of hazel. "Yes, yes, I would love for you to call on me. Someday, I might just say yes to that other question."

He wrapped his arms around her and swung her in the air, not regretting the pain it caused his ribs when he heard her giggles. "That makes me a very, very happy man."

As he stopped, she rested her hands on his shoulders. "Are you sure I won't bring more trouble into your life?"

"You bring sunshine, Mindy." He brought her close to kiss her again. "Will I bring trouble into your life?"

"The best kind." She cupped his cheek. "Together, we can face it. Isn't that what it's all about? Together?"

"Sí, sí." He moved his head to kiss her palm. "We are stronger together, with God. With Him as our shelter, we can face anything."

Mindy beamed. "I like this plan, Dr. Matrone. I like this plan a lot."

# EPILOGUE



*Thursday, September 10*

Nick stood in front of the mirror that sat atop his bureau in his newly finished attic apartment and adjusted his tie. Already sweat beaded on his temple. September was supposed to usher in cooler months, most welcome after one of the hottest summers Wisconsin had seen. However, summer wasn't ready to give up just yet.

He slipped into his vest, hooked his timepiece to his button, and adjusted his collar. He looked the part of a respectable doctor about to open the Whittlebush Clinic. Mrs. Whittlebush had been full of scolding when he called to tell her the name he, Mindy, Buck, and Adaleigh had agreed on. Nick refused to budge because, even over the long-distance line, he'd detected the emotion in her voice. She was honored.

Shrugging into his coat, he released a pent up breath. Ever since he'd bought the ring he planned to offer Mindy his respiration had been off. Three days and he still hadn't gotten the nerve up to ask her. What if it caused her to come to her senses and realize he wasn't the knight she insisted he was?

He forced more air from his lungs. At this rate, he'd hyperventilate before his first cup of coffee.

A knock preceded David's voice. "Ready, Doctor?" David grinned at him from the doorway.

"First patient arrives in …" Nick checked his watch. "Fifteen minutes. Wait, why aren't you on the lake today?"

David leaned on the doorjamb. "A captain can take a day off occasionally, can't he?"

Nick raised an eyebrow. "You never take a day off during fishing season."

"Fine. Though the official opening party isn't until next Saturday, I wanted to be here for your first day at the clinic." The man shrugged as if it wasn't a big deal. But it was. Adaleigh had even purchased train tickets for Mrs. Whittlebush and Samantha Martins to visit for a month.

"I'm not getting all emotional, if that's your aim." Nick cleared the telltale thickening from his throat. "I'm sure Adaleigh has wedding stuff for you to do today anyway."

"Just over three weeks." David's face beamed the light of a man completely in love. "Adaleigh will finally be my wife. I can't fathom it. Three weeks."

"Out of my way, you big sap." Nick pushed past him down the hall.

As Mindy had suggested, they had turned the attic into three bedrooms, giving Nick the one with the best view. She also suggested creating a living area so Nick could relax away from the clinic area. He passed the space on his way to the stairs, her touch all over the brightly colored pillows that adorned the couch, and the warm blanket draped over his favorite high-back chair. They'd even installed a coal stove and ran the pipe out the roof to keep it warm in the winter. Didn't need anything like that today.

David followed him. "When are you going to ask Mindy to marry you?"

Nick clomped down the stairs. Mentioning his plan to David had been a mistake. "Soon enough."

David stayed on his heels. "Having doubts? Because if you are, as Mindy's friend—"

"No doubts." Nick spun at the base of the stairs. "A man needs to be sure of these things."

David studied him for a moment, and Nick retreated down the second-floor hall. This level had rooms for patients who would stay overnight, or longer, while he treated them. Mindy, Adaleigh, Bella, and Mabel had made them homey rooms to make patients comfortable, while also keeping them easily cleanable to maintain a healthy environment.

Nick stopped at the top of the steps leading to the main floor. "How did you know Adaleigh wouldn't say no?"

"Mindy is crazy about you, Matrone. Trust me."

Nick nodded, absorbing David's confidence. "I love her." Then he hurried down the stairs, uncomfortable revealing such inner thoughts.

Thankfully, David didn't say another word as they headed toward the kitchen.

No sooner had they poured coffee than Buck arrived with treats from The Barn, compliments of Mrs. Collins, and news from Detective O'Connor. "Emisher pleaded guilty to the counterfeiting charges. The ring is officially shut down."

"Does that mean Mindy is out of danger?" Nick asked as he selected a banana muffin.

"She is." Buck leaned on the kitchen table. "But the trouble isn't over."

"Your brother." David sipped his coffee.

"He's clammed up. Won't see me. Won't talk." Buck shoved his hands into his pockets. "He's not the mole in the Conglomerate."

Nick and David stared at Buck.

"Detective O'Connor and I—"

David choked on his coffee. "You and my uncle?"

Buck rolled his eyes. "In dealing with my stepbrother, we discovered he planned to bring counterfeiting into the Conglomerate. We stopped him in time because Mindy was caught in the crossfire. None of that solved what's been going on the past couple years."

"Mindy said you knew a lot about counterfeit bills." Nick tossed out the statement, fishing for more. He'd been around criminals enough that a suspicion had taken root since Mindy told him all that had transpired after he'd been falsely accused.

Buck rubbed his clean-shaven jaw. "Sebastian has had me questioned multiple times for that. Doesn't help that the only thing Joe has done is implicate me."

"Is any of it true?" David eyed him over his mug.

"No." Buck dropped his chin. "At Mindy's suggestion, I told Detective O'Connor more information. Things I can't tell you. If things don't improve soon, however, Sebastian is going to send me to jail, or I'm going to find myself in someone's crosshairs. If only I could figure out who."

"What can we do?" Nick asked. The man had been on Nick's side. He'd be on his.

"Pray." Buck's gaze roved the room. "I might need to face someone I never thought I'd see again."

Nick and David exchanged glances, and Nick found his own questions echoed in David's expression.

"It's thanks to Mindy, you know. She planted the idea." Buck pushed off the table. "Enough about me. Who is your first client?"

Nick smiled. "Mrs. Bindle, of course."

Mindy let herself into the new clinic ten minutes before Mrs. Bindle's appointment. She meant to arrive earlier, but Bella had insisted she wear something other than a serviceable brown skirt and white blouse. It's how she ended up wearing the light blue dress she now wore. It made her feel self-conscious. A nurse shouldn't draw attention. Bella had simply waved off her concerns, and Mabel silently handed her an apron. Her little sister hadn't spoken again since the last time Mindy wore the blue dress, but smiled more, and that was enough.

The apron was not just any apron. Bella explained she had helped Mabel sew it, and that Mabel was working on more of the same. The white panel on the bottom stretched to her knees and would protect her skirt. The top panel covered her front and was framed with ruffles that swept over her shoulders. She wore it now, and it felt like a hug from her little sister. It made her proud to wear her sister's handiwork.

"Hello?" She closed the front door of the clinic behind her. Tomorrow, Mrs. Whittlebush would arrive to see the transformation her house had undergone. Samantha was joining her as a companion. However, Mrs. Whittlebush was also serving as chaperone, so Samantha could attend David and Adaleigh's wedding in a couple weeks. It would be excellent to see them both.

"Morning, Mindy." David strode down the hall. "Congratulations on your first day as a nurse in the new clinic."

Mindy couldn't contain her smile. "Can you believe I'm a nurse?"

David cupped her shoulders, his own smile lighting his eyes. "I'm so proud of you."

She sniffed the emotion away, but couldn't find her voice.

David pressed a friendly kiss to her cheek. "You like working with Nick?"

"Of course I do." She pushed him away. "Go spend your day off with your future bride."

David grinned. "Three weeks."

"As if I haven't heard that *all* morning." Mindy rolled her eyes. Adaleigh was giddy, and as her maid of honor, Mindy heard how eager she was multiple times in a day. It made her happy for her friend, also a tad envious. She loved Nick ... would their love be anything like Adaleigh and David's?

Mrs. Bindle's arrival ended the conversation. Nick and Buck emerged from the kitchen, and Mindy had to work hard not to stare at Nick. This was time to be professional, not a love-sick ninny.

David took his leave after offering another round of congratulations. Buck did the same. Then Nick led Mrs. Bindle into the exam room.

"I'm thrilled to be your first patient in the new clinic." The older woman clapped her hands, then frowned. "What's going on between you two?"

Mindy glanced at Nick just as he looked at her. Her stomach swirled, and she rushed to the table where she'd set out the day's charts the night before.

"You know I'm calling on Mindy." Nick brushed Mindy's shoulder as he reached for his stethoscope. "But in the office, we are doctor and nurse. Professional."

Exactly Mindy's thoughts.

Mrs. Bindle cackled. "Nonsense. You can be professional and still keep the spark alive. I know, because I worked beside my husband for forty years. He ran a shop, you know. I was a shopkeeper's wife and helped him plenty. People loved to come to our shop because we worked it together."

Mindy sought Nick's expression, wondering about his reaction to Mrs. Bindle's statement.

He scratched his cheek. "You would not be offended by a doctor-nurse team like that?"

Mindy's stomach swirled even more. Did he mean a husband-and-wife doctor-nurse team?

"I think it would be perfect." Mrs. Bindle jerked her chin in a decisive nod, then allowed Nick to help her onto the exam table. "In fact, I chose to be your first patient in order to tell you that. I do not need a medical appointment. I wanted to reserve this time for the two of you."

Mindy's jaw dropped. Nick sputtered.

"What?" Mrs. Bindle brushed lint off her skirt. "Since Rose Whittlebush left and Elaine Ward passed away, God rest her soul, someone has to take over helping Marie Martins with the matchmaking around here."

"Uh." Nick blinked, looking from Mrs. Bindle to Mindy, then back again to his patient. "You're serious?"

The older lady raised her thin, gray brows. "You going to do something about this opening day present I'm offering you?"

Nick laughed. "Yes, ma'am. I think I will. Come with me, Mindy." He wove his fingers through hers and tugged her down the hall, through the kitchen, to the backyard.

"What ..." Mindy's confusion was silenced by Nick's finger on her lips.

"Wait here, il mia *amore*." Nick winked and dashed back into the house.

Completely bewildered, yet hopeful, she wandered closer to the edge of the cliff that looked out over Lake Michigan. Crow's Nest had been her home her entire life. Her parents finally wrote that they'd settled in California, yet asked her to keep watch on Mabel. When they had enough money to support her, they would send for her. Did Nick realize marrying her would mean bringing Mabel into the family, too? Then again, he had Bella under his care. Though the young woman was coming into her own.

She turned when she heard Nick's steps coming toward her. Determination set his jaw. Right hand fisted at his side. Her pulse increased. Was this good news or bad news he meant to impart?

As soon as he reached her, he took her hand, his expression softening, and rested her palm over his pounding heart, eyes glued to hers. Yet, he said nothing. If anything, his heart rate increased. Dangerously.

"Nick, you're worrying me. What is it?"

Panic flickered in his eyes.

"Nick?"

He opened his fist to reveal a simple gold ring. The warm sunlight glinted off the metal, making it sparkle like the lake beside them. Mindy covered her mouth with her free hand. Was this a proposal? She searched Nick's expression, willing him to speak, but he had turned pale.

"I don't need flowery words, Nick. Just ask." She moved her fingers from her lips to his cheek.

His throat convulsed, and his voice emerged like a croak. "Marry me?"

Mindy grinned and threw her arms around Nick's neck. "Sí, sí. I will marry you."

Nick wrapped her in a hug, burying his face in her neck. "Truly? You, the most beautiful soul, will marry swarthy old me?"

Mindy laughed, pressing her hand on his head to keep him close to her. "Absolutely, my love. Together, with God as our shelter, we can face anything."

Hooting came from the house, and Mindy glanced over to see Mrs. Bindle giggling like a schoolgirl. Matchmaker indeed.

Nick's laugh joined theirs, and he swung Mindy around, calling over his shoulder. "Close your eyes, Mrs. Bindle. I'm going to kiss my nurse."

"You waited long enough, Dr. Matrone!" Mrs. Bindle hollered back.

Love radiated from Nick's brown eyes. "Yes, I believe I have." And he kissed her.

Continue the series in ...
*Investigation of a Journalist*
Read on for an excerpt.

# INVESTIGATION OF A JOURNALIST



*Monday, September 14, 1931*
*Chicago, Illinois*

Buck Wilson did not deserve a second chance. He knew it down to his marrow, yet here he stood, outside Chicago's Union Station, in the very town where he'd left all his hopes and dreams. The detective who wanted to arrest him at his side.

He tugged his fedora lower. "If they find out I'm here, you know what they'll do."

"I reckon so." Michael O'Connor braced his hands on his belt and looked around, neck craning to see the tall buildings around them. "You liked it here?"

"Let's go, O'Connor. Quit acting like a tourist." Buck tugged at his collar. The heat was more oppressive here in the city than up in Crow's Nest. He couldn't wait to leave, to return to the small Wisconsin town that had become home. But first he had to face the one person he thought he'd never see again.

"I could have done this by myself, you know." O'Connor kept up with Buck's brisk pace.

"I know." Buck turned his back on the Chicago River and headed west down Jackson. He needed the walk, even if it meant arriving looking wrung out. Frankly, he wasn't entirely sure he wouldn't be tossed out on his rear. He deserved nothing less. But he needed to face her like a man, not send the detective to do his dirty work.

Detective Michael O'Connor was close to seventy, with blue eyes that could see into a man's soul and a gray mustache that seemed to be a living thing at times. Buck scratched at his own usually clean-shaven chin. The travel down from Crow's Nest hadn't afforded time to shave, and the scruff provided a measure of anonymity. However, showing up, looking like a hobo, wouldn't win him any good graces.

He halted. "We need a cab."

"Finally. He has some sense." O'Connor grumbled.

"Yeah. Yeah." It was a longer walk than he remembered and the Windy City, Chicago was not today. He'd give anything for a fishy breeze off the lake. And just as much, he wouldn't breathe a word of that sentiment to his companion. Though, as the older man folded himself into the hansom cab with a twinkle in his eye, Buck suspected the good old detective knew more than Buck wanted.

"Did you tell Matrone where you were going?" Detective O'Connor broke the silence that settled once they were on the move.

Nick Matrone was an Italian doctor who befriended Buck this past summer. He was one of the few men in Crow's Nest who saw Buck as a person instead of the head of the Crow's Nest Conglomerate. They sparred every morning, except this one, of course. Matrone's fiance, Mindy Zahn, was the first to prod Buck about facing his past.

"They can't know the truth." Buck watched the old buildings go by. "Telling you is dangerous enough."

"I wish you would have told me two years ago." The man huffed. "Two heads and all. We could have solved this before people got hurt."

Could they have done so? He'd been reluctant to risk it. But now, with children getting caught in the cross-hairs, and his own step-brother in jail again, the counter-risks were piling up, too. "I guess we'll never know."

Before too long, he recognized the spire of St. Mark. The sun reflected off the cross that rose high above the surrounding buildings, including the one where the cabbie stopped. Buck paid the driver and sent him on his way. O'Connor stood silently beside him. He appreciated that about the detective. The man didn't rush into things. For a moment, Buck let his eyes linger on the Catholic Church across the street, where a man in a flatcap unloaded crates of food to carry inside.

On the edge of one of the Italian neighborhoods, smells of sausage and basil wafted through the air and punched him in the stomach. They reminded him of the blissful life he'd been forced to leave behind. O'Connor gripped his shoulder and Buck shook himself out of the memories. If he wanted to make his sacrifices—*her sacrifice*—worth it, he needed her help. There was no other choice.

"We're being observed." O'Connor's gravelly voice rumbled.

Buck turned toward the old brownstone, nearly stumbling over a newsboy as the kid darted by, a package of newspapers tied with twine in his arms. Sometimes he missed the hustle and bustle of the city, but most times he did not. And there were plenty of children to trip over on the wharf in Crow's Nest.

He scanned the windows, spotted the flutter of a curtain. The Di Stasio Giornaliste Agency was home to some of the most dogged female journalists he'd ever met. Curious women who would have no trouble tossing him to the street for what he'd done to one of their own.

*Enough stalling*. He fortified himself as he climbed the five steps to the brownstone's door, O'Connor to his left. *Lord, please let me find favor in her eyes. Grant me this grace, though I know how undeserving I am of it.*

He knocked and stepped back, arms loose at his sides. The confident arrogance he wore in Crow's Nest had no place here. It was but a disguise. One he wore so long, now he wasn't sure what to do with his hands. Maybe he should have brought flowers? No. This wasn't a date. He wasn't even here to apologize. Though he surely would. Maybe he should begin on his knees in penitence. Begging for her help.

"Take a breath, Wilson." O'Connor spoke nearly silently. "You're going to Lindy Hop your way out of here."

A laugh jerked up his throat, and his shoulders relaxed. He stuffed his left hand in his pocket and raised his other to knock again—only for the wood to vanish before his fist. He stumbled a step forward, catching himself on the doorframe. For there, before him, stood the most beautiful woman in the world. His heart stuttered, and an ache bloomed in his chest as the realization of all he gave up crashed in on him.

"Caroline." Her name on his lips emerged broken, just like him.

A variety of emotion danced across her round features before she shuttered them away. She was not overly tall, but neither was she short. Indeed, diminutive, she was not. Dressed in her typical white blouse and black skirt, a tie at her throat, and a black eyebrow cocked, she looked like the warrior he knew her to be. Her dark hair was exactly as he remembered, pinned up with combs to soften the bob. She shifted. With one hand she held the door open, but she relaxed a hip, resting her other hand on it as it jutted out in her signature stance. Still, not a word left her unsmiling mouth.

He'd rehearsed this moment in his mind since they left Crow's Nest. No, since he'd made this ridiculous plan with Detective O'Connor, his nemeses-turned-partner. Though if this didn't work, the man beside him might have to arrest Buck like he had surely dreamed of doing the last few years. He could picture the older man's bushy mustache twitching in glee as he secured Buck's wrists in cuffs.

"Did you have something to say?" Carrie spoke firmly, neutrally, showing the skills that made him first admire her. Her gaze took in his companion, but focused on him. "Or are you going to stand here in a daze until supper?"

"I need your help." Dunderhead. Those were not the first words he'd planned. Beside him, O'Connor sighed.

The index finger of Carrie's right hand bounced against her belt, the only sign he'd caught her off guard. "The girls think I should slam the door in your face."

"I deserve it."

She huffed and threw the door closed.

"Your eloquence leaves something to be desired." O'Connor growled.

Buck cringed. But before his brain engaged, Carrie flung it open again. "Get your *posteriore* in here, Wilson. And shut the door." She spun on her heels, leaving him gaping on her front step and O'Connor laughing like a crazy old man.

Caroline Wagoneer had used those exact words the first day they met over six years ago.

"I like her." O'Connor pushed into the house.

Yeah. So did he.

And, for the first time in two years, his heart gave a pitiful thump of hope.

Continue reading

DANIELLE GRANDINETTI

*Investigation of a Journalist*
daniellegrandinetti.com/investigation-of-a-journalist

# From the Author

Dear Reader,

Thank you for joining me for Nick and Mindy's story. Ever since I wrote the conversation between Mindy and Adaleigh in *Confessions to a Stranger*, I knew Mindy needed a happily ever after. But who could be her hero? An outsider? Buck? And then came Nick Matrone.

Of course, he left Crow's Nest at the end of *Refuge for the Archaeologist*, which meant finding a way to bring him back.

Research into the anti-Italian prejudice of the late 1800s-early 1900s gave me insight into his story. Returning as a gallant doctor was not enough, however, the inner wounds he would have developed based on his past made him the perfect main character to star across from naive, cheerful Mindy. I also loved bringing more weather related phenomena into the story. A heat wave worked perfectly with the grumpy-sunshine pairing.

From the first time Mindy entered the series, I knew she struggled with reading. Dyslexia has been a long-misunderstood learning disorder and I encourage you to read the historical note on this, if you haven't yet. I also pray that I have represented both Dyslexia and Childhood Mutism in an honoring way. Please forgive me if I have not. My desire is to bring awareness and show that those who battle these challenges are strong, capable people who are loved by God just as they are. This is why it was important to me not to have Mabel "healed" by the end of the story.

Thank you for joining me this far into the Harbored in Crow's Nest series. There is one book left, and I know many of you have been highly anticipating discovering Buck Wilson's story. I cannot wait to share it with you!

You can also discover the story of Bella's Italian friend. Margherita Vicienzo, crippled in the recent earthquake, is forced to flee her home when her former fiancé, an Italian Blackshirt, aims to purge her from the earth. Now an illegal refugee, she is given sanctuary in Eden Cove, England, with the Ferryman family, who live in 1 Sycamore Street. Hunted by one man, can she open her heart to another? Find out in *The Italian Musicians Sanctuary*. Visit daniellegrandinetti.com/the-italian-musicians-sanctuary for details.

I hope you enjoyed *Sheltered by the Doctor*. I'd be honored if you would leave an honest review on your preferred retail site. As always, I'd love to keep in touch. Visit my website at daniellegrandinetti.com for where to follow me. And be sure to sign up for my weekly newsletter at daniellegrandinetti.com/fsn for all the bookish news.

Thank you for reading!

Danielle Grandinetti

# HISTORICAL NOTE

The temperature data shared in *Sheltered by the Doctor* is based on true meteorological data from those dates. That includes June 30, 1931, recorded as being the hottest day that year, and, as far as I could ascertain, the first time the temperature reached over 100 degrees Fahrenheit in recorded history for that portion of Wisconsin.

The struggles Nick faced as an Italian immigrant were not uncommon. While the prejudice was more blatant in the late 1800s, it continued through World War II since Italy was part of the Axis Powers. The prejudice against Italians was one of the impetuses behind the immigration laws that curbed immigration in the early 1900s and set up the battle over welcoming Jewish refugees from Germany during the coming war. To learn more about Italian prejudice, I recommend the following from The Michael Schwartz Library at Cleveland State University: *Italian Americans and their Communities of Cleveland*, chapter six, "Anti-Italian Sentiment in America."

Nursing in the 1930s was in a state of limbo. At the time, being a nurse did not require registration. As long as a woman did not label herself as a Registered Nurse, she could still operate as one. During the 1930s, there was a push to change that, and in 1938 New York became the first state to require a license for all nursing practice. The state law allowed for two levels of nursing, a practical nursing license and a registered nursing license. A year later, the American Nurses Association put their stamp of approval on the New York state law. Find out more from Penn Nursing at the University of Pennsylvania, Nursing Through Time, 1930-1959.

Mindy and Mabel battled two different learning challenges. Mindy suffered from dyslexia and Mabel from Childhood Mutism. Mutism in children is divided into two causes, physical and psychological. Mabel's was psychological. To find out more, visit the Selective Mutism Center, What is Selective Mutism.

Dyslexia, at the time, was a very misunderstood condition. At first, it was called "word blindness" because it was thought to be a vision problem. Over the course of the late 1800s and into the 1900s, much theory was suggested about the cause. From psychological problems to mental defects. Find out more in the article, "Dyslexia debated, then and now: a historical perspective on the dyslexia debate." Now, according to Mayo Clinic, they believe this learning disability is a genetic condition that affects the area of the brain that processes reading and language.

Bare Knuckle Boxing is still considered a lesser sport than regular boxing, possibly because it was practiced by Irish immigrants rather than in the more educated arenas. Read more in the USA Today article, "Fight club: Legalized bare-knuckle boxing may be next big show in ring."

As for Martial Arts, they were brought to America in the late 1800s with Chinese immigrants, though Native Americans had their own form of martial arts. Chinese and other Southeast Asian Martial Arts did not become popular until after WWII. When they returned home, servicemen who spent time in Japan and the surrounding nations brought this "new" fighting technique back with them. However, it wasn't until the 1970s, with the movies of Bruce Lee and Chuck Norris, that martial arts became as well-known and accepted as they are today.

Wound Care is something I have personal experience with, having suffered from one myself, and having to endure days and days of having it packed and irrigated. Fortunately, I had topical lidocaine, though it still hurt horribly! For Nick, he would not have had access to the same pain relief. I cannot imagine. Praise God for modern medical advances.

# THE LORD'S PRAYER

Padre nostro che sei in cielo, sia santificato il tuo nome.

Venga il tuo Regno.

Sia fatta la tua volontàqui in terra, come in cielo.

Dacci anche oggi il cibo necessarioe.

Perdona i nostri peccati,

come noi abbiamo perdonatoquelli che ci hanno fatto dei torti.

Fa' che non cediamo alla tentazione,

ma liberaci dal male.


Our Father which art in heaven, Hallowed be thy name.

Thy kingdom come,

Thy will be done in earth, as it is in heaven.

Give us this day our daily bread.

And forgive us our debts,

as we forgive our debtors.

And lead us not into temptation,

but deliver us from evil:

For thine is the kingdom, and the power, and the glory, for ever.

Amen.

# ITALIAN-AMERICAN GLOSSARY

Amica/amico—Friend

Amore—love

Bella—beautiful

Bene—good

Caramelle—candy

Cosa—what

Cuore mio—my heart

Dolce—sweet

Dolcezza—sweetness

Fratello—brother

Grazie (mille)—thank you (very much)

Il mio/la mia—my

La tua/il tuo—your

Lo so—I know

Macché—nope

Motlo—very

Non ho capito—I don't understand

Padre nostro—our Father

Paperotta—duckie (pet name)

Per favore—please

Puzzolente—smelly

Sí—yes

Signora—missus

Signorile—elegant/lady-like

Sorella—sister

Stupido—stupid

Torta—cake

Uno, due, tre—one, two, three

# Join My Fireside News

Grab a spot on my virtual hearth and receive a weekly email filled with bookish content. As a thank you for subscribing, you'll receive a digital copy of my historical romance novelette: *Fire and Water*.

**Subscribe Here**

# Harbored in Crow's Nest

Welcome to Crow's Nest,
where danger and romance meet at the water's edge.
daniellegrandinetti.com/harbored-in-crows-nest

## Confessions to a Stranger

Harbored in Crow's Nest, #1
*She's lost her future. He's sacrificed his.*
*Now they have a chance to reclaim it—together.*

## Refuge for the Archaeologist

Harbored in Crow's Nest, #2
*Will uncovering the truth set them free*
*or destroy what they hold most dear?*

## Escape with the Prodigal

Harbored in Crow's Nest, #3
*Only a Christmas miracle will save*
*an unwed mother and the lumberjack protecting her.*

## Relying on the Enemy

Harbored in Crow's Nest, #4
*She's protecting her children.*
*He's redeeming his past.*

## Sheltered by the Doctor

Harbored in Crow's Nest, #5
*A fake relationship might keep her safe,*
*but will it break their hearts?*

## Investigation of a Journalist

Harbored in Crow's Nest, #6
*A second chance to set the record straight,*
*and rekindle a lost love.*

# Di Stasio Giornaliste Agency

La Verità con Integrità. Truth with Integrity.
The Legacy of a (Girl) Stunt Reporter.
daniellegrandinetti.com/di-stasio-giornaliste-agency

## Undercover Wish

Di Stasio Giornaliste Agency, #0
*Alessandra Di Stasio*
*Chicago World's Fair: World's Columbian Exposition*

## Eyewitness Sketch

Di Stasio Giornaliste Agency, #1
*Gabriella Salatino*
*Prohibition*

## Sabotage Games

Di Stasio Giornaliste Agency, #2
*Emma Hancock*
*Summer & Winter Olympics: Lake Placid & L.A.*

# Shrouded Trail

Di Stasio Giornaliste Agency, #3
*Lena Carney*
*Presidential Election*

# Fraudulent Progress

Di Stasio Giornaliste Agency, #4
*Klara James*
*Chicago World's Fair: A Century Of Progress Exposition*

# Pursuing Dust

Di Stasio Giornaliste Agency, #5
*Tabitha Jóhannsson*
*Dust Bowl*

# Hostile Ally

Di Stasio Giornaliste Agency, #6
*Liesl Kaufman*
*Berlin Olympics*

# OUR HOUSE NOVELLAS

**As the world marches toward what will become WWII, visit Our House as we join the resistance.**

**The Italian Musician's Sanctuary**
Romance, history and intrigue at Our House on
Sycamore Street.

*Hunted by one man, can she open her heart to another?*
Eden Cove, England, 1931—Margherita Vicienzo flees Italy pursued
by her former fiancé, a member of Mussolini's Blackshirt. Smuggled
illegally into England, Margherita is a foreigner at the mercy of strangers.
Her limp from an improperly healed broken leg means she has nothing
to offer the Ferryman family, who offer her sanctuary, and nothing to
appease their son who resents her presence.

Luke Ferryman needs a wife. He wants to marry for love, but carries
the weight of his family's generations-old expectations on his shoulders.
Though he inherited the role of both baker and ferryman, he knows
he can't fulfill both needs once his aging grandparents retire. A wife
would help, but not an illegal one like the refugee his matchmaking
grandmother is harboring.

As opposite as night and day, Luke and Margherita forge a tentative friendship that grows despite the constant threat of Margherita's discovery. But when strangers appear in the close-knit seaside town, threatening Luke's livelihood and Margherita's safety, the choice between justice and mercy becomes harder. And sacrifice proves the only answer.

## The Recluse's Vindication

### Rumors, Monsters, and Second Chances at Our House on Heather Wynd

*The Loch Ness Monster isn't the only recluse seeking a Scottish haven.*

Bieldfell, Scotland, 1933—Falsely accused of murder sixteen years ago, American cowboy Benjamin Ford has chosen to hide out in the Scottish Highlands. Reclusive and not afraid to die, he rescues children out of an increasingly dangerous Germany. When his childhood best friend appears at his door, he's not the boy she remembers.

Eleanor Finch's life ended sixteen years ago. In one horrible day, she lost her dreams, her reputation, and her heart. However, she never gives up the hope of finding her friend, so when she learns of Ben's whereabouts, she leaves all that is familiar to convince him to return home.

But Eleanor isn't the only person searching for Ben. Hunters follow her trail. The thin veil of gossip and rumor may be their only chance of a future ... unless the Loch Ness Monster is real after all.

daniellegrandinetti.com/our-house

# Unexpected Protectors

**Visit small-town Wisconsin during the Dairy Strikes of the Great Depression in these three historical romances.**

For details, visit:
daniellegrandinetti.com/unexpected-protectors

## To Stand in the Breach

Strike to the Heart, #1
She came to America to escape a workhouse prison,
but will the cost of freedom be too high a price to pay?

## A Strike to the Heart

Strike to the Heart, #2
She's fiercely independent.
He's determined to protect her.

## As Silent as the Night

Strike to the Heart, #3

He can procure anything, except his heart's deepest wish.
She might hold the key, if she's not discovered first.

# FAIRYTALE RETELLINGS

### HEART OF BEAUTY

stand-alone origin novella

*Discover the origin of Crooked Tooth Ranch in this 1870s western retelling of Beauty and the Beast.*

daniellegrandinetti.com/heart-of-beauty

### HIS BOSS'S LITTLE SISTER

stand-alone novella in the Apron Strings Tea Tale
multi-author series

*A touch of fairy tale, a spoonful of history, and a teacup of hope … a 1930s historical romance retelling of Hansel and Gretel.*

daniellegrandinetti.com/his-bosss-little-sister

**UNDERCOVER WISH**
stand-alone novella, part of the Di Stasio Giornaliste
Agency series

*A Di Stasio Giornaliste Agency origin story and a retelling of Aladdin
and the Magic Lamp.*

daniellegrandinetti.com/heart-of-beauty

# ABOUT THE AUTHOR

**Danielle Grandinetti** is an award-winning author of 1930s historical romance, where mystery and suspense intertwine with hope. Her work has received recognition including a Distinguished Faith in Writing Award, two National Excellence in Storytelling Awards, and finalist honors in the FHLCW Reader's Choice, Selah, and Daphne du Maurier contests.

A second-generation Italian-American rooted in Midwest traditions, Danielle draws inspiration from tea, books, and the creative beauty of nature. Holding a master's in communication and culture, and driven by a lifelong love of stories, she crafts tales that celebrate resilience, diversity, and belonging. Danielle lives along Wisconsin's Lake Michigan shoreline with her husband and two sons. Find her online at daniellegrandinetti.com.

www.ingramcontent.com/pod-product-compliance
Lightning Source LLC
Chambersburg PA
CBHW061632190726
48289CB00006B/1578